Glenn Myers is a fan of D(
Terry Pratchett, P G Wodehou
wanted to write a comic nove
soul, and this is it.

www.glennmyers.info

www.fizz-books.com

With love
to you all
Glenn Myers
July 11

Paradise

Glenn Myers

Fizz
Books

Copyright © 2010 Glenn Myers

First published 2010 by Fizz Books

www.fizz-books.com

ISBN 978-0-9565010-0-4

British Library Cataloguing in Publication Data
A CIP catalogue for this book is available from the British
Library

Cover design by Sam Richardson

Printed by Lightning Source UK Ltd, Chapter House, Pitfield,
Kiln Farm, Milton Keynes MK11 3LW UK

This book is for Cordelia
who has always believed.

THE PAVILION AT THE EDGE OF MY SOUL

'So this is my soul?'

'I've seen worse sir,' said Stub.

'You'd better lead on.'

We tramped through cans, bottles and takeaway cartons around the outer edge of a large Dome. It was raining. The tall spirit ahead of me wrapped his overcoat around himself and pulled his hat further onto his head. I followed his long strides rather like a Yorkshire terrier trying to keep up.

Stub's moody stride across the landscape lost a bit of dignity each time he sank into the rubbish. Sometimes he set off a mini-avalanche and went *whoa* with flail of skinny arms.

He didn't find it funny.

Eventually we put most of the rubbish behind us and started climbing out of the valley that housed the Dome.

'It will be all right, won't it?' I asked.

'So I am led to believe sir,' Stub replied.

Looking back I could see it was a pleasure-dome, brown at the edges, tacky with a swimming pool and restaurants. Beyond the Dome lay the stain of a town and further hills.

Climbing onto the ridge, we came out from under the shower-cloud and for the first time got a clear view of the sky above and the landscape beyond. I gaped.

The landscape that was my soul was floating between two waterfalls of colour that stretched from the horizon almost to the top of the sky.

'This region of the heavenly places is called Vanity Fair, sir,' said Stub.

It took a while for the colours to resolve themselves.

'It's a mall,' I said eventually.

'Yessir,' said Stub.

What a fantastic place. Shops were piled on top of each other, layer after layer, filling the sky on both sides. Signs jutted out. Goods spilled onto marble ledges. Vast open doors beckoned. 'In a way, it's *The* Mall, sir,' continued Stub.

'It's like the Grand Canyon for shopping,' I said.

All the famous high street names were there. They were sliding past on either side as the great landscape that was my soul glided forward.

'*Osama's*!' Back on earth, my favourite Afghan restaurant had closed down. Here it seemed to be thriving. The wide frontage of the shop stretched back into dark depths where, under whirring fans, a celestial version of the Giant Surly Bread Chef conjured Afghan flat bread called *murtabak* from doughballs and meat. 'Can't we go in?' I asked.

'No sir,' said Stub.

'Just put my nose in the door?'

'That's not why we're here, sir,' said Stub.

'Some aren't even shops at all,' I said, my eye still ranging up and down the levels of Vanity Fair. A shopfront was busy with editors and journos playing with gadgets, and I recognized it as a 3-D version of one of my favourite magazines. A political review was next door. I spotted a theatre and a camping exhibition.

'May I suggest you look straight in front of you?' asked Stub.

'But this is fantastic.'

'Sir.'

'If we must.'

I pulled my gaze away from the Old Fashioned Internet Sweetshop which on earth only existed as a website but here in the heavenlies took up three candied storeys.

'The task in hand, sir.'

Below me my soul-landscape sloped down to a cricket pitch and a cliff edge. A wooden pavilion stood at the edge of the cliff. Three ropes stretched from under the pavilion into the sky. These ropes led to a penguin-like creature which was pulling my soul through this canyon of colour.

'That's my Pengub.'

'Yessir.'

Pengubim—*Pengubim* is the plural, like *cherubim* and *seraphim*—are the workhorses of the heavenly places, towing souls through the ether.

'Keziah told me about the Pengubim,' I explained.

'This is where you steer your soul, sir,' said Stub. 'In principle.'

'You mean, if I did ever actively steer my soul, that pavilion is where I'd do it from?'

'That is the theory sir.'

'How does the Pengub know where to go if I don't steer it?' I asked the gaunt spirit.

'It feels the impulse of your heart and tries its best.'

I glanced again at the bright canyon of shops that filled the sky on both sides.

'So my soul came back here as soon it could.'

'This is it's natural habitat, sir.'

'What you're saying,' I said, as I followed him towards the pavilion, 'is that my soul is never happier than when mooching aimlessly on a consumerist whim and fancy.'

'It's a default setting, sir. When you can't be bothered to do anything else.'

'And now I have to break out of it.'

'Indeed, sir.'

The pavilion on the edge of my soul was wooden, musty and empty. We inspected its echoey depths: a large room for cricketing teas. Changing rooms for the two teams and the umpires. A room at the back where a grounds-keeper could brew cups of tea.

'What's with the pavilion?' I asked Stub.

'You built it, sir. Think it through.'

'It's not coming,' I said. Stub sighed.

'As well as reflecting your love of the game of cricket—and perhaps a generally playful outlook on life —it also says something about the deep conservatism that lurks in your heart. You cling to its old-fashioned simplicity.'

'I do?' I said. 'I thought I was a radical, creative thinker.'

'You are not a radical, creative *doer*, sir. There is a difference.'

A picture-window occupied the back of the pavilion facing out over the cliff to the Pengub. A ship's wheel allowed me to steer. Stub told me my Pengub was called Henry.

'So this is where I'm supposed to take command of myself.'

'Yessir.'

I sat in a captain's chair in front of the wheel.

'OK,' I said. 'OK. Now what do I do?'

'You break out from all of this,' said Stub, his red eyes on me. 'You break the shackles of the past. You move on.'

'I do?… *All* the shackles of the past?'

'As many as we can manage, sir.'

'I feel quite nervous about this,' I said. 'Now that it comes to it.'

Stub gazed down at me. His heroin-addict face was barely visible between the turned-up collars of his overcoat and the turned-down rim of his hat.

'See that thin strip of sky?' he said. By straining my neck I could see a purplish ribbon far above us. Lights pulsed in it. Lazy golden meteors slid across like crayon strokes. The weather blew down from there. 'Head for that.'

'OK.' I pulled gently on the wheel.

Henry the Pengub flapped his earnest wings, and we climbed.

It was a long way. We rose through layers of shops and eventually emerged from the canyon.

'Finally. The end of Vanity Fair,' I said.

'No sir,' said Stub. 'Just the limit of the retail space.'

'What's up here, then?'

'You can never tell,' said Stub. 'Moods. Lusts. Irrational Emotions. Sudden Whims.'

'Wild Dreams? Forlorn Hopes?'

'In all probability.'

'Abandoned Principles?'

11

'Certainly.'

'Ideas Whose Time has Come?'

'Not unless they're very lost, sir.'

'My soul swims through this stuff all the time?'

'Yessir.'

'How will I find the *Diner*?'

'They said they'd put a light on for us, sir.' Stub was scanning the sky.

'What's that dark patch?' I asked.

'Some kind of slick,' said Stub. 'The heavenly places aren't as clean as we might like.'

'Is it dangerous?'

'Merely unpleasant.'

'Can we avoid it?'

'Sir, we've hardly started. We're in the bowels of Vanity Fair. This is just the beginning. It's the beginning of the beginning. We need to keep to our course. The best thing to do is put Henry onto auto-pilot.'

'How does the auto-pilot work?'

'There's a bit of string for tying the wheel down.'

'Ah.'

I tied the string and watched apprehensively as the black cloud grew to fill the picture window.

Stub wrapped his coat around himself and pulled his hat further down.

'Let's walk around for a bit, sir.' We left the pavilion, crossed the cricket pitch, climbed the ridge again. All was gloomy. The rain-shower had passed, and I could look down on the brightly lit Dome. Inside the Dome, I knew, were sweet memories: a swimming pool, friends—some wearing bikinis—and a selection of restaurants.

'That's where I used to go at times like this,' I told Stub. 'Gloomy times.'

'And at all other times,' said Stub.

Near the Dome I could see the lights of Keziah's black Mini and also those of the Polish truck called *Zlotcwicvic Enngerrgrunden Transportowicz, Krakow* (I never did quite catch the spelling)—driving around the rubbish outside the Dome: traumatic memories I'd never managed to purge.

The blackness was now all around us, clammy and cold.

'I feel I could start writing French existentialist poetry,' I said.

'Resist the urge, sir.'

'It won't help?'

'Not in my experience, sir.'

'What's that?' Over the cricket pitch, a patch of darkness was thickening and taking shape like a giant black raindrop. Having gathered itself, it slowly fell.

'Melancholy is lumpy in the heavenlies, sir,' said Stub. 'It condenses out. Brace yourself.'

The blob landed, wobbled on the cricket pitch and exploded.

'What is the point?' I exclaimed suddenly. 'Really. What is the *point?*'

'No point at all!' snapped Stub.

'I don't know why I go on. I don't want to go on. I don't.'

'Nobody's forcing you,' said Stub.

'And you're no help!' I said.

'I'm *no help?*' snarled Stub. '*You're* an albatross around *my* neck!'

'No.' I said. 'You're an albatross around your own neck!'

'Oh yes?' yelled Stub.

'Yes!' I shouted.

13

We were standing toe-to-toe, looking each other in the eye. I coughed.

'Sorry,' I said.

'It's all right, sir.'

'That was the blast wave, wasn't it?'

'Yessir. They pass.' I brushed gobby bits of melancholy off my shoulders and face.

More dank minutes passed before the slick began to break up around us. I returned to the pavilion, untied the wheel, and steered Henry towards the purple sky.

We were higher now, but my eyes struggled to make sense of what I was seeing. Bubbles drifted by. Shower clouds blew over. Patterns of light lit the sky—shafts of light breaking into fragments. Schools of silvery light like fish coalescing back into lightening-like shafts. Lights strobed. I saw huge fat golden raindrops on solitary journeys; in the distance, odd beings (animals? machines?) on paths not aligned with mine. Smoke-like waves curled by. Sometimes I glimpsed distant landscapes pulled by almost-invisible Pengubim.

I looked at a vertical grey line that seemed suspended in the middle distance.

'What's that thing?' I asked.

'Navigation aid,' said Stub.

'It's followed us ever since we climbed out of the Vanity Fair mall.'

'That's a trick of perspective,' said Stub. 'It's always present. It helps people steer through the layers of metaphor and imagery in the heavenly places. A lot quicker than using the Pengub. You'll get training.'

Up we went.

Finally, a steady point of light high in the sky, the colour of brass. As Henry the Pengub pulled, the light expanded, unfolded and became a tiny city, which grew.

I eased Henry out of the climb so that we approached the city almost horizontally. I picked out skyscrapers nestled together, basking in their own golden glow. The city rested on a cloud, pulled by a six-winged Pengub.

'I've never seen anything like this,' I said. 'Even with everything that's happened.'

Strange beasts flew round the city, flapping their great wings. Some of the skyscrapers were connected by high walkways. Vast, not made by humans, the city shone with its own quiet light, sliding across the sky like a cruise liner.

'Er... that's not where you want to go,' said Stub.

'It isn't?'

'I think that's an administration block.'

'Oh.'

'The *Diner* can't be far.' Stub was still scanning the sky. 'I'm sure they'll have put it somewhere nearby. There!' he said finally.

'That light there?'

'Yessir.'

We rose above the great city and flew on.

It's not easy to measure time in the heavenly places, since time passes at different rates depending on the neighbourhood. Even after we spotted the light, it was a long pull towards the *Diner* through the busy purple sky.

'Steer just so as you miss it, sir,' said Stub. 'The navigation light is swinging underneath the *Diner* itself.'

'OK.' I adjusted my path slightly. We passed the light, which was hanging down from the porridge-coloured clouds on which the *Shepherd Diner and Lido* rested. We came to the lip of the cloud; and over.

Henry, slowing now, flapped leisurely along the length of a low white wall, which was topped with terracotta tiles. We followed the wall until it enlarged into a two-storey building in the same white and terracotta. Friendly arches in this building gave glimpses into a garden and pool within. In front of the building was a pavement cafe, which offered a spectacular view of the high heavenlies.

The cafe was nearly empty. Seated at one of the tables, with a fresh smoothie in front of her, was Keziah. She wore her familiar black top and jeans. Her face was as white as ever, her hair as straight and black as ever, the eyeliner overdone as usual, the lips sulky. She did seem, though, slightly more relaxed than the Keziah I was used to.

We glided past. I waved. She appeared to sigh and I noticed green eyes watching me steadily.

'How do I park this thing?'

'Fly out, then approach the *Diner* head on,' said Stub, 'Get your Pengub nice and high, to keep out of the way. And *dead slow*.'

I still maintain that I *was* going dead slow and the bump was just what happens when two things with momentum meet. Hardly any chairs fell over. A bartender did poke her head out of the entrance to see what was happening, but she soon went away, after putting the chairs back up.

Keziah was standing up with smoothie splattered on her T-shirt.

I tied the wheel, left my pavilion, walked with Stub to my soul's edge, and stepped neatly onto the *Shepherd Diner and Lido*.

'Hello,' I said to Keziah.

'Thanks for this, Jamie,' she said, holding her T-shirt so the orange juice, passionfruit and mango didn't stick to her.

'Sorry.'

With a flick of thought, Keziah changed into identical clothes that were clean.

'Never mind.'

'Hey, where's Henry going?' I asked, seeing my pengub flapping away, towing my soul behind him.

'The *Diner* has its own Pengub, sir,' said Stub. 'Customers' pengubim enjoy swimming with her. Henry will be OK.'

'I see.' Then I said to Keziah. 'I hope I'm doing the right thing.'

'If you don't think you're doing the right thing, you shouldn't have come.'

'I'm just not totally sure what I'm letting myself in for.'

Keziah glared.

'Jamie.' She grabbed my shoulders and spun me around, so that I was looking out over the heavenlies, my feet overlapping the edge of the *Diner*. 'Look at it!'

'Ow,' I said.

'*Look at it*. Billions of souls. Down there, swimming in that soup, a soup they're blind to. I can see it. You can see it. Because of what we've been through. And up here, a team, friends. Jonah and Corrie Bright and Stub, and others. Turning the world upside down. Turning it the right way up. Replanting Eden.'

'Well, yes.'

'Not many people get to do this.'

'I suppose—'

'We live in the margins, Jamie. And it's what life is *for* Jamie. It's what life is *about*.'

'For you maybe.'

'No. For you too.'

'Perhaps.'

'Not perhaps. Not this time. Jamie, what *you are doing* is re-starting your sad, smug, hedonistic, self-obsessed life.'

'I am?'

'And to start with you might like to practice your steering, which is *lousy*.'

'Keziah,' I said, wriggling out of her grip, which was hurting, 'if we're talking about *driving* we might like to remember how we got here in the first place.'

'That was not a driving problem. It was a head problem. And it was a long time ago.'

'It was two months and three days ago.'

TWO MONTHS AND THREE DAYS
EARLIER

It began with a bonbon, just out of reach.

I admit it wasn't the most sensible thing I've ever done, stretching for this sugar-coated toffee while gunning the car at its whining maximum.

On the opposite carriageway traffic flowed towards Cambridge. A lone black Mini was flitting in and out of this line of traffic, heading for me, angry as a bluebottle.

I don't borrow my sister Lizzie's car often. Partly for the environment. Mostly because it's an eggshell, powered by a lawnmower engine, with sunflowers painted on the side.

Lizzie had snaffled all but one of the bonbons. Fingers scrabbling, I tried to manoeuvre the bag.

The oncoming Mini tucked itself safely behind a Polish container truck, *Zlotcwicvic Enngerrgrunden Transportowicz, Krakow*, I didn't catch the spelling.

The sun came out, low and directly behind me, lighting up the January slush.

I looked down quickly at the bag. The car clock, I noticed, just flipped over to 9:46.

Lizzie's flower-painted car whined.

A single bonbon.

I glanced up—to see a white-faced girl, in the black Mini, filling the windscreen.

My fingers touched icing sugar.

By the time *9:46* ended, the bang from the collision had travelled nearly thirteen miles. Our two cars had spun to a halt, horribly splayed across the carriageway. The Mini was upside down. My car was a twisted bale of metal in a muddy field, soon to start dripping with my blood. *Zlotcwicvic Enngerrgrunden Transportowicz, Krakow* was a mile away, rushing for the container port at Felixstowe and anonymity.

My spirit, calm as a balloon, was rising quietly above the crash site. Below I could glimpse the straight black hair and the scrawny figure of the Mini driver, her spirit also rising. Far below us, cars had stopped, traffic was backed up, people had emerged and were circling the wreckage.

I had no sense of anything.

It was silent up here. Minutes passed. As I watched, the traffic started tentatively to rearrange itself. An ambulance arrived. A cloud rolled over, blocking my view.

Above me in the greyness I glimpsed godlike beings in white Arran pullovers. Behind them in the sky was a tunnel.

For a second I felt a spasm of complete fear, the first thing I'd felt since the crash.

The godlike beings grabbed me—they had many arms, as well as sucky things like sink plungers—and threw me up the tunnel.

Things happened in that tunnel that I don't have words for. I was bumped about. I thought I heard some arguing, possibly a punch thrown. I was left on my own in the dark, for what seemed like hours. Then some more bumping and cursing, and finally, a soft blue light.

It didn't stay that way for more than a second, because that was how long it took to start thinking.

My first thought must have been *bacon sandwich* (I had entered the afterlife without breakfast) because one appeared in front of me.

It looked perfect: freshly sliced white bread, bacon grilled until it was not quite crisp. The bread looked like it had been swabbed in the fat and blood that had dripped out of the bacon. The sandwich was hanging in the air in front of me, oozing with contentment at being itself.

I examined this wondrous sandwich from all angles, and then sniffed it. Still perfect. I took a bite, and it was exactly as I expected, every note of taste in place.

I thought I'd try imagining some coffee—Costa Rican, freshly ground, steaming. It too winked into existence in front of me.

Not too shabby so far, I thought.

For my next course I created a quarter-pound of toffee bonbons in a white paper bag. These were, like the single one left far behind in Lizzie's mashed car, toffees boiled just enough to be soft, then dragged through a dust-bath of icing sugar. You can still buy bonbons like that in internet sweetshops—sometimes I included fun links in my client websites.

You need to put four bonbons in your mouth to get the full blessing, and I did, and after that I thought I might like another coffee.

OK, I concluded after several more experiments, *I am on my own in a faintly blue world. I have access to all my*

memories. And I can build with them. Perhaps this is what you
do when you are dead.

Four days later I was playing a cricket match—just
about to bowl England to victory, with several former
Prime Ministers calling out encouragement from the
stands—when a black Mini drove onto the pitch.

Black Minis had appeared fleetingly already,
horrible phantoms that seemed to conjure themselves up
just as I was falling asleep, but they were usually easy to
erase.

This Mini, however, was driving across the pitch
with a pointed disregard for the hallowed turf, the
legendary players, and the state of the match.

Behind the wheel was the pale-faced girl with dark
hair. The Mini stopped in front of me with a little lurch.

The girl climbed out of the Mini and walked over to
me. She was just below my height. She didn't have a
friendly face and was wearing too much eyeliner.

'Is this cricket or something?' she asked.

'Yes,' I replied.

'What a waste of time.'

'I was just about to bowl England to victory.'

'So you can reset it.'

'It took me all morning to get it to this point.'

'Stupid.' She stretched out her hand. 'I'm Keziah.'

'Hello Keziah.'

'I'm real.'

I took her to Osama's, which I had created the day
before on a tropical beach at the foot of a white cliff, just
outside Lord's Cricket Ground, not far from the
lighthouse where I made my home.

I decided to have Male Film Stars from the Golden Age of Movies as the hospitality team. (I thought I'd give the Brazilian Ladies' Olympic Beach Volleyball Squad the afternoon off.)

Gregory Peck took the order and Jimmy Stewart served it. I only wanted a snack so I had my usual two lamb murtabaks, washed down with coffee made with sweetened condensed milk. She had date and banana muffin, fresh fruit and coffee.

(The real Osama's, when it existed in an insalubrious but life-affirming corner of Cambridge, didn't do date and banana muffin. Imagine asking the Giant Surly Bread Chef for date and banana muffin. But this was my dream-world and Osama smoothed things over. Perhaps he sent Jimmy Stewart out to a bakery.)

Louis Armstrong and his Hot Fives were the band.

Keziah was dressed in black jeans, a black top and a leather jacket. We ate in silence. Sneaking a glance from my murtabak I couldn't decide whether she was sad or angry. She had full lips and a mouth that curved slightly downward. Dolphins seem to be smiling all the time: Keziah's normal expression, I decided, was sulky disapproval. She looked hard and aggressive and unfeminine and worn down. Skin wasn't great either. Nothing sparkled.

'Why didn't you swerve?' she asked abruptly.

'What?'

'You could've swerved off the road. I can't believe you didn't take evasive action.'

'Funnily enough I wasn't expecting somebody to jump out suicidally from behind a truck.'

'You should be ready for anything on the road.'

'How thoughtless of me.'

23

'You could have thought, *the sun's just come out, that driver can't see me.*'

'And *you* could've thought, *perhaps I shouldn't drive at high speed on the wrong side of the road into oncoming traffic.*'

'It takes two to crash.'

'Technically.'

'It was so stupid, you dying. You didn't need to.'

I put the murtabak down.

'Do you know, funnily enough, when we were sitting here, not talking, I thought to myself, *she might be wanting to say sorry.*'

'I just can't believe you were so *lax.*'

'She might be wanting to apologize. Just when my life was getting nicely warmed up. She might have the decency to put her hand up and say, *oops.*'

'That's what I am trying to do.'

'You're not doing it very well.'

'I didn't expect you to be so difficult.'

I tore off a large piece of murtabak, swabbed it around in the curry sauce, and folded it into my mouth.

'I am sorry you find me difficult,' I said.

'And I am sorry for the crash.'

'So am I.'

We ate in silence for some time.

'So this is what you've been doing since we died?' Keziah asked, looking round at the formica tables and red-tiled floor, with Osama himself smiling in the background and, behind the stainless steel counter, the Giant Surly Bread Chef cracking eggs with one hand and slopping and twirling the flat Afghan bread with the other.

'Any fool can be uncomfortable,' I replied. 'We might be here a long time. It's amazing what you can build out of your memories, don't you think?'

Keziah seemingly didn't think. 'Obviously I've mashed them up,' I continued. 'There isn't really an Osama's Afghan restaurant at the foot of a white cliff near Lord's Cricket Ground. There was an Osama's on Mill Road near where I live, but it's been taken over by ayurvedic Vegans.'

'I don't remember it.'

'Very bad Korma.'

'You haven't thought about what's happened to us? Or where we are?'

'No,' I said.

Green eyes surveyed my face like a building inspector weighing up a condemned bus-shelter.

'Pathetic.'

'My choice. What do you do by the way?'

'Before I was dead, I was a lawyer.'

'So things are on the up, then.'

She sighed. We then had that little interchange that's like two computers finding a shared comms protocol or perhaps two dogs sniffing bottoms in the park. We both had a home in Cambridge. I'm a web designer, running my own business, clearly a more bohemian character than a *lawyer*.

As lawyers went she was interesting, however. She defended people in magistrates' courts, specializing in the hopeless.

We explored all that and then the conversation fell away.

'Do you want to see my beach gadgets?' I asked.

'What?'

'Now you're here, you might as well see some of the stuff I've built.'

'No, I don't want to see your beach gadgets.'

25

I picked up the murtabak and then put it down again. 'My sister Lizzie says, and my ex-girlfriend Caroline confirms, that when guys want to talk they go and play with their toys. If they ever do talk, they find it easier in a garage somewhere when there's an engine spread all over the floor. For example. So that they always have something to change the subject to.'

'I see.'

'The quad bikes are out here.' We nodded to Osama and walked out onto the beach.

I'd spent half an hour engineering fine detail on this bike. I copied it with a moment's mental effort so we both had one, and we set off across the beach. I quietened the engines.

'So what have you been doing,' I asked, 'since the crash?' Keziah looked across at me, as if deciding momentarily whether to be honest or sarcastic.

'Trying not to drown in a sea of regret and rage.'

'I recommend fantasizing.'

'I'm not asking for advice. Don't offer it.'

'Sorry.'

'Have you found the HELP system?' Keziah asked.

'There's a HELP system? How does that work?'

'It's a set of questions and answers that you can personalize however you like.'

'I gotta try this.' I stopped the bike and copied a palm-roofed bar from one I'd built ten miles further down the beach. I considered. 'I think I'll have my HELP system as a bartender.' With a few deft thoughts I fashioned a small, Spanish-looking barman with a white apron and a stunning moustache, put him behind the bar, and went up to him.

'Red wine OK?' I asked Keziah.

'I've stopped.'

'Hm,' I said. 'Don't you think because you're dead and a million miles from home you might start again? It's not going to kill you, is it?'

'I'll have water with a hint of something. *Sin gaz.*'

'One glass of red wine, please Pablo, and one glass of non-fizzy water with a hint of... I dunno, lime, passionfruit and mango. Go steady with the passionfruit.'

I passed her the glass.

Thank you,' I said to Pablo. 'So you know everything?'

'You are too kind, *Señor.*'

'OK.' I took a deep breath. 'Let me start with a few simple ones: Where am I, Why am I here, and when will I leave?'

'OK Jamie.' (He pronounced it *Hymie* doing the Spanish throat-clearing thing) 'After the crash your spirits ejected from your bodies. You were seized by collectors, haggled over, bought, packaged again and transported to where you are now—'

'Which is?'

'You and the *Señorita* are in—'

'A cage,' said Keziah.

'Paradise,' corrected Pablo. 'The truth is, in here you have complete access to every thought or memory you have experienced. All the universe you ever knew is yours. You're freer than you ever were on earth, free to roam through a universe built from your memories.'

'But we can't leave,' Keziah pressed on.

Pablo the HELP system shrugged. 'What is leave? Where would you go? Outside this habitat the universe is hostile, washed with dangerous radiation. It burns. You would not last. In here is the world of your minds—

27

which was your whole universe before you left the earth
—and you can go anywhere.'

'One thing,' I said. 'Why are our memories so much
more vivid than they were on earth?'

'Because they are stored here,' said Pablo. 'Here, in
the heavenlies.'

'They weren't in my head, then?'

'Of course not, *Señor*. There was no room. No
room! Your brain was just the machinery for translating
true memories into chemical and electrical signals. Your
memories built up here, in the heavenlies. Now that you
have left your body, your spirit can experience them
directly.'

'Without having to port them onto a different
platform,' I said, understanding it now I could use a
computing metaphor. 'So where are they, these
memories?'

'They cruise through the heavenlies, *Señor*,' said
Pablo, 'like clumps of seaweed, pulled and pushed by
many influences. It doesn't matter where they are. Your
spirit has perfect access to them because they are your
memories, bound to you by Life.'

'Wild,' I said. 'And how did we get here? Does this
happen to everyone?'

'Certainly not! It is a privilege. You and the *Señorita*
now belong to two spirit beings who care for you and
have a wonderful plan for your ongoing death. If you
listen to them and obey, all will be well. If not...' He
shrugged a Latin shrug.

'And what do these spirit beings get out of this?'
asked Keziah.

Pablo put the glass down and raised himself to his
full height, which wasn't very high.

28

'There are still parts of the universe, *Señorita*, where some beings find fulfilment from caring for other beings. You should be glad that you have arrived in such a place.'

'I see.'

'Why can't we see them?' I asked. 'These spirits?'

'All in good time, *Señor*. They are busy and important spirits. They want you to make yourselves comfortable first. Before the training starts.'

'The training?'

'It's mild and pleasurable.'

'So how long do we stay here,' I asked. 'In all?'

'How long?' asked Pablo. 'Given the alternative, *Señor*, I would stay as long as possible.'

I digested this.

'So correct me if I'm wrong. Keziah and I are trapped in this cage forever, with only our memories and each other for the rest of time? We are also due for—training—by the spirits who have captured us.'

'That's an unfortunate way of putting it, *Señor*. All you need for happiness is here.'

'In that case I'd like a large bowl of salted cashew nuts.'

'Why cashew nuts?' asked Keziah.

'Because I like cashew nuts. Would you like one?'

'Nuts from a bar?' said Keziah. 'Are you kidding?'

'Let's go.'

I snatched the glass bowl of nuts.

'In the last few days,' I asked, placing a cashew on my tongue and sucking off the salt, 'have you ever thought about what's happened, and felt a blanket of gloom descending on you?'

'Durr, Jamie.'

29

'Well I don't do blankets of gloom.' We walked away, back to our quads. 'Goodbye, Pablo!' I called. Then I whistled to the sky, and called, 'Come on then!

'I built this yesterday,' I told Keziah.

Seconds later, a B-2 Stealth Bomber appeared low over the horizon. Its shadow flicked over our heads. The bomber released a precision-guided weapon which dropped deep into the thatched roof of Pablo's bar.

It exploded with a blast that warmed our faces and bent some distant palm trees.

We watched the rubble and palm-thatch fall.

'Happiness,' I said.

'I'll see you around, then,' replied Keziah, revving up the quad.

'Where are you going?' I asked.

'Home.'

'How do you do that?'

'I drive to the edge of the world you've created, fly across the intervening ether, and park on my world.' She twisted the throttle and buzzed away.

I reclined in my male-ish white leather armchair, the one with the footrest, the inbuilt magazine rack and the drinks holder. The log fire, spitting and crackling, lit up the white-painted walls of my lighthouse.

Tucked onto the nearby sofa, reading a novel, was Caroline. It had only been a matter of time.

'That armchair is totally gross,' she said.

'You don't think it goes with the lighthouse?'

'It doesn't go with anything.'

It's true, at the time of the crash I was not Caroline's official boyfriend due to some inexplicable girl thing she had been going through. I hadn't seen much of her for some weeks before the accident. But in memory of eighteen happy months of dating, I'd created her from my memories, along with the armchair that both she and my sister Lizzie had prohibited me from buying, my 1970s-retro lava lamp, and my collection of Laptops I Have Loved.

Next to the door was a nacho-and-dips dispenser that I'd lashed together from recollections of vending machines.

'Caroline,' I said. 'Could you help me make some notes?' She was taller than me, thin, glasses, curly yellow hair. Long flowery skirt today—she was given to drastic changes of clothes and image. She was, however, consistently earnest and strict and clumsy and entirely lovely.

'I'm not your personal slave you know,' she sniffed.

'I know, I know. I just thought, *possibly*, here am I, dead... all alone... needing a helping hand... and I thought, who better—'

Caroline sighed. 'Just get on with it.'

'Is that enough grovelling?'

'For the time being.'

'OK. Stardate 04 01 01—no, don't tut, Caroline, tutting is a bad habit—I need some way of keeping track of the passing days, and the Star Trek system is out there. I think I've been here about four days. Which makes it Stardate 04 01 01. Who knows how long I've been here really or what time it is on Earth.

'Positive things:

'1. Despite being killed in a crash, I am well.

'2. It has been fun creating a new world—including you Caroline—and I can look forward to more of this.

'Negative things:

'1. I am sharing a cage with just one other living soul, and she has issues.

'2. I haven't met our mystery owners and I have absolutely no idea what they plan to do with us.

'3. Gloom and depression threaten to fall on me at any moment.'

'Do you want a view on that?' Caroline looked up from her notebook. She had a bookish primness and I'd long thought she needed to be unprimmed (or perhaps, de-primmed). I had, however, never quite managed the needful ravishing.

'No I do not,' I said.

'You should go see Keziah again,' she said.

'Why?'

'Because there's only two of you and you need each other.'

'But I've got you, Caroline.'

'For one thing, you haven't *got* me, and for another, the me that you've cut-and-pasted together is an anaemic hotch-potch of your memories and fantasies.'

'You are?'

'Believe me.'

'You can still be pretty withering.'

'Nothing like the real thing.'

I considered this.

'You couldn't by any chance wash up the mugs?'

'Jamie, even if I'm a figment of your imagination, I'm not putting up with you being chauvinistic, self-absorbed and bone idle.'

Perhaps I've recreated you too well, I thought.

'I heard that,' said Caroline.

'All right, I'll do the mugs,' I said. 'Perhaps you could add a note to the log. "Even in the privacy of my own private head, figments of my imagination are getting at me." That's another one under negatives.'

'The point is—' said Caroline.

'Sorry.' I said. 'Sorry sorry sorry.'

You could, I found, hold yourself together pretty well through the days. But my spirit was somehow still locked in a sleep-and-wake cycle, and the evenings were tricky. At any moment a recreated Mini might appear from the depths of my memory, heading for my head. This wasn't Keziah paying a visit; it was just the bad memories rolling around.

Even when Slumber finally did his stuff, sleep was tricky too. I wasn't in control. My unconscious spirit seemed to kick around among mental debris like a bored teenager. Then—also like a bored teenager—I always seemed to end up hanging around the same place, a holiday resort covered by a large Dome. It was pleasant enough—it seemed to hold all my happiest memories—but puzzling.

The following day—I'd spent the morning gliding the Space Shuttle into Edwards Airforce Base, one-handed, while eating a Thai Red Curry—I thought I'd visit Keziah. The Space Shuttle seemed overkill for crossing the small gap between our worlds, so I built a small biplane and buzzed off from Edwards.

Soon after I left my landscape, Keziah's cloud-covered world came into view against the soft blue. I slowed the plane, enjoying the cloud-surfing.

I emerged from the clouds into a storm and a battlefield. Water was sluicing from the sky. But even through the curtains of rain I could see this wasn't a coherent landscape. Everything was the wrong size. Bits of cities. Giant syringes and razor blades. Big greyish blobs like fish eggs, that contained huge people-shapes haranguing each other. Several gallows. Lizzie's car. Everything was swaying up and down and jostling against everything else, as if were part of an ocean.

Bonfires burned. Each bonfire had a person on it: sometimes an old man, sometimes a middle-aged woman, sometimes a version of Keziah herself.

I did fly over a couple of parks—in one I saw a very young version of Keziah being carried giggling on someone's shoulders, perhaps her dad—but that only served to make the jumble look lonelier than ever.

I quickly decided I was not going to land and declare myself willing to be offered a drink and a little snack (which had been Plan A). I was going to get out as fast as possible and hope Keziah never noticed I'd come.

I swung the plane around to head for home and caught a glimpse of a building like a temporary office alone in a parking lot. It was defended by high fencing, floodlights, dogs and barbed wire.

My quad bike was parked next to the building. As I flew by, I thought I glimpsed Keziah at the window, working at a desk. I saw her get up, perhaps disturbed by the clatter of the plane, and she looked out of the door.

It seemed best to circle the plane, smile and wave.

The plane was quite noisy, so I didn't catch all the swearwords, but I got a general impression.

Some hours later, I was part way through writing Keziah a letter—going through several drafts, because I didn't know what to say—when I heard a banging on the door. Since my lighthouse is a few hundred metres offshore, built on rocks, accessible only by rowing boat in calm seas, this was a surprise.

'Who is it?' I asked.

'Funny.'

I turned the wrought iron latch in the wooden door, got a brief glimpse of rocks, tossing foam and seagulls, and ushered Keziah in. She was windswept and wearing an oilskin.

We looked at each other for a moment.

'You look like you need some chocolate.' I magicked a blue-and-white striped mug of hot cocoa. 'Marshmallows and whipped cream?' She accepted this silently. 'I'll leave a bar of chocolate here, if you need it,' I said, placing a 400g bar of the darkest stuff on the wooden table.

Rain was dripping off Keziah and her hard expression had not moved. 'My sisters always liked chocolate,' I said lamely.

'House rules,' she said icily, sitting down. 'Never come to my place uninvited.'

'OK.'

'It's private.'

'Absolutely.'

'And personal.'

'Fine.'

'And I haven't got round to sorting—'

'Fine. Sorry. *Sorry*. But *you* of course come to my place—'

'Yours is clearly a fantasy playground. And we needed to make contact.' She snapped off one row of chocolate, broke it into three, and put one piece in. Not that it seemed to be lightening her mood.

Neither did the next two pieces. Keziah, I thought parenthetically, must be one of those skinny people who can mainline on sugar and fat and never change shape. Me, I only have to look at three onion bhajis, a meat biriani, a chicken dhansak, a portion of rice and some

naan bread and I put on weight. 'My thoughts are still...
jumbled,' she went on.

'It's interesting the way you were in an office,' I said.

'I had some paperwork to finish.'

'I see. And the people burning to death outside—'

Keziah snapped off another row of chocolate and
looked at me, green eyes defiant.

'The paperwork was the cases I was working on
before I died. I wanted to put my mind to rest about
them.'

'Fine,' I said, hastily. 'Good idea. Look, all I wanted
was maybe set up some system so that we could
communicate without intruding on each other.'

'That's what I came over to say,' said Keziah.

'I had this idea,' I said. 'I made some mobile
phones. I'm not sure how they work, but they do work.' I
passed one across the table. 'They don't need charging.
We can fix up times and places to talk.'

'All right,' said Keziah, picking up the phone.

'Also, I've been making a library of my books and
music. I created my friend Caroline, who's a librarian.
She's putting them in order. If you want to borrow any of
them.'

'Thank you,' rising to go.

'It might take your mind off things.'

'It won't.'

'I'll contact you. We'll have a meal or something.
Take the chocolate. How are you going to get home?'

'I'll walk.'

'Across the water?'

'And across the ether. If you want, you can hover a
few inches off the ground.'

'Hmm.' I thought for a moment, then checked my ship's brass chronometer. 'Not so easy. I've booked a force 19 hurricane in a few minutes.'

'Can't you delay it?'

'Not without reprogramming. I've got a better idea.' I opened the door on a world of tossing sea and screaming wuffs of wind. 'Oh Dumbo...'

A wave crashed against the rocks at the base of the lighthouse, spotting the air with salt and dampness.

Dumbo the elephant flapped into view, wafting his big ear wings, steady in the air despite the gale. He stretched down his trunk, hugged her with it, and lifted her gently onto his back.

'Bit more fun,' I said.

Keziah appeared to be bearing this wearily.

'Jamie,' she called down as Dumbo rose into the sky and the wind gusted. 'Have you talked to the HELP recently?'

'Isn't he a bit damaged?' I called up.

'Mine isn't,' she called down.

'No, I haven't.'

'Tomorrow.' Keziah's voice was indistinct across the moan of the storm.

'What about tomorrow?'

'Induction Day.'

Induction Day

An uncomfortable night. A few random dreams. But inevitably back inside the enigmatic Dome.

This time I was lying on a poolside sun lounger. Caroline was next to me, reading a novel, but generously allowing our feet casually to brush against each other. Fountains splashed into the pool.

The place wasn't busy, and everyone I could see was a friend: Caroline's house-mates, the guys from the pub quiz team, old mates from college and clients from work.

My blonde-stereotype sister Lizzy was wearing a black bikini tied on with fragile-looking bows. She was tossing a ball around the pool along with three Computer Studies guys from college. They were almost limp with unquenched lust. From the anxious looks on their faces I guessed they were wishing they had mobile internet access sewn into their beachwear so that they could secretly google Witty Things to Say to Girls.

It was all perfect, except for the sense that something deadly was lurking outside the Dome.

I clambered off the sunlounger and inspected the edge of the Dome. Outside it looked like November, dank and grey. An evil-looking rain, yellow-tinged and sticky, was dropping steadily from the sky, splattering against the glass like bird-lime.

Rubbish was piled outside. As I focussed my eyes in the greyness, I wondered if shapes were moving among the heaps.

This Dome looked like the last bright place in the world. I walked round its entire edge and the view hardly changed: hills of rubbish on the outside and the lurking sense of danger, just out of sight.

All I could think was, *they're not getting in. I'm not letting them in.*

I was completely disoriented when I did wake up in some kind of holiday resort the next morning.

This wasn't the Dome of my nightmare, happily, but nor was it anywhere I ever remembered. I watched dark green palm trees sway against a bright sky. I sensed, rather than felt, a female presence next to me.

I glanced out of the corner of one eye and saw in a moment of terror that the female was Keziah, sleeping in a bikini. With skin as chalk-white as hers, not a great choice, I thought.

We were at the side of a swimming pool.

In panic I looked down at my own body: a thong. Somewhere down there, nestled amid my gentle and congenial contours—so reminiscent of the Yorkshire Dales—a thong.

A further shock: my arm had a tattoo, a heart with the initial J in one corner and K in the other. Little turtle doves were flying round the heart.

At that moment Keziah also opened her eyes. She blinked, rolled over, puzzled for a second.

'O Keziah,' I said.

Keziah sat up. 'Completely not funny,' she snarled, looking down at herself.

'I'm sorry?'

'Jamie. What are you doing?'

'What am *I* doing?'

She looked around 'This is the *Hotel Splendide*! You've been messing around in my head!'

'I haven't done anything!'

'And find a towel or something. You look disgusting.'

'Look—'

She herself had summoned into being a piece of African cloth, which she was busy folding around herself.

'Over there,' she pointed. 'In the changing room.'

I jumped up and trod over the 1930s rose-and-white concrete slabs, which were hot to the touch.

'It's locked.' I rattled the changing-room door. No, not locked. Not even real. Just a piece of stage scenery, a fake changing room.

'Can't you magic up a towel?' she called over.

'Give me a minute to concentrate,' I said. 'I'm not having a good morning.'

'Honestly Jamie,' she said, finishing tucking in the African cloth with one hand and with the other holding out a pink bath towel that she had just imagined into being.

I trudged back and took it off her.

'Thank you,' I said.

'Jamie!' she said. Not with an ellipsis, indicating entreaty (*'Jamie...'*). It was a 'Jamie!' with an exclamation mark, wielded like a baseball bat. 'This is a precious' (*thwack*) 'place' (*thwack*) 'of memory' (*thwack*) 'for me—'

'It's not his world,' interrupted a voice. 'It's mine... and I bring peace.'

A tallish, erect man of late-sixties in appearance (late-sixties both in age and in the last time his clothes were fashionable) was walking across the swimming pool. He wore jeans, an open-necked shirt and a ponytail. The twist of fabric in his ponytail was a scrap of the same flowery material as his shirt. An earstud gleamed. His skin was the shade of orange that says on the packet *Burnished Bronze*, but looks and smells like Extra Value Fake Tan. The stuff was thicker in his wrinkles. His feet, curiously, were on backwards, the heels pointing towards us.

'Peace!' He said again, splashing over the swimming pool. 'Peace from you to me. My peace to you. Hello and welcome to Paradise.'

'This is the *Hotel Splendide*,' said Keziah, sullenly.

'... Where you used to come with your dad. I retrieved it from your memories. A little taste of Paradise. Also a unique example of French West African modernist colonial architecture.'

He reached the side of the pool and stepped out. He kept trying to twist his feet the right way round, but they wouldn't go.

He looked Keziah and me slowly up and down. 'I see you're not ready for the full beauty of the human form. Shame.' He pointed at our swim things which glowed slightly, and then turned into our normal clothes. 'I am your god! One of them, anyway.'

The tattoo disappeared as well, thank goodness.

'Hello,' said Keziah.

'Hello,' said I.

We stood around awkwardly. He had a glittery look in his eyes and I thought he was going to put his arms around us. 'You can call me the Lord.'

'The Lord?'

'Convention,' he said. 'Also recognition of genius. I'm the Lord. You're my people. May as well start off on that footing, loosen up later.'

'What if we don't?' asked Keziah.

'Ah. Outside your habitat'—he waved vaguely—'is a boiling mass of hot yellow rain that rots you down. Bones into glue, that sort of thing. And out there are evil spirits who will enjoy sucking out your life as you twist and turn in pain. Some of them are artists which is something. But most of them, just brutal. No class. We've saved you from that.'

'Why have you messed around in my memories?' asked Keziah.

'To make you feel at home. The *Hotel Splendide* has fond memories for you, Keziah. Jamie likes swimming pools. I built a place for you to become friends. Paradise. It connects your two worlds. I built it in your sleep. Your world is over there,' (he pointed to a door marked GIRLS in the wall) 'and yours, Jamie, is on the other side.' I noted a door marked BOYS. 'I expect this is where you will spend most of your time. We're going to extend it together. Your Eden.

'My partner and I will help you. He's called Gaston but is happy to be known as the Overlord.'

Keziah looked him up and down.

'No thanks,' she said.

The Lord glared at her.

'What do you mean, *no thanks?*'

'What do I mean? Go away, leave me alone. I'd rather be dead. That sort of no thanks.'

The Lord seemed to have an unfathomable expression on his face. It might have been shock. Eventually he spluttered,

'This is Paradise! This is *your idea* of Paradise! I fetched it myself from your memories. Hurt me too. Look at these burns here on my arms and legs.'

'I don't do *lecherous old men*,' said Keziah, steadily, planting herself right in his personal space.

'No?' asked the Lord.

'No.'

'I can end this *right now*,' spat the Lord, twitching slightly as if about to sprout a claw. 'One snap of my fingers. One snap. You impossible little cow. One flick of my head and you're out in the yellow rain. Out there—' he pointed vaguely to the sky—'You'll beg to die and you won't be able to.'

Keziah didn't take her stare away from him, and stepped closer.

'Do it then. I don't care.'

Expressions were chasing themselves across the Lord's face like shadows across a hillside on a windy day.

'I might,' he said eventually. 'I really might. The fact is *young lady*, my partner and I understand you've been under stress, and that you may say things you regret, and so we're going to make allowances. You might like to think things over.' As he finished the sentence he reached out, picked up Keziah by the scruff of the neck, walked to the girls' side of the pool and tossed her over the wall. I heard a crumpled landing, followed by a curse.

He looked over the wall for a few seconds, then turned to me. A smile was stuck on his face. It looked like one he'd got out of a book.

'Jamie,' he walked towards me, still with the rented smile. 'She certainly has spirit. I'm sure I can talk sense with you.'

I gulped.

'*Me?*' I said. 'Erm—yeah. I'm open. You know. I—I —I'm obviously grateful that you... rescued us. Yeah. You have to have an open mind.'

'Excellent,' said the Lord. 'Open mind. Very good.'

'What will it involve?' I asked.

'Happiness. The adventure of your lives. Your dreams coming true.' His smile was still hanging on his face, like he'd forgotten to move it. 'However. We weren't expecting all that trouble from *Madam* over there. I think —um—my partner and I will reveal ourselves to you further in due course. Visit us tomorrow morning, after breakfast. Here in Paradise.'

Then a cloud came—a bit oily, like an exhaust fume —and hid him from my sight.

I watched him disappear, then called over the wall to Keziah. 'Are you OK over there? Would you like a drink?'

I heard a curse.

'I'll take that as a no,' I said.

Back in my side of the habitat, with the care of one doing an oil painting, I recreated the River Cam, Cambridge's compact little river, complete with one of those flat-bottomed boats called *punts* on which generations of students and tourists have propelled themselves using a pole to push against the riverbed. Punting has long been the best way to waste an afternoon, see the sights, drink wine and flirt with girls. I sat with the reconstituted Caroline while her house-mate Mel stood barefoot on the back of the boat. Mel was a sturdy, athletic girl, a secondary school games teacher, a bit dim, whom I'd also called into being. Her painted toenails were slightly chipped, as is the way with hockey players. She pushed the pole against the riverbed and we slid along.

I'd done the picnic. Caroline's idea of a picnic involved salad, prawns, tiny sandwiches with the crusts cut off and obscure upper class things called 'devils on horseback'—not your authentic English cuisine: pies, nachos, dip, samosas and bhajis.

'Do you think being a pet is a bad thing?' I asked her.

'It would be if *you* owned it,' replied Caroline, rummaging in the hamper.

'If we could for once,' I suggested, 'not turn every conversation onto my failings, I might enjoy the change.'

'But you're such an easy target,' said Caroline.

'I'm trying to work something out,' I said. Mel poled us under the stone Trinity College footbridge, and we became echoey for a moment. 'If creatures more powerful than us wanted a human being—me, say—as a pet, which I think is what is happening, and offered to look after me very well, so that I was happy, should I say yes?'

'I'd say they were mad,' said Caroline, who had been horsey in her youth, and like many well-bred English girls, seemed to have a touch of *equus* in her ancestry. 'Think of the mucking out.'

'Assume that was taken care of.'

'A big assumption.'

'Assume it anyway.'

'I can see it would probably suit you,' said Caroline, disapprovingly. 'Fodder. Sleep.'

We glided under another bridge, Mel choosing the middle span to avoid hitting her head.

'I am dead,' I protested. 'What choice do I have?'

Caroline found what she was looking for. 'Ah, a tomato. How good of you to think of me.'

'I'm dead and beings out there are bigger than me. What else can I do?'

'You could put up a fight, like Keziah is doing.'

'I get the feeling they will win.'

'She stood up to them.'

'Not really. As far as I can see, she was just being herself. She treats everyone the same way. Say hello, bite their head off.'

'No,' said Caroline, thoughtfully. 'She gave them the chance to get rid of her, and they didn't. That's a win.'

'I think they were being patient.'

'Perhaps they were bluffing. Perhaps they need her for something. Perhaps they even need *you*.'

'Hard to see what for,' I said. The girls both nodded thoughtfully. Mel poled us towards the Mathematical Bridge on the Cam, where you have to turn the punt. 'They may want to show me as a prime specimen of a human male,' I said. 'I could understand that.'

Very late that evening, I was watching the fire in my lighthouse lounge. Caroline had gone to bed (she still insisted on her own room; even I couldn't believe in a Caroline who would alter the habits of a lifetime). I was concentrating on the fire and the turn of the lighthouse-beam.

'*Jamie.*'

The shock of hearing my name in an empty room made the hairs on my arm stand on end.

'Lizzie!' I said, looking round.

'*Jamie…* ' The room was empty.

'Great,' I said aloud. 'Now I'm hearing voices.'

'*Jamie, what have you done?*' At the sound of her voice, my carefully constructed world flickered out, then flicked back, like a candle-flame in a gust.

'Lizzie!'

Spooked, I walked through the lighthouse—up to the light, outside and around the balcony, back inside, all the way down to the kitchen, out of the door. Silvery moon, calm sea. No Lizzie. I returned inside and took some slow breaths.

I cut a slice of fruitcake from my pantry and took a chunk of Wensleydale cheese from the fridge. Then I climbed the stairs back to the lounge, banked the fire, and fired up a movie. Somewhere part through *Blade Runner* I managed to swap my waking world for my sleeping one, without hearing any more voices. But I did, of course, return to the mysterious Dome.

And somebody was still trying to get in. I looked up and scanned the top of the Dome for any weaknesses. Then I started to pace again slowly round the edge.

Other things being equal, this Dome was a resort you'd never want to leave. Perhaps my subconscious was trying to create a Paradise of my own. In which case, many thanks, subconscious. But something *was trying to get in*.

I was now sure that people were moving among the piles of rubbish outside the Dome. Worse, they were people I'd spent my life avoiding: the air-headed, the boastful, the in-your-face, the stupid, the depressed, the anxious, the neurotic, the boring and the mad.

Halfway round the Dome I found a leak. This was new. The noxious yellow rainwater that fell against the Dome was seeping in. A trickle ran all the way into the pool. None of my friends were looking out for this. With a quick thought, I created a roll of duct tape and carefully taped over the crack in the floor. Then a second time, then a third and a fourth.

I was wondering whether I shouldn't create some concrete and pour it round the Dome as an extra seal, when I noticed a bulge in the duct tape. A knife-blade poked through, then sliced back and forth.

I watched it move.

I'm not letting them in. I imagined two high voltage wires, one in each of my hands. Crouching down, I touched the knife with them. I heard a crack, then one of those humming-power-station noises.

A cadaverous figure scrambled up and looked at me through the glass of the Dome, clutching his hand. He was over seven feet high, heroin-addict gaunt and wearing a Sam Spade raincoat and hat. The little I could see of his face was white and streaked with welts. The eyes were hollow and glowed a dull red.

'No!' I said, even though I knew he couldn't hear me because of the Dome. 'No! You're not getting in!' I called out of my mind a concrete mixer and started pouring concrete over my duct tape.

I vaguely noted that I was being quite reckless. Being terrified helped, as did being separated from the ghoul by a concrete wall and thick glass. The ghoul didn't seem to know what to do.

I slopped concrete over the leak and willed it to solidify.

The ghoul glared in frustration. 'Go away!' I mouthed.

He let his hands fall back by his side, looked at me for a further second, then scrambled over the rubbish and out of sight.

I re-lined the whole Dome complex with my concrete. I saw this wasn't the first time repairs had been made. This place had been patched up often.

Around me, the funfair wheels turned, the fountains spurted, the wave machine stirred the pool and my friends screamed and bellowed. A rock anthem filled the air: someone had found the juke box. I returned to the lounger. My hands were still shaking.

When I woke up, I had breakfast, left my lighthouse, gingerly stepped back into the *Hotel Splendide*—in swimming things of my own choosing this time—and chose a deckchair, ready to meet the Lord.

I took one of my favourite books, that 600-page epic *Total Javascript*, one of my favourite books, containing absolutely no ghouls, no car crashes, no nightmares. Blessed, blessed computer manuals. I was engrossed until I heard a cough.

'Oh hello,' I said, shutting the book. The Lord was standing in front of me. Next to him was a short, bulky figure with a brown suit and a bristling moustache. He looked like one of those ancient pedigrees of pig that were bred to produce candle tallow.

'Jamie!' this one barked, looking me up and down. 'Name's Gaston. CEO, chief dealmaker. You can call me the Overlord.'

'Er—thank you,' I said.

'Need a little chat.' I think Gaston meant this as a fatherly whisper, but it came out like the thunder of those bull elephant seals that the BBC likes to film in the Weddell Sea and show in lush documentaries on Sunday nights.

He ushered me to the middle of three deckchairs set in a kind of arc at the poolside, with a table of nibbles and drinks in front of us. My deckchair was midway between upright and reclining, so I had to shuffle into it. With Gaston clambering into his deckchair next to me, I felt there were chins and folds of skin everywhere.

'Leopold. Do your stuff,' said Gaston the Overlord.

'Jamie,' said the Lord, also known apparently as Leopold, 'what do you know about nuclear physics?' He was sitting on the edge of his deckchair, looking keenly at me.

'What?' I said. 'I—er—the maths was a blur. I've read bits.'

'Your scientists know about a Universe filled with matter and energy. That's only part of it. If you're going to include everything (we call it the Omniverse), you have to include all the spirits—a whole other creation. Fortunately, nuclear physics is a good guide. Atomic particles and eternal spirits have a lot in common.'

'OK,' I said.

'This isn't the place to go into detail,' put in Gaston.

'I was merely outlining the general principles,' said Leopold, a little testily.

I was having to swivel my head from one to the other. It was like watching a tennis match.

'Jamie,' continued Leopold, 'the things that make up atoms last forever. So do the things that make up spirits. Atoms bounce off each other. Spirits also bounce off each other. Matter and spirits, of course, don't bounce off each other. They pass through each other.

'The Overlord and I are spirits—godlike spirits. Inside your body when you were alive was a human spirit. That's the part that's really you; the part that has survived death.

'Humans, of course, don't know much about the spiritual world because you spend all your days in the

51

material world. We, however, do live in a spiritual world, so we can help you. Is that clear?'

'Fair enough,' I said.

'If your friend Keziah had listened to us, she wouldn't have wasted a day and set us all back in your programme,' grumbled Gaston.

'I'm coming to that,' said Leopold. 'Now, Jamie. What do you think you lack? Most of all?'

'It would be nice not to be dead.'

'Irrelevant.'

'I miss my ex-girlfriend a bit. I was trying to get my web-maintenance contract with the hospital renewed. And my favourite Afghan restaurant has shut down.'

The Lord and the Overlord looked at each other. The Lord continued.

'These are all examples of a general principle. Think what all humans lack. What is the cry of the human heart from birth to death and beyond?'

'It's difficult when I'm put on the spot like this. Not curry, I suppose.' I said. 'Obviously not. Could you give me the first letter?'

'Happiness,' snapped the Lord.

'Right!' I said. 'Happiness. Of course. Happiness.'

'Moments of happiness,' said the Lord, 'exist as tiny sub-spiritual particles. Like the neutrino in physics, they're essential to the universe. Like the neutrino, moments of happiness barely interact with anything. They're elusive. They slip through your fingers. That's cruel irony, since all spirits need them. All spirits yearn for them.'

'I didn't know you were going into all this detail,' muttered Gaston. 'I think you just might be confusing him.'

'We haven't confused him. It's an essential part of the teaching,' insisted the Lord. 'Are you confused, Jamie?'

'Erm,' I said. 'It's beginning to come clear. I—obviously...'

'You see, he understands it perfectly. Every spirit needs Happiness. But Happiness is rare. What strikes you about your Western culture?'

'It's unhappy?' I guessed. I didn't believe this myself, but you know how it is when a teacher is in full flow. You just go with it.

'Exactly!' said the Lord. 'For all that everyone is surrounded by things that genuinely promise happiness, there's a poor return. That great concert doesn't quite deliver. That new thing you buy, disappoints. That meal leaves you feeling fat rather than fulfilled. You sit around and think, "Am I the only one feeling this way, pretending a happiness I don't feel?" You aren't.

'Yet you're on the right lines. You need to improve things a bit—extract more happiness from the opportunities around you. Squeeze more value out. Up your percentage of happy moments. Which is where we come in.

'There's something else that you may not have noticed. *No spirit beings*. Aw, you have people dabbling in horoscopes. You have people hugging trees and wearing crystals, but it's all fringe. They don't know what they're doing. They wouldn't know a spirit guide if he appeared in front of them and breathed on bread and made toast. It's one of the tragedies of Western cultures over the past 300 years that you've ditched the spirits. You abandoned formal religion, fair enough, had its day, but you chucked out the baby with the bathwater. Out went the spirits. Out went Happiness.'

I began to think there was a flaw here but I couldn't put my finger on it. 'So how,' the Lord went on, 'do you find Happiness?'

'You could earn money if you knew that,' I said.

'I intend to,' rasped Gaston.

'Get back to following the spirits,' whispered the Lord, leaning forward, his mouth closer to my ear than I would have preferred. 'Why? Because the spirits know. Billions of years surfing through space. We see interactions between Happiness and spirits. We show you how. We add value. We improve your odds. Every little helps.'

He looked pleased with this. 'It's an art though,' he added. 'Not certain. Still mysterious. Nevertheless. Do what we say—and you get happier.'

'OK,' I said, not knowing what else to say.

'Do you believe it?' asked the Lord.

'Er—yeah,' I said shrugging. 'Yeah. OK.'

'You see,' said the Lord to the Overlord. 'You simply have to lay it out. I told you he'd get it. Anyway,' he turned back to me. 'You'll be wondering what your first instruction is.'

'Will I?'

'It isn't good for man to be alone,' barked Gaston. 'That's it.'

'Look,' snapped the Lord. 'Who's doing this? You or I?'

'Time management,' insisted Gaston. 'Get to the point.'

'I am coming to the point,' said the Lord with dignity. 'Not everything is about efficiency. Relationship isn't about efficiency. Jamie, *spirits need to be in community*. Like subatomic particles. Humanness is manifested in pairs. It's not good for man to be alone. We made sure we put two of you together in this habitat. It cost us quite a bit. Jamie, you have to get Keziah on board.'

'I what?'

'You and Keziah need to follow us together. As a single spirit on your own you might as well not bother. You have to get into a relationship with her before we can do much with you.'

'I think that might be impossible,' I said.

'I don't see why,' said the Lord. 'Male spirit/female spirit; proton/electron. What's hard about that?'

'You've had plenty of time,' harrumphed Gaston.

'*Time!*'

'Yes,' said the Lord. 'There was pressure to speed things up, even from the Overlord here, but I thought, no, they'll have transplantation shock to overcome, then they need to find their way around the habitat, and I hope they'll find each other. "We just have to be patient," I said to myself.'

'We gave you six full days,' said Gaston. 'Six full days, everything you wanted. The whole world of your minds to explore. This wonderful safe habitat. Six days, no return on our investment.'

'You didn't seem to manage that,' said the Lord. 'So we gave you a bit of help. Do you like Paradise? The swimming pool here? I designed all that. Her memories; your desires; a romantic setting. There you were, next to each other on sunloungers. Somehow you managed to mess even that up.'

I was aware of my jaw going up and down and no sounds coming out.

'These things might be a bit more subtle than that,' I protested. 'You expected... I mean *good grief...*'

'We manage,' said the Lord with a glance at the Overlord. 'The Overlord and I. And we're much more incompatible. Aren't we?'

'The point is,' said the Overlord, 'we can't keep faffing around. You have to sort it out between you and Keziah, or the whole thing won't work.'

'That's the end of the lesson,' added Gaston. 'We need the cloud, Leopold.'

A cloud enveloped them. 'I hope that will get things back on track,' I heard Gaston the Overlord mutter before his voice was gone.

'They can totally stuff that idea,' I said to Caroline. It was the afternoon of the same day. I was shooting clay elephants on a grouse moor. Mel was firing off the clay elephants using a trebuchet and I was blasting them out of the sky with rocket-propelled grenades. When they blew up, *whamsplat*, I had them dissolve into a firework display.

'There's relationships and relationships,' said Caroline, who was wearing outdoor-girl shorts, hiking boots, and pink thermal layers.

'Caroline. Please don't be so free with the R word. I've spoken to you about this before.'

'Don't be infantile,' she replied, not passing me an RPG to better make her point, and pushing her glasses back up her nose. She'd be a lot better with contact lenses. 'It's ridiculous for you and Keziah to be sitting at the opposite sides of your cage and both sulking.'

We heard the *yoink* of the trebuchet and watched a clay elephant trace out a parabola over our heads. Mel was a hardworking girl who liked the simple tasks.

'Your point?'

'You might as well be friends. You might as well work together.' The rain and wind was flicking at Caroline's hair and she brushed it out of her face.

'It wasn't my fault that we're not.'

'That's arguable.'

'I was just being me. I am what I am. She's the one who's insufferable.'

'Really.'

'Anyway that's just what Gaston and the Lord—*Leopold*—want us to do, be friends. It's playing into their hands!'

'Which is why they won't stop you.'

'Mel!—would you stop sending these things over for a minute? That one nearly took my head out.'

'Sorry,' shouted Mel cheerfully from behind the trebuchet.

'Call her up,' said Caroline.

'I don't want to.'

'Call her up.'

'If I wanted to be nagged, I'd have created my mother,' I grumped.

We shot off a dozen more clay elephants, which gave me an appetite, and I was wondering about creating a takeaway Osama's booth there on the grouse moor, when I heard this:

'*Well, I'm here again, Jamie.*'

Lizzie. Out of nowhere.

'*It's my lunch hour, so I thought I'd pop in.*'

'That was Lizzie!' said Caroline.

'I know that's Lizzie. This happened to me last night. I heard the same voice.'

'You didn't create her from your memories?' asked Caroline.

'Caroline. Who in their right mind would create another Lizzie? I need help to *solve* my problems. It's just her disembodied voice keeps coming out of nowhere.'

'That's what disembodied voices do, come out of nowhere. Otherwise they wouldn't be disembodied,' Caroline was saying pedantically, but something was going wrong with the world. The sky, I noticed, had turned from grey to black.

'*I bought you some grapes,*' continued Lizzie. '*They wouldn't let me bring them in, so I had to eat them outside. Which is why I'm a bit late.*'

Something was happening to my chest—a deep pain, ballooning up.

'You all right?' asked Caroline, but she, the grouse moor, Mel, the trebuchet, the clay elephants and everything were fading rapidly to black. My chest was in terrible pain and I had to keep heaving it up and down just to get air in my body. I could only feel one leg. It was itchy.

Everything flickered off. *System crash*, I thought. *Fantastic.*

How had breathing been so easy all my life? It was nearly impossible now.

Lizzie's voice was still speaking, blonde and relentless. '*Jamie, I hope you're still in there, bro. It's Monday today. You had your crash on Friday. They cut you out and they've been trying to stop the bleeding. Then they said you had a punctured lung, which made me think like a burst balloon, you know. Pssshsht! I'm surprised you didn't go flying round the hospital.*

'*Anyway I think they've mended that.*

'*They also said there's not much brain activity, and what there is is chaotic. I said that sounded like you. There's some things—haema-somethings—that they're a bit worried about.*

58

That's because of the fractured skull. They were trying to explain it all to me but I said, don't worry, I'm sure you'll sort it. It was so icky. *I'm telling them definitely not to switch anything off.'*

I tried to say, *Lizzie, I'm here,* but like in a nightmare, I couldn't.

'What else can I tell you? I got a couple of nice new tops, but I don't suppose you'll be interested.'

Suddenly the pain and darkness disappeared.

The grouse moor rematerialized. Caroline's upside-down face was peering down at me. Grey eyes: a beautiful oval face, especially if she'd take the glasses off and pay for a haircut every so often instead of clipping her curls in front of the mirror.

'You all right?'

'You all disappeared,' I said confusedly. 'Lizzie started telling me about some tops she'd bought.'

I looked at Caroline for a long moment, my head spinning and beads of sweat still on my face, trying to order my thoughts. 'I need to phone a lawyer,' I said.

We got back to the lighthouse as quickly as we could. I snatched the mobile phone and texted Keziah.

'Please can I c u? Important.'

She texted back:

'v busy.'

I tried again:

'Life & death! Honest.'

She texted back:

'u r contemptible.'

'I am sorry 4 being c.'

There was a pause in our texting. Finally she wrote,

'r u decent?'

To which I replied,

'No thong.'

Then on second thoughts added: 'ie thong + + +.'

After a lengthy pause I heard her knocking on the lighthouse door. I let her in and we were quickly sitting round the wooden table with mugs of tea. I introduced Caroline, then told Keziah about my blackout.

'I was in my body again, in hospital. What if we're not dead, Keziah?'

'After I was thrown out of that *Hotel Splendide* place I heard you sucking up to the Lord,' said Keziah, not having listened. 'Why did you do that?'

'Because we don't have many options, that's why.'

'Can't you see what he's like?'

'I happen to think you can't fight all the time. You have to pick your moment.'

'Oh, right! You're really going to pick a moment.'

'I might just be being realistic.'

'Or you might just be being spineless. He's going to abuse us Jamie. It's all over his face.'

'He's called Leopold, the Lord. I met the other one, Gaston. He seems all right. Bit gruff.'

'You being a reliable judge of character.'

'Well, you're right about them wanting us to get together,' I said.

'That's why you called me over...'

'No, Keziah, I'm telling you that because that's what they told me. That's how the land lies. I called you over because when I blacked out I thought I heard my sister Lizzie speaking to me. We might both be still alive in hospital. On life support or something.'

'I don't want to think about that,' said Keziah.

'You might have to. Look,' I said. 'There's a certain pragmatism in going along with Gaston and Leopold isn't there? While they're not harming us?'

'There's also a certain pragmatism in fighting them, every moment, every inch, all the time.'

'Because you've taken against them.'

'Because I know what abusers are like.'

Another knock at the door disturbed us. Caroline said, 'I'll get it,' and opened the door on the Lord, who strode in without invitation. He looked like he had dressed hastily.

'I've just been watching what's happened,' he said. 'I was away for a bit.' He ran his fingers through his greying hair, as if collecting his thoughts. 'Jamie, I'm guessing you might have been troubled by dreams and hearing voices? They're just a hangover from death—false memories. It's like when you behead something and it starts twitching. Same with the mind.'

'Lizzie was saying things I've never heard her say before.'

'That's normal. Things get jumbled. Nothing to worry about.'

'I could feel pain, like I'd had a car accident.'

'Yes, yes, perfectly normal. Did she mention any days having passed?'

'Yes she did. She told me it was Monday on earth… three nights and four days after the crash.'

'How long do you think you've been here?'

I totted up. 'About a week.'

'Precisely,' said Leopold. 'You see, your spirit's had a trauma. You are most definitely dead and Keziah's right. You've got to move on, get over it.'

Then he turned to Keziah.

'Miss Mordant, I know you don't want to cooperate with us. I want to tell you that the Overlord and I are eternal beings of incredible power. You do have a choice: you can do what we say now. Or you can do what we say later. We will break you in, Keziah. We always do and we will.'

Keziah's green eyes were staring him down, furious, like when a teenager is told off.

'That's that, then,' said Leopold. 'Glad to clear that up. Nice to see you two together. I'm off. We'll meet for breakfast tomorrow.'

'Breakfast?' I said. 'Let me do that. I can do breakfast.'

'Don't make it early,' said Keziah.

EVERYTHING YOU BELIEVE IS WRONG

Sleep. Dome. No intruders. Bikinis. Better.

'Right,' said Leopold, the next morning. 'It's time to talk some sense.'

I'd offered to be host, because it gave me an excuse to re-create one of the great life experiences: the all-you-can-eat hotel breakfast. This particular meal bore a resemblance to the buffet at the *New Directions in Public Service Web Administration* conference that I'd attended (at my own expense) in Frankfurt the previous November, part of my plan to give my contact at the hospital the ammunition she needed to persuade her boss to come up with the budget to keep me on.

The organizers had been wise enough to lay on an extravagant junket to make up for the lack of content in the conference itself. That, they guessed rightly, would draw in the punters. I had missed the morning plenary two days in a row due to needing a lie-down.

Keziah took a bowl of fresh fruit. I started with that, plus cereal (got to look after yourself, even when dead), then planned a route through the sausages, bacon, tomatoes, mushrooms, baked beans, potato wedges and eggs, finishing in the croissants and chocolate-bread. Leopold wasn't eating, having confessed in a petulant moment of self-disclosure that he'd suffered from severe dyspepsia since at least the Ice-Age-before-last.

'I'm not sure you realize how lucky you are to have us working with you,' said Leopold.

'I'm sure we don't,' I replied, looking down with a humble and serious expression. Across the table from me, Keziah had tuned out.

'It's yourselves that suffer in the long run,' he said.

'OK,' I said carefully. 'What do we do?'

'We need you happy and normal,' said Leopold. 'A couple. Home. Garden. Some routine to life. An occupation. The basics. That's the start.

'Then you go forth and multiply.'

'We what?' I said, dropping a German sausage.

'He wants us to breed,' said Keziah with a sigh.

'We can't,' I gasped, after a long moment while I fully grasped this point about breeding and then a further moment which I spent becoming aghast. 'Can we? You know. Even if we wanted to. Which I don't. With all due respect.'

Otherwise, why would I have been playing fantasy cricket matches and creating restaurants? A series of experiments had already underlined the point. Everything seemed to be present and correct up here, but nothing worked.

'You refer to the Chastity of the Heavens,' said the Lord. 'It's true. None of us can.'

'Why is that, then?' I asked.

'Why? It is one of the mysteries of the universe that even we spirits haven't totally fathomed yet.' Leopold gave a bitter little twitch. 'Of course *some* spirits claim to know. Some spirits float around with smirks on their faces saying, "Just wait for the Great Consummation." But they don't know. They can't know.'

'I see,' I said.

'Meanwhile on *earth*'—he spat the word out—'two fish or pathetic little insects or even plants—plants I ask you—dandelions! Japanese knot-weed!—can multiply sexually at the drop of a hat and flower and be fulfilled whereas here in the heavenlies beings like us—great beings, superior beings—can have all the urges and desires and even the equipment but somewhere deep down there's some missing piece. It's stressful, I can tell you. You don't know what stress is. Thirteen thousand eight hundred and nineteen million, four hundred and twenty-three thousand, six hundred and nine years, two months and twenty-four days, earth time, and still I *haven't*, not really—And we're all growing *old* and you wonder sometimes *what is the point*. What kind of malicious beast would create us... Excuse me.'

He rushed out of the restaurant, squeezing the sides of his head.

Bumping and banging sounds came from the men's room. I retrieved the German sausage and took an invigorating mouthful, then another. Keziah spooned in a couple of grapes and some shredded grapefruit, neat as a cat.

Leopold crashed back in, smoothing his clothes. 'We are fine about it, actually, and what we mean by *multiply* is build a world together. You've got all your memories here. Mix and match them. You've got your imaginations. Be inventive. You can build a whole world. You can even create new people, mashups from friends you know. A whole beautiful world.'

'So really you're talking about making a fantasy world by combining own memories?' I asked.

'Paradise,' said Leopold. 'The start, maybe, of a whole new way of being human.'

'I have a slight problem with that,' I offered. 'What if we're incompatible?'

'Nonsense,' returned Leopold. 'Look, name me a creation myth from your planet—and I should know because I *wrote* some of them—where the hypothetical first Father and first Mother say to their Creator, "sorry, no can do, we just don't belong together"?'

'Technically that doesn't prove anything,' I pointed out. 'Obviously, if a primaeval pair didn't get on, they wouldn't reproduce, and the Creator would have to try again with someone else. There might have been dozens of primaeval pairs that never made it. Only the winners get to be in the Creation Myth. It's natural selection...'

Leopold was not looking amused.

'To be sure of success,' I said, emolliently, 'we need our own time and space. It's not like we haven't been busy already. You must have seen my Lord's Cricket Ground and Edwards Air Force Base and Osama's and all the miles of coastline. This restaurant.'

'No-one's really interested in that,' said Leopold. 'It's the life you build together—the life we train you to build—that's what matters. That's where true happiness lies. I thought we'd explained that.'

'All the better to let it develop slowly and naturally, then,' I said. 'If Keziah and me are going to spend eternity together, er, we need to have plenty of time to get used to the idea.'

Leopold looked uncertain. 'I suppose we should listen to what our pets are telling us. It adds to the pressure on me though.'

'Gaston doesn't approve?' I hazarded.

'Never mind what Gaston thinks. I'm not his slave. I'm the expert animal trainer. I dictate the pace.'

'So I'm sure you'll do what's right then,' I said smoothly.

'Hmph,' said Leopold. 'Look. I'm prepared to work with you in the mornings and give you the afternoons to —'

'Adjust and acclimatize,' I suggested. 'To our new lives.'

'Very well. But we're still going to have our first training meeting today. Meet me in the centre of the habitat in half an hour.' He left.

After the door banged, I looked at Keziah.

'Well?'

Keziah sighed.

'I think there might be something in going along with him a little,' she said.

'I'm glad you're seeing sense.'

'I don't care whether I die or live,' she said quietly. 'But I've started building something in my habitat. I want to see how all my memories and feelings fit together.'

I thought of the people being burnt alive, the gallows, the razor blades.

'How do you know they *do* all fit together? Aren't they just randomly—'

'I see something in my sleep,' she said. 'I want to build it.'

'That's interesting. I see something in *my* sleep,' I said. 'I wouldn't want to build it exactly, though.'

'So I need time and space,' continued Keziah.

'I get it,' I said slowly. 'Gaston and Leopold want us to have a relationship. You want to understand yourself or bring closure or something.'

'And you want to do anything rather than suffer.'

'You mean, I have pragmatically assessed the best survival options. We each need time. So we go along with Leopold.'

'For a bit. And the minimum we can.'

'All right.'

'You know Jamie,' she added thoughtfully, 'if you got past your stupid jokes, total self-obsession and craven cowardice, you might find inside you a kindly person trying to get out.'

I was hurt by this.

'Unlike you,' I said.

'For sure.' She left.

'Right,' said Leopold, half an hour later, in the middle part of the habitat. He had been adding fresh scenery to create a clearing in light woodland.

'This landscape,' said Leopold, 'is empty. A wide canvas to paint your dreams on.'

I could hear a stream. The meadow-grass was soft, the sun was shining, you could fiddle with buttercups.

Leopold had changed into some extremely ill-advised white shorts, white socks, trainers, T-shirt, and baseball cap. You just had to look away, but then you kept being drawn back. He was sitting on a tree stump.

'Now, your first lesson together: everything you believe is wrong. That isn't necessarily a problem.'

It would have been nicer to lie down, smell the meadow-grass, watch the clouds, sleep off breakfast and think of nothing, especially not loopy nonsense from an eternal being with uncalibrated fashion radar. He went on. 'Can a fly understand its place in the universe? Of course not. It hasn't got the mental capacity.

'Can humans? Of course not. Same reason. Your puny minds and limited senses haven't a hope. So all ultimate human explanations must necessarily be wrong. All religions must be wrong. The Universe will always be puzzling and mysterious because you cannot grasp what's happening any more than a fly can.'

He shifted his position on the tree trunk slightly, trying and failing to straighten his feet which forever swung backwards like a compass pointing north.

'However. All is not lost. You still have yourselves. You also have all the things that previous generations have built and left lying around the Omniverse.'

'Such as what?' I said.

'Such as everything. On earth, you're used to driving on roads you didn't build, in cars you didn't invent. You write with an alphabet you didn't think up, eat food you didn't selectively breed, and on and on. You can inhabit ideas that other people have worked on, if they work for you.'

'Even if they're not true?' I asked.

'Everything that has been invented was made for the same reason—to satisfy ambition and be popular with girls,' said Leopold. 'Truth is nothing to do with it. It's out there, it works for you, you can use it.

He clambered to a standing position, not entirely smoothly, bit of arthritis in the knee. 'So here's what we're going to do. I've set up this place—' He gestured around—'as the perfect place to start. Ready to be filled with your dreams.

'*Then* we discover that whatever life you choose to build together—you can improve on it by getting help from the spirits. Working with us gives you that bit extra to get ahead.

'I shall wander in and out among you, sometimes here, sometimes there, ready to strengthen, advise, counsel. Lead you into greatness, into Art.'

'Will you be wearing those shorts?' I asked.

'Why should I not?'

'Well it's—er—easier to think of you as one of the lads if you dress like that,' I lied. (No friend of mine would last ten seconds at the gym in those.) 'We might find it easier to think of you as a god if you were more, you know, robed in splendour.'

'Ah! That's where you make a mistake, you see. I am both great and I dwell with humans. Both.'

'Fair enough,' I said.

Leopold looked over at Keziah. 'You've been quite quiet this morning. Are you happy with all this?'

'It's still the morning,' said Keziah, not looking up.

'You may have to buck up, my dear girl,' insisted Leopold. 'If you're to benefit from the training.'

Keziah didn't reply.

'If there's anything you need to say before I leave, say it.'

'I'm not "your dear girl",' said Keziah.

Leopold gave her a stare, then buzzed off, a lazy streak in the sky.

Keziah and I were still sitting on the grass. I rolled over to look at her.

'I thought you said you were going to cooperate?' I asked.

'I was.'

'I'd like to see you being difficult.'

'No you wouldn't. And listen,' she went on, 'when I said you were kind-hearted I was trying to be nice. You just trampled on me.'

Keziah, I noticed, had this female knack of restarting a conversation from the last time offence was taken, no matter how much has happened since. I can imagine men coming home after fighting their way through the Second World War and their wives saying to them, 'Did you know, six years ago, you left the toilet seat up?'

'You accused me of craven cowardice and total self-obsession,' I continued.

'Yes.'

'My point is that it isn't true.'

'Really.'

'No,' I said defiantly. 'Not true at all. Ask anybody. Ask Caroline. You've met her. Former girlfriend. Librarian. Reads literary fiction. Knows about character.'

I summoned her from my mental store and she appeared.

'Hello, Caroline,' I said. 'Now listen, Keziah here—whom you've met, Caroline, Keziah, Keziah, Caroline—she says I suffer from craven cowardice and total self-obsession.'

'Your point is?'

'My point is you're going to say, "what a fatheaded remark. You clearly don't know the lad."'

Caroline thought for a moment.

'Nope,' she said. 'I think she's got you down pretty well.'

'I can send you back to where you came from, you know.'

'But you're not going to because Keziah and I are going to go for a coffee and a triple-chocolate muffin. You can build something or something. Would you like to?' she asked Keziah.

'Chocolate's important,' replied Keziah.

'Good,' said Caroline. 'Can we borrow the elephant?'

'If you must,' I said, and whistled for Dumbo.

71

I watched them go, feeling a bit left behind. *Right if you want me to build something*, I thought, a little grumpily, *I will*. A maglev. A superfast train thumping through the countryside, resting on concrete supports for an extra-smooth ride. I started clearing some forest and installing the track.

It wasn't unlike a sim game, of course and, as many have discovered before me, large-scale industrialization is fun. It was soothing to extend the track, put bridges in, decide on the route round a mountain. You could forget your troubles. I chopped down trees, slotted in concrete supports and laid track, and rode up and down on the bits I'd finished, at speeds of 300 klicks an hour.

The girls came back.

'Enjoy your nosebag?' I asked.

'Yes we did,' said Caroline. 'But neither of us could believe how one-dimensional I am as a character. Honestly, Jamie. We went out for *eighteen months*. I'm your complete memory of me. It's pathetic.'

'Well I'm very sorry,' I said, peeved.

'It was a terrifying insight into the male mind.'

'While you were away drinking coffee,' I said, with dignity. 'I started to construct a state-of-the-art railway. Look at it.' I waved my hand at the slim line of concrete and steel curving into the distance.

'Marvellous,' said Caroline.

'It'll eventually link the whole country.'

'There's only you and Keziah here!'

'And a lot of trees. True, but it's good to have the infrastructure in early. Avoid the strategic planning mistakes of the past.'

'I'm sorry, that won't do at all,' said another voice. It was Leopold's, who was walking towards us, busy and fussy. 'Is this what you've wasted your time doing? Won't do.' He waved at it and it vanished, telescoping in on itself.

'I spent all morning on that,' I protested.

'Won't do at all,' he sighed. 'I want you to build a *home* together. Taking the best resources of both of you. Not a technology theme park. The man-woman-home thing is fundamental. That's how you'll be happy. Trust me. I'm a spirit and I know.'

'Well, that's tomorrow's job.' I said. 'Look where the sun is! Lunchtime.'

Leopold glared. 'We've wasted a whole morning. Be on time tomorrow.'

That afternoon I rebuilt the maglev in my own part of the habitat, though it didn't have anywhere to go except up and down the coast for a few miles. It had stops at the lighthouse landing stage, Lord's Cricket Ground/Osama's, the River Cam, and Edwards Air Force Base.

Truth to tell, it was a bit boring riding up and down, especially at 300km/hr, as the time between the stations was about 1.4 seconds, and the acceleration and deceleration made you fear for your lunch.

So instead I built a funfair. I took Annie, Caroline's other house-mate. I'd often shared a kitchen with Annie while, upstairs, thumping noises indicated that Caroline was on an expedition through her wardrobe, on a quest for the elusive magic clothes that made her feel good about her body.

Annie was a round-faced, brainy, long-haired Singaporean Chinese girl, a postgrad, a cellist. She had a good line in smiling shyly but not much conversation, which was just as well, because the gentle exterior hid the most terrifying right-wing opinions. Among the unspoken rules in Caroline's household was *never talk politics with Annie*. Anyhow, there were Annie and me, silent Annie and me, going round and round on the Big Wheel in an empty fairground, not talking politics.

Half an hour of this was plenty. I erased Annie from the scene (she said she didn't mind), rowed to the lighthouse, cooked myself a curry, watched a movie.

Still not sleepy. Phoned Keziah. It rang for a long time before she answered.

'Were you asleep?' I asked.

'No,' she replied. 'Just busy.'

'I can imagine,' I said. 'Would you like a snack or something?'

'Alright. Just give me some time to finish.'

Shortly afterwards, we were sharing two hot chocolates on a rickety plastic table in my habitat. We overlooked the cliff and the lighthouse with the hot chocolate stall and the funfair behind us. It was warm and star-spangled and I had arranged a soft breeze. Not because I wanted to be romantic, not with Keziah, you jest, she's scary, but because it was pleasant and because I could. The smell of fried potatoes and candy floss also drifted on the air. I had honky-tonk organ music playing in the background as an empty carousel whirled. Keziah had piled her hot chocolate with marshmallows and squirty cream.

'How's your building project going?' I asked. I paused while she swallowed a marshmallow. 'You shouldn't put so many in at once.'

'I got rid of everything you saw,' said Keziah, stirring her chocolate. 'Started again.'

'Remind me what you are trying to do?'

74

'I'm pulling out every memory I've ever had. I'm looking at how it felt. Then I'm filing it.'

'I never knew filing could be so much fun.'

'Do you know what forensic scientists say?'

I was lost by this apparent change of subject.

'Er—"Hello, I'm a forensic scientist"?' I suggested, then made one or two rude suggestions about what forensic scientists might say, involving rubber gloves.

'They say, "Every contact leaves a trace",' said Keziah. 'So I think every experience leaves a trace in your personality. By looking at them one by one, you can build a model of your whole self.'

'There must be millions of memories.'

'That's why it's so engrossing. Of course you can pick the most important memories first and then work down.'

She swallowed another marshmallow. 'I'm still trying to get it all to work the way I want. I've had the same dream several times. It might be a clue from my subconscious—a landscape. That's what I'm building.'

'I told you about *my* dream, didn't I? It's a beach resort that's full of old friends and my sister Lizzie. There's a big Dome over it to keep the elements out. Oh, and there's constant pressure to break into the Dome, led by all the people I've ever disliked, which is a lot, some corrosive acid rain, and a seven-foot-tall ghoul. I could imagine it's my subconscious sorting itself out.'

'What's he like?' asked Keziah.

'What, the ghoul? Big and ghoulish. He's tall and thin, covered in welts and he has bony, jabbing fingers.'

'Hair?'

'Short and lank, probably, but hard to see under his hat. He dresses like someone caught in a rainstorm in the 1930s.'

'About seven feet tall? I've seen him too.'

'What? Weird. Do you think we should mention this to Leopold?'

'No. Tell Gaston and Leopold as little as possible.'

'You really hate them, don't you? For me, I think you have to get along with people.'

'Well, tomorrow you'll be happy, because we have to be all domesticated.'

'I know. Build a home. Why does he want us to do that, do you think?'

'Oh that's easy. He's just like every sex attacker I've ever met. A home is always what they want. Husband brings wife a bunch of flowers every Friday. Wife is cooking a pie. Rubber boots and plastic tractors in the hall. He can't have it himself but he wants to somehow create it through us.'

'Do you meet many sex attackers?'

'All the time.'

'What a nice job you have.'

'Keeps me on the straight and narrow.'

'So anyway,' I said, wanting to change the conversation, 'tomorrow it has to be flowers and pies.'

'Please don't gush tomorrow, will you?' said Keziah. 'I'll be sick.'

THE SNAKE

'Morning,' said Leopold, as we assembled in the clearing again. Keziah had brought a cup of coffee with a lid on it. Scowling at the morning sun, she settled herself next to a tree trunk.

I'd already been for a jog along the beach and watched the sun come up twice, at different speeds. I'd caught the maglev back, and then had a balanced breakfast at Osama's that contained all five important food groups: carbs, trans fats, sugar, salt and MSG.

Leopold was wearing a kilt and he stood on the brow of a hill, with sunlight suffusing the mist around him. 'Do you like it?' he asked. 'A momento of past triumphs. I was involved in the re-invention of Scottishness. It was a kind of bet. Find the coldest, gloomiest, wettest, most midge-infested place on earth and get grown men to bare their thighs. Nobody thought we could pull it off.'

'You invented Scottishness?'

'Not just me. Big team. Puritan traditions gave us a good start. It just needed a nudge. Anyhow,' said Leopold, 'can't talk about that now. It all fell apart, infighting. Got to look forward. You can summarize what I'm trying to say as Three Spiritual Laws. Very simple. Totally foundational. Here they are:

'The Three Spiritual Laws:

'1. Happiness is out there, and you sometimes meet it.

'2. There is no meaning, just useful models.

'3. Spirit powers will help.

'Isn't that simple? Isn't that brilliant? Isn't that life-changing? Isn't that a foundation for all your lives with us?'

Keziah took a long drink of her coffee, with the air of a garden being watered after a long drought, or a girl being kissed after half a lonely lifetime. 'You see how it explains everything,' Leopold went on.

'Er, yes,' I said. 'I think.'

'It explains your human condition. Alienation. Moments of happiness. Spirit guides needed to fill the gap. So do you believe it? Jamie?'

I was on the spot.

'I suppose.'

'Absolutely. Absolutely.' Leopold was quite animated this morning, almost hopping. 'And Keziah. Keziah do you believe it?'

Keziah took another long draw on her coffee, then looked up and blinked.

'Whatever. Just don't talk so loud. It's the crack of dawn.'

'This is life and death...'

'But, she's thinking about it,' I said hurriedly. 'You're thinking about it, aren't you Keziah?' I was looking at her with what Paddington Bear would have called his 'hard stare'. Keziah grunted.

'See!' I said.

'I suppose you have worked out what this all means,' said Leopold. 'It means you follow me. It means you follow me, like a good shepherd.' He was striding around now. 'I find you the green grass. I find you the still waters. I give rest for your souls. Plenty of fakes around, but I'm the real deal. Gaston and I, that is. The real deals.'

He was beaming. And, in truth, almost slavering too. 'Questions?'

'Love,' I said, somewhat to my surprise. I think Caroline would have been surprised too. Fortunately she wasn't there. 'Doesn't that come into it somewhere?'

Leopold looked weary for a moment.

'What do you mean by love?' he asked.

'I dunno… Love. You know. Love.'

'What,' asked Leopold patiently, 'is love?'

'Well it's… everyone knows what love is. It makes the world go round.'

'Define it then.'

'I can't off the top of my head.'

'The place of love,' said Leopold, 'is overblown. That's one of the deep things wrong in your culture.'

'That seems a bit harsh.'

'Well listen up. This is important. Love is OK for getting two people to breed. Unfortunately, your society has raised it to some kind of Great Universal Principle. And that's asking too much of love. Look. Boy meets girl —they fall in love—epic love story, Darcy and Lizzie, Romeo and Juliet. With me so far?'

'Yes.'

'They drool over each other, they drip with powerful chemicals, they go through a pre-breeding ritual. Whatever. They are "in love". They can't bear to be apart. Obstacles arise—no matter. They move mountains, cross deserts, mortgage their futures. Anything to be together. Finally they succeed. They breed. A baby comes, the darling of their hearts.

'So far so loving?

'Fast-forward fifteen years. I've seen this so many times. They can't keep it up. Their teenage son—the little baby they "loved to bits"—can't bear the sight of them. On a Saturday, Romeo goes to the football. Juliet goes shopping. Romeo may once have moved mountains for Juliet, now he won't move his socks to the laundry basket.

'They naturally think they have failed. But they haven't failed. Love has failed. Love *always* fails in the end. The Grand Idea has let them down because too much was asked of it.

'Even so, they can still live happily—and for ever after. How? By investing in things that—unlike love—*are* designed for a lifetime of heavy use. Football. Shopping. In the case of the son, heavy metal. The football and the shopping and the heavy metal are what they turn to when love fails.'

'But you want us to build an ideal home together, Keziah and I. Isn't that love?'

'No. It's an algorithm. It's a widget.'

'I'm sorry?'

Leopold sighed. 'Over the years, humans have found the least worst option for co-existing is to breed in pairs. But you mustn't take that biologically-determined convenience and extend it to a grand unified theory of everything. Love isn't the secret of happiness. *Things* are the secret to happiness, and breeding successfully—love, if you like—is one of the "things".

'The only thing that can be said about "love" (or let's say for clarity "companionship and breeding") is that it's one of the staples. Like food or sleep. That's why it was so important for you and Keziah to "fall in love" and get set up together.

'Do you see? Now look, I've got to go. Other duties.
But do as I urged yesterday. Build your ideal home. Build
it together. See if I'm right!'

He streaked into the sky and out of sight.

I looked over at Keziah.

'Well that doesn't seem too bad.'

'Jamie. It's still the morning.'

'You'd rather I just built a house while you finished
waking up?'

'So long as you can do it quietly.'

So a little distance away I built a *house*: whitewashed
walls, thatched roof, picket fence, rambling roses
bestriding the front door, chocolate Labrador sniffing
round, children's toys scattered on the lawn, a jumble of
boots outside the door, woodsmoke curling from the
chimney. I was busy planting up the cottage garden at the
front when Keziah wandered over.

'Ms Mordant,' I said. 'How nice of you to turn up.
I'll show you round the property. You'll notice the
original oak front door opening onto a flagged hallway.
Note the boots, various sizes and colours, scattered
round flagged hallway in homely fashion. The property
benefits from a large kitchen off the right (26ft x 28ft),
also flagged and with many original and unusual
features: oak table, large fireplace, utensils hanging from
ceiling on butcher's hooks along with onions and dried
herbs. Walk-in pantry. In *here* we have the dining room,
seats 12 comfortably, for those nice county-set dinner
parties and bridge evenings. Over *here* a cosy little living
room... 42-inch panel TV and a sound system... and
next to it, here, a library-cum-study with a fine view of...
what would you like a fine view of?'

'Now I know what hell is like,' said Keziah, looking round.

'I thought it was quite nice,' I said.

'You would.'

'I take it you don't want to see how the first floor benefits from four good-sized bedrooms, including a magnificent master bedroom with ensuite and dressing room and fireplace—remember this is for Leopold. Not for us.'

We returned to the 26x28ft flagged kitchen with many original features. I took a kettle off the Rayburn, found some coffee, filled a cafetière. '*Pain aux chocolat* in that breadbin there,' I said. 'Just out of interest, what would your ideal house be?'

She fetched some chocolate-bread, put it on a plate and sat at the oak table, breaking the bread absent-mindedly. 'My ideal house... Nobody's ever asked me that. I had a little top-floor flat in Arbury... No, I know what I'd have. A pub. I'd rent out the rooms to homeless old men. They'd buy heavy furniture and velvet curtains and thick rugs. Downstairs we'd have a pool table and darts. Smoking would be *compulsory*. During the day we'd have chiropodists and social services and a doctor and probation coming in. A big screen TV for the football. We'd serve pub food, greasy as you like. I'd be behind the bar helping them to keep to a couple of pints a night. It would be the first home for some of them.'

'So Keziah's idea of paradise is long nights on her own with a roomful of grizzled old criminals?'

'Lovely.'

'But sadly not Leopold's stereotype of the domestic ideal.'

'I think I'll go out and do the vegetable garden,' said Keziah, popping in the last piece of chocolate bread. 'We used to grow vegetables. We had chickens, too. My dad wanted to demonstrate sustainable living.'

'Er... there is one other thing. Do you think we should offer Leopold lunch?' I poured the coffee.

'Me and you, entertain him for lunch?' she asked, narrowing her eyes.

'Yes. Make him happy.'

Keziah wrapped her fingers round the coffee mug. 'You mean me cooking it, don't you? And you choosing the wine.'

I coughed. 'Anything to get him off our backs. I keep trying to remember, we need to survive here.'

Keziah sighed. 'Doesn't have to be anything special,' I added. 'Game pie? Maybe with mange-tout and a little —'

'I suppose I can do soup. Soup can't be hard.'

'There are nice soups. I think I've got a *bouquet garnier* hung up here somewhere. Caroline's mum's big into those, but they're not too bad.'

'I meant, like, from a can.'

'Oh.'

'Or a cup of soup.'

'OK,' I said. 'I'll make lunch. And you can—some vegetables maybe, from the garden? How did you survive college and law school?'

'Subways, Starbucks, cigarettes and chocolate,' she said simply, counting them off on her stubby fingers. 'A few illegal substances. Red wine for breakfast.'

'I'll make some bread,' I said. 'You ever made bread?'

'You *make* bread?'

So Keziah went out into the garden and I started baking. Oh, I'd missed this. I used to start early and put in a couple of hours' work. Then, when I was fed up with lining up words and pictures, mix the flour, yeast, fat, water. Knead it. Smash it against my worktop. Punch it, squeeze it, feel it live. Go back to work refreshed, while the smell filled my little house.

With my bread sprawled in a polythene bag on the top of the Rayburn, I took Keziah some more coffee.

She was sitting on a sunlit patch of lawn where the grass ended and the vegetable patch began. Her back was turned to me. She never sat straight, slouching like a gambler rather than shoulders-back like a supermodel. On one side of her was an empty cane trug (a sort of basket) to carry the vegetables. On the other was what looked like a coil of greenish-white rope, which she was talking to. A couple of steps closer and my mind suddenly issued a recall notice. *That's not a coil of rope. It's a snake.*

'That's a snake!' I said.

'Coffee!' Keziah said, shuffling round. 'Thank you.'

'And pecan and maple plait.' I was a little lost for words. 'Is this one of your memories?' I sat down, keeping a distance between both Keziah and the snake.

'No,' said Keziah. 'I found him here. He's been telling me some interesting things.'

The snake looked directly at me.

'Good morning, sir. I hope you are well.'

He blinked twice. The tilt of his head spoke of somebody with a cap in his hands.

'Did you just say something?' I asked.

'Yessir.'

'Who are you?'

'My name is Stub, sir. I am one of the damned.'

'The damned… not the band?'

'No, not the band,' said Keziah. 'Of course not the band.'

84

'Ah.'

'Damned, sir,' explained the snake calmly, 'as in condemned to eternal destruction in the Lake of Fire.'

'Ah,' I said again. 'That kind of damned.'

'Yessir.'

I was still holding the tray of coffee and bakes, so I set it down on the smooth lawn.

'Bit of a conversation stopper,' I said.

'Yessir.'

I told Keziah to help herself. She took her cup and a plate. I asked the snake, 'would you like...'

'A kind thought, but not for me, sir. Thank you. Food turns to ashes in my mouth.'

'I see. Do you... is it... must be a bit of a problem. Being... being—'

'Damned. Yes.'

'Like being nine wickets down with 400 still to get on the last day of a Test Match.'

'With all due respect, sir,' said the snake patiently. 'It isn't anything like that.'

'Fine. Well I mean not fine, obviously... Is it something you get used to, being... damned?'

'No not really sir. I find I can maintain composure for intervals but then at unpredictable moments I plunge into long periods of despairing introspection and self-harm, sir.'

'Jamie,' interrupted Keziah, 'Stub here was telling me about Gaston and Leopold.'

'Are you a friend of theirs?' I asked.

'No sir,' said Stub. 'We are immortal enemies.'

'Tell him what you told me,' said Keziah.

'Well sir,' said the snake. 'You may not be aware of this, but your accident caused a stir in the heavenly places. Normally, departed human spirits disappear from the scene quickly after death. Your spirits are still tethered to your bodies—'

'I knew—' I said.

'Because you are all but dead, sir, but not quite dead. There are two of you, male and female, and you are young. It turns out you are a rare prize. Sir, there was a considerable fight over who should have ownership of you, which Gaston won, but at some cost to himself.

'Gaston and Leopold now have to spend the majority of their time flattering other evil spirits as payment. (The only currencies that work here are bullying and grovelling.) For example, several times a week, sir, they have to worship the beings who collected you, which is a strain on their mental welfare, since they regard these collectors as far below them in the social hierarchy. That is what they are doing at this moment, which is why it is safe for me to visit.

'They also have to spend time, sir, grovelling to their line manager, a powerful evil spirit called the "Almighty Toad".

'These particular heavy burdens are of course in addition to the social debts they have accumulated over the past 13.8 billion years, which are severe, sir.'

'And why would they—'

'Sorry, didn't mention that. They want to experiment on you, sir. It's clearly something very important, given the level of social debts they have incurred. We just haven't found out what it is yet.'

'Great,' I said.

'You said, "we",' said Keziah. 'Who's "we"?'

'Therapists, miss,' said Stub. 'Part of a regional structure. I belong to the Cambridge Area Neighbourhood Soul Repair Team. Known internally as the CANSORT, miss.'

'Wild,' I said.

'Inevitable if you think about it, sir. In this part of the Omniverse—which includes your earth, of course—everything is mixed and nothing is settled. Nothing final like perfect happiness or endless death, sir. Not till the Lake of Fire.' He looked moody for a moment, so far as a snake can. 'No place of desolation without any hope at all; no place of exaltation without any sorrow at all. Every garden, if you like, has a snake. Every snake has its garden, for that matter. Inevitably, the heavenly realms need therapists, sir.'

'So, you've come to rescue us. Tell me you've come to return us to our bodies,' I said, hope rising.

'Not so simple, sir. My goal is to tip things in a healing direction.'

'Oh.'

'I can illustrate... Perhaps you'd both like to move back for a moment. Just if you could clear a bit of space.' We shuffled backwards. The snake shrunk and slithered in on itself. Momentarily it was just a dim fuzz of dancing green-and-white light. Then, rapidly, it expanded out again, big and white. A person—skinny, white-skinned, lank hair, red welts. Seven feet tall. Raincoat. Feet the wrong way round.

'You!' I said.

'Yessir,' said Stub.

'You were trying to break in. In my dreams.'

'Yessir.'

'How can you be in my dreams and also not in them?'

'Welcome to the heavenlies, sir. The distinction between sleep and wakefulness is less marked, as indeed is the distinction between reality, dream and metaphor, sir. Living in your world of matter forces these distinctions to have a sharpness they do not have elsewhere.'

'But you were trying to break up my Dome.'

'Certainly, sir. It's not healthy.'

'In your opinion.'

'We will have to differ there, sir.'

'Forgive me for saying so, but you're not exactly the picture of well-being yourself.'

'Sir, I fully accept I am not the best advertisement—'

'Exactly.' I said. 'Look, that Dome, that's like my subconscious saying that's all I've got left. So nobody gets in, and nobody changes it, because it's all I've got.'

'Even if it means your healing, sir.'

'It's nothing to do with my healing. My healing is all about the people in Intensive Care getting my body back in working order. You're not trampling over the few shreds of myself that I have left. If I let you in… it feels like I will die.'

'You will not surely die, sir,' said Stub, with irritation. 'With the greatest respect, I don't think you know what death is.'

'I seem to have been on a learning curve recently.'

'A crash course, perhaps sir?' Stub suggested.

'Not actually all that funny.'

'I apologize,' said the ghoul, with the same humble nod of his head as when he'd been a snake. 'I made the judgement that you communicate in silly jokes when you are feeling insecure, sir.' Out of the corner of my eye, I saw Keziah wince.

I felt angry all of sudden. 'Oh, I'm insecure am I? Need to be treated in a special way because I'm insecure —'

'Jamie,' said Keziah.

'What?' I snapped. 'What is it now?'

'Shut up.'

I stared into her green eyes, which were angry. 'He's trying to help.'

'I don't appreciate being told to shut up—'

'Stop saying stupid, idiotic, fatheaded things then. That might cut it right out.' She looked at the ghoul. 'In my dream I saw you going around with a wheelbarrow and some building materials.'

'Yes, miss. In the months before you crashed you'd been flooding yourself with memories. You broke the walls down yourself.'

'I did?'

'Driven by self-loathing you tend to smash down the barriers that normal people erect. I'm doing a little rebuilding.'

'Oh. Thank you.'

'It's my job.'

'Why did you now appear to me as a snake?'

'I made the judgement, Miss Mordant, that in a garden full of birdsong and fruitfulness, you'd warm most to the snakes. It was only a guess, miss.'

'Good call,' said Keziah.

'Thank you.' He bowed. 'I have to go in a moment —Gaston and Leopold may return—but I need to give you some advice. Miss Mordant. You have realized that being on earth or being here in the heavenlies hasn't really, down at the roots, made any difference to your basic problems?'

'Yes,' said Keziah. 'Same me.'

'That's because it isn't changed circumstances you need, none of us do. It's a changed paradigm.'

'"Make a heaven of hell",' I said.

'You've read Milton?' said Stub, looking at me. 'I thought you were a computer engineer, sir.'

'I'm a *web designer*,' I said sniffily. 'Anyway, I used to go out with a librarian who'd read Milton. Or at least shelved him. Before she shelved me.'

'I knew him.'

'Milton? *John* Milton? Seventeenth century English epic poet? Author of *Paradise Lost*?'

'Before he was famous. When he was at Christ's College. Had a big interest in our world. Sir, I must, must go. Miss Mordant, people are like stories. You're not at the end of yours yet. That thing you're building in your spare time, keep going. It's vital.'

'Yes, yes. But what about Gaston and Leopold?' I asked. 'Should we fight them? Or go along with them? Keziah here—'

'I haven't any advice for the short-term. I'm so sorry, sir. There is a case for passive acquiescence to your captors and an equal case for militant opposition. I could be wrong advising either course of action.'

'So we just have to—' I said.

'Also, Miss Mordant' said Stub firmly, 'it probably is therapeutic not to cut yourself off completely from Mr Smith here. An irritant is another word for a stimulant.'

'That's nice,' I said. 'So what should I do?'

'I'm afraid, sir, there's not a lot I can do for you at the moment,' said Stub. 'With respect you wouldn't take my advice if I gave it.'

'I might. You never know.'

Stub sighed. 'My advice sir, is to take your head out of the sand.'

'Shan't.'

'You might find more than the pain you fear.'

'Touchy-feely hoopla.'

'Quite so, sir.'

He turned back to Keziah. 'Another thing you could try, Miss Mordant. Look out for things that seem unnecessary or wasteful or pointless. They're probably not part of Leopold's original garden. Mushrooms, for example.' He pointed into the wood. 'You don't know which are poisonous. They don't look particularly nice. You have to tramp through dark forests to find them. What's the point?'

'And Leopold likes everything nice.'

'Chocolate-box nice. You might like to discreetly try eating one. I will come back when I can safely do so. Goodbye.'

He spiralled in on himself again, turning into the dancing blob of pale light, which shot rapidly into the sky, and out of sight.

'You are such a total prat,' said Keziah.

'He's a snake,' I said wearily. 'He's a condemned criminal. He looks like a heroin addict who's been injecting his own eyeballs. And he's recommending we eat magic mushrooms.'

'I liked him,' said Keziah.

'Which is why I don't.'

Keziah walked off. 'I'm going back to do the bread so that it's ready for when Leopold gets back.' I continued, a little lamely. 'I'll magic up some vegetables since you haven't managed to collect any.'

'I'm going to find some dark places,' said Keziah, over her shoulder, 'and root around.'

Both Gaston and Leopold showed up at lunchtime. I ushered them into the lounge, stoked up a fire and sat down. They looked a little drawn and tired.

'We're happier without the fire,' said Leopold, blowing it out. 'It's quite warm already. But this looks

91

OK.' Leopold looked around. 'I think you've made a great start. What do you think, Gaston?'

Gaston grunted. 'Where's Keziah?'

'She said she might be late,' I said. 'Because she was going to pick some things fresh for lunch.'

'You know we won't be eating,' said Leopold. 'Doesn't agree with us, food.'

'No, shame,' I said.

'But we'll enjoy watching you.'

The fire crackled. In my flagstoned hall, a long-case clock sounded out the half-hour with a dither of clanks and whirrings, like an Aunt woken.

'Don't you think it's so very homely?' said Leopold to Gaston.

'I can think of a few improvements,' muttered Gaston. I heard the rattle of the back door latch and Gaston and Leopold followed me into the kitchen. Gaston took a long look at Keziah, like a race-horse owner running his eyes over a likely filly. Keziah ignored him and hoisted the trug onto the table. I introduced them and they said a brief hello.

'Mushrooms,' she said.

Leopold gave a light laugh. 'Oh my dear girl,' he said. 'You've picked the one thing you really can't eat!'

'Really?' she said.

'You didn't tell them before?' asked Gaston.

'It may have slipped my mind,' hissed Leopold back. 'I've been a bit busy... Unfortunately,' he added smoothly to Keziah and me, 'you can eat anything that grows in this habitat. Everything except the mushrooms. I was going to mention it. They're mind-altering. We try to keep the habitat clean but you how it is. Stuff blows in.'

'Well,' I said breezily, 'it wouldn't go with the soup anyway. Er, if you guys want to sit at the table I'll bring it over. I've baked some bread. I thought since it was only lunch we can eat in the kitchen.'

I served a bowl for Keziah and another for me. We started eating. She was a bit distracted.

'I didn't need to give them much guidance,' Leopold was saying to Gaston. 'Just the "three spiritual laws" and then I let them do what comes naturally. But these little wisps of truth get completely intermingled in their lives. It's organic development. Slow but steady. You see Jamie,' he said to me, 'in setting up this home, you and Keziah are just doing what comes naturally, aren't you?'

I avoided Keziah's gaze, but she looked a bit out of it anyway.

'Yes, in a way,' I said.

'And what we've got to do now is just keep adding to it, beautifying it, extending it, peopling it. Building a whole world, founded on the light-handed guidance of Gaston and Leopold.'

'Not enough,' spat Gaston suddenly.

'I thought we'd discussed this before,' hissed Leopold in a low voice. 'Gaston, dear, we'd discussed it.'

'I am not prostrating myself any more in front of those spotty Collectors without getting something back,' Gaston muttered. 'I am just not.'

Leopold looked across the table at us. 'Gaston and I have to sort a couple of things out, don't mind us. You carry on with your soup. It's a project thing we're involved with. Terribly high-level. Nothing for you to worry about.' He turned to Gaston, 'Gaston, darling, we agreed, this is building for the long-term. The time will come. I want them to want it, I want them to beg for it.'

'I want something now,' insisted Gaston. 'Now.'

'You just don't have any idea,' Leopold paused in his hissing to say across to us in a light voice, 'Don't worry about us! Creative tension you know!' Then carried on: 'You've got to let it ripen.'

'Leopold! Sort it. We don't know how much time we've got. We've got to be ready.'

'Do you want it thorough? Or quick? Darling, please, let's talk about it later.'

'I want both.'

The rest of the meal passed in silence. Gaston left first, with a taut nod. After he'd gone, Leopold said, 'You're doing very well. Both of you. Yes. Well done.'

He left.

Keziah and I looked across the table at each other.

'Well, I think we did OK,' I said. 'Not sure what Gaston was going on about.'

'Whatever,' said Keziah. She looked a little uncertain. 'I ate a mushroom.'

'What?'

'It frightened me.'

'I didn't think anything frightened you.'

'This did.'

'I said you shouldn't have eaten it.'

'I didn't say I shouldn't have eaten it. I just said it frightened me.'

'What was it like?'

She thought.

'Does music ever make you cry?'

'All the time,' I answered. 'You wouldn't believe the schlocky stuff that gets me going. *Abba* has been known to.'

'It was like that.'

'Like *Abba?*'

'No, you dork. Like… awe. Like standing on the edge of the Grand Canyon.'

'That doesn't sound very frightening.'

'You try then.'

'I like to stay in control of my mental processes,' I said. 'No telling what they'd do if I let them off the leash.'

'I'm going back to my side of the habitat. Do some more building.'

'Would you like some chocolate tonight?'

'I suppose I can fit it in,' she said. She put the mushroom-filled trug over her arm.

That afternoon I built this amazing circular cinema underneath the lighthouse—you could distantly hear the waves pounding above the ceiling, but somehow, a film wasn't quite hitting the spot. So next I built a gym underneath the cinema, and challenged Mel to a bout of kick-boxing. Bad idea. Only lasted one round. She's strong, Mel. I forgot.

'No, no, I'm fine,' I told her. 'I just lost interest after the first round.' Lost a tooth as well. Toyed with the idea of creating some nubile Tooth Fairy to climb in through the lighthouse window and rummage lightly under my pillow at night in some floaty fairy-skirt, but couldn't be bothered.

So instead I arranged a tropical storm—a knack to this, getting the clouds to roll, the banana trees to bend, the waves to roil. I walked arm-in-arm with Caroline along a promenade between the maglev and the beach. We'd put oilskins over our beach things.

'I'm beginning to think,' I said to her, 'that I'm not being imaginative enough. The beach and Osama's and even the maglev, they're all very well, but it's a bit unsatisfying. Shallow.' I paused to pick up a flat stone and skimmed it across the sea—*bounce, bounce, bounce*. I counted seventy-two skips before it disappeared out of sight.

It was cosy walking with Caroline through the storm. I glanced across at her. She had beautiful clear skin and sweet, perfect lips. Pity about the I've-starched-my-knickers way she walked. But perhaps that was nerves. Which you can't blame her for.

'Have you ever thought *shallow* might be your problem?' asked Caroline.

'No I haven't,' I said patiently. 'In case you haven't noticed, being something like *dead* is my problem. Being captured by evil spirits is my problem. Being forced to share the sky and all eternity with a feral lawyer and a condemned therapist is my problem. Being *shallow* is the key to survival.

'I'm just beginning to realize the power I have. Don't you think there's something in what Leopold has been saying? *Think of what we can build!*

'You know what I'm thinking of doing? Warming up the North Sea.'

'Jamie—' she said, about to embark on a conversation that I knew would be about us and not good. She'd increasingly got this way over the months. Getting too involved in her Reading Club, I suspected.

'What's the worst thing about Cambridge?' I asked hurriedly. 'The way an East wind settles in about November and doesn't stop blowing till April. You may have noticed this. Well, not this Cambridge. Think of a chain of fusion reactors under the sea. Pumping out hot water. Think of the sea life we'll attract. Maybe we can install some coral reefs. Imagine putting your feet in the

North Sea in January and it's *warm*. It'll be a whole new experience.'

'Jamie.'

'And the climate will change with the sea temperature. Steamy winds from the East. Banana farming. You can redevelop the whole coastline. "The Lincolnshire Riveria".'

'Jamie—'

'I know,' I said. 'You're going to say it's too mind-boggling.'

'Never mind.'

We continued to walk, but it wasn't the same. She didn't have *vision*, Caroline. I began to wonder if she and I weren't indeed incompatible. Had she not dumped me, I might have considered letting her go myself by now.

Keziah and I were both in a subdued mood when we met for our evening chocolate with our backs to the funfair, facing the sea.

'Eaten any more mushrooms?' I asked.

'Of course,' she said.

'And still building your thing?'

Keziah didn't answer for a long time, looking out to sea. Eventually she said,

'Do you think life passes more intensely here?'

'How do you mean?'

'It's so concentrated. Instead of thoughts being so shadowy, you can pin them down.'

'I suppose,' I said. 'I've certainly had some good meals.'

'Most of the people I worked for had things in common. Broken homes. Abuse. Self-hatred.'

I shifted uneasily. It would be much more fun to talk about how I was rearranging the constellations in the sky to some more modern configurations, such as *The Christmas Tree* and (my particular favourite) *The Apple Logo*. Much more fun than *Orion the Mighty Hunter*. Keziah said, 'Please don't make a stupid comment or change the subject.'

'Nothing was further from my mind,' I said quickly.

'I had a rocky time at university.' She sipped her chocolate.

'Who doesn't? Some friends and I once decided to take the Eurostar to Ashford for a joke. Except they tied me to the seat and I couldn't get out till Belgium. Cost me a hundred and fifty quid to get back.'

'I had an abortion and six weeks in a psychiatric hospital in my first year.'

'OK. That sort of rocky.'

'What saved me was the night I volunteered at the night shelter. I was doing it to show off, an edgy student thing. Anyway. I found the people in the shelter were exactly like me. We'd all come to the same place, though by different routes. I was home, Jamie.'

Keziah was looking out over the sea. I opened my mouth. 'Please don't give a long talk about how you, too, found fulfilment from deep involvement with the needy,' she said.

'I wasn't going to,' I said, abandoning a mention of how I did a street collection for Kidney Research each year. Actually, what I used to do was empty my small change into six of the envelopes and mail them back.

'Really.'

'No, I was going to make a sympathizing noise,' I improvised. 'I learnt that girls have to solve problems out loud and at length. Men are obliged to be present but mustn't talk and aren't allowed to read the paper.'

'Good. Until then I'd hardly known anyone else like me. Here was a houseful.' She sipped her chocolate. 'Jamie if you make a stupid comment or a joke at this point I will give you reasons to believe that I did not go to Women's Advanced Self Defence classes in vain.'

I felt my knees pressing themselves together.

Keziah continued: 'Me and my sister were brought up in West Africa. My mother ran—still does run—a mission hospital. My dad built solar fruit dryers. We had a goat for a pet. Her name was Clarissa.'

'Clarissa. Nice.' I said.

'My sister's black. Jemima. They adopted her. Then three months later my mother fell pregnant with me. It was so obvious Jemima was adopted that my mother spent all my childhood overcompensating.'

I don't do parental compensating, never mind overcompensating. 'My mother is the most fearing and controlling figure I've ever met,' went on Keziah. 'And when I was seven my sister and I were sent to a boarding school. That's the way you do it in Africa—that or come home. It was an abusive context.'

'The man who you were burning on the bonfires.'

'The head teacher. Yes. Abuse is the most destructive thing you can do to a person. My mother would not move us out. By then my dad was so broken with his depression that he didn't stop her. My sister seemed to be in denial. She floated through school. I fought every day. Seven years.'

'Quite surprising,' I said.

'What?'

'That you fought. So out of character.'

'So here, at college, I'm in the night shelter with guys with the same self-hatred as me, the same powerlessness and the same sense of being evil and of being victims. We were the same. Except I could turn the world round for them.

'My life changed. I had been planning to be a city lawyer, really rich, breaking my mother's heart as many times and in as many different ways as possible.' Keziah spooned in a marshmallow quite calmly, a bit like a minor celebrity saying her life ambitions were to care for small animals and work towards world peace. 'But now I wanted to fight for these guys for the rest of my life.'

I thought, but didn't say, that a twenty-six-year-old talking about 'the rest of her life' was a little, well, teenage. I long ago stopped having a Purpose. Unless you count Consuming with Finesse. But mostly I was just wishing we could talk about something else.

'You mind if I ask you a question?' I said. 'Of course, that itself is a question, so really I'm asking if I can ask you two questions... anyway... here's the second question ... why are you telling me all this?'

'It's called sharing. It's what human beings do,' said Keziah.

'Not the ones I know,' I snapped. What is it with girls, I thought, that they have this urge to hold serious, in-depth conversations? What have I done to deserve this? Do I not look like just the sort of person *not* to have serious, in-depth conversations with? Isn't this what reality TV is for, so that girls can get it all out of their systems and we guys can watch the cricket without them interrupting at crucial moments to discuss somebody-at-work's ectopic pregnancy?

'One other thing,' said Keziah. 'When I crashed into you... I get these waves of depression sometimes. My head was in a mess.'

'No, really,' I said.

'I wasn't quite trying to kill myself, but I didn't much care what happened.'

'I already said it's over,' I said.

For a moment I felt a little stab of sympathy for her. So bleak, her life. But you can't get dragged into these things. And please could we stop talking like we're trapped in daytime TV.

'That constellation up there,' I said. 'It's called *The Christmas Tree*.'

She walked away into the night.

Almighty Toad

A good way to stop *Zlotcwicvic Enngerrgrunden Transportowicz, Krakow* rampaging through the door and across my duvet as I tried to sleep was to think systematically about food. Treat it like an exam question: *List the foods of Singapore* (as taught us by Annie, and as discovered through several research trips to the hawker centres in London's Chinatown):

Hainanese Chicken Rice

Fish Head Curry

Mee Goreng

Laksa

Nasi Lemak

I was thinking so hard I kept accidently creating these dishes which materialized in front of me.

Chai Taw Kway

Rojak

Fishballs

Yong Tau Foo

Slept finally and in my dreaming slipped from roti prata and curry sauce, to chocolate, to Keziah, to marshmallows, to Mel dislodging a tooth to—where was I now?

It wasn't the Dome.

I was propped up, half-sitting, half-lying. Every breath hurt. I was thirsty. Something was pumping oxygen up my nose. Lizzie's voice.

'*Me again!*

'*Mum and dad are still trying to sail to Madeira so that they can get a flight home. They sent their love as does Helen from work. There's all kinds of people been popping in.*

'*Alison said to call if your situation got worse. I said, "Alison, if his situation gets worse, I might as well just email you with the date of the funeral." I thought you'd think that was funny. Anyway, she'll come on Sunday if she can fit you in. The kids are with Oh-*Hugh!* this weekend. She doesn't want to upset them by bringing them to see you. Exams, you know.*

'*You'll like it in Intensive Care when you wake up. Every time you go through a door you have to wash your hands with alcohol. They said you're not meant to lick it off, but I mean…*

'*You gotta stay positive.*

'*I've been telling your customers that you're ill but that I know how to maintain your websites.*'

('*Nooooo!*' I thought to myself, in my sleep, my panic rising. Helen and Lizzie made up the two-woman graphic-design house *Wizzy Graphics* and they often produced material for my sites. Lizzie also knew where I kept my list of clients' site passwords, in case something happened to me.)

'*I've always fancied having a go at that. You've never let me. Anyway, "It's a good job," I said to myself, "that he's got his sister."*'

The hospital faded away after Lizzie's voice stopped and my dreaming spirit made its way back to the Dome. I clearly needed a drink and possibly a large bowl of Bombay Mix.

O you beautiful Dome, I thought, with your splashing fountains, your fake sunshine, your girls, your lack of stress. I soon settled in the Shallow End of the pool to watch a demonstration match from the Brazilian Ladies' Olympic Beach Volleyball Squad.

Until, that is, I heard someone tapping at the outer wall.

I wasn't sure I wanted to know who it was. I turned my head.

'Caroline!'

She continued tapping. Water dripped off me as I clambered out of the pool.

'What are you doing out there?' I mouthed. I signalled for her to meet me at the main entrance. I was fairly sure I was in trouble of some kind, and began unpacking some excuses—not easy, since I wasn't sure what I would be adjudged to have done wrong. Best get out a random selection:

'Just having five minutes off, Caroline. After the day I've had.'

'I'd no idea I was supposed to have phoned.'

'No, of course I didn't mean {*whatever it is you thought I meant*}.'

Maybe I should plead innocence: 'Can I help it if the Brazilian Ladies' Olympic Beach Volleyball Squad wants to practice some moves in my dreams?' Innocence rarely worked with Caroline, however: you could usually only appeal the sentence, not the verdict.

The main entrance was heavily padlocked. Beyond was a row of polythene strips to keep the heat in. I undid the locks and pushed my head through the polythene strips. Outside, the wind was howling and the rain had lumps of ice in it. The gusts that whipped through the polythene strips were enough to cause storm damage to any naked extremities. Caroline's hair was flat against her head—she looked wetter than I did—her lips slightly blue, her face white. Underneath the anger, in a soggy summer dress, was a vulnerable Caroline, perhaps, a Caroline who's tried her best to look good but was feeling an idiot instead. A Caroline who wanted a hug.

'What are you doing out there? You'll freeze! Come in!'

'I can't,' said Caroline.

'Yes, you can. Come in.'

'No, I can't.'

'Why not?'

'You've already let in the Caroline you let in. I'm the Caroline you never let in,' said Caroline.

'You're being enigmatic.'

'I'm being perfectly clear.'

'Caroline. Come in.'

'Just go back to the Shallow End, Jamie.'

I sighed.

'If you weren't going to come in, why did you knock?' (Why are you *always* making *pointless gestures*, Caroline, that I'm supposed to *get*?)

'You don't get it,' she said.

I thought of the Bombay Mix back at the poolside.

'Look,' I reassured her, 'this is just a dream. We'll be OK in the morning.'

'The Overlord and I have taken the view you're doing very well and we've decided to fast-track you,' said Leopold the next day. 'We're going to deal with the most important topic of all. The tools for relating with spirits. Quite a privilege, this. I hope you're ready.'

This new day was a hot one in Paradise. I was dangling my feet in a fast-flowing stream at the edge of the clearing. Keziah was sitting crosslegged next to me, meditating on her cup of coffee. An orange sun was climbing through the pines. Leopold was perched on a log across the stream from us. A lesson on how to sit in a kilt would have been a good move, I couldn't help thinking. 'There's really just one basic tool,' he told us.

He looked at us. It may have been a trick of the rising sun, but I wondered if Leopold wasn't perspiring a little. He crossed his wizened legs—on balance, a good thing. 'It's a tool that most people instinctively understand. But a tool that Western cultures have abandoned. Any ideas?'

I was avoiding his gaze and Keziah was still evolving her way out of the primaeval swamp called Morning. Leopold cleared his throat.

'When we look at the research, we see that if these humans are going to be happy, they have to worship us.'

He looked at us sharply. 'I know,' he added hastily. 'You may ask *why?* It's so absurd. What can you give us? Nothing. But the research is clear. We lead you in worship, life for you gets a bit better. Happiness increases. There it is. A finding.

'We say to ourselves, if we have to be the subject of their adoration and worship, if that's what it takes, we'll pay the price and do it.

'With me so far?

'So.' Leopold glanced at Keziah and started rubbing the side of his neck very hard. 'I thought we'd make a start today by worshipping Gaston.'

He coughed again. 'Obviously, he is a senior spiritual being. That's why he's called, "The Overlord." It's quite appropriate. Trust me in this.

'Clearly we're going to have to do this in a way that is true to your cultural values. You have to worship the spirits with postmodern chic and sophistication rather than pre-modern ignorance.

'Think of what the pre-moderns made to represent their gods. Strong things, like bulls. Goddesses with massive child-bearing hips. They worshipped the statue and that helped them worship the spirit behind the statue.

'That idea obviously needs updating. Here's my stroke of genius. This is what's going to change the world. What do *you* make to represent your god? Any thoughts?'

He looked at us each in turn, legs still crossed.

'No? I'm not surprised. This will stretch many great minds. What you make is a piece of Art, representing all that makes you happy. An expression of thanks to the Overlord Gaston. Your own, personal, patchwork god. This is the revelation. Deep down, you know it's true. It's your heart's desire. Thus saith the Lord.'

Leopold was so excited that he suddenly stood up and started to pace around.

'Just imagine if this took off on earth itself! An end to branded gods! No more buying a religious franchise! Everyone with their own distinctive patchwork god looking over their house!'

The dyspeptic Leopold was looking ravenous. 'Imagine the way it will bring families together, weaving and stitching a family god! Imagine the cottage industries springing up, helping people with design!

'Some of these patchwork gods aren't going to be physical artifacts at all—some will be pure creations of software and music. Imagine the town fairs to which people bring their gods! Imagine the renaissance in art and society!

'Spirituality and creativity and humanity—buried for so long under a weight of rationalism, mass-production and branding—unleashed again in the world! And you're the start!'

'You couldn't just run this by me again?' I asked.

'Just build a god of your own design and use it to worship Gaston,' spat Leopold fiercely. 'How hard is that?'

'Well, I'll give it a shot,' I said.

'Er,' said Leopold, scratching the back of his neck. 'Er—we do need you both.'

Keziah was holding the coffee mug to her lips as if it were a dear friend needing a hug. She looked up, green eyes steady and level. 'It's one of these basic things,' continued Leopold. 'Live together. Worship together. Basic.' He swallowed.

'Worship Gaston? Worship you?' Keziah asked, eyes narrowing over the coffee mug.

Leopold massaged his chin. '*Technically*, you give devotion to very personal works of Art, that *represent* the spirits, so in a way...'

I said, 'Keziah, I think it's just one of those things we have to do. You know. To cooperate. Like we said.'

Leopold said, '*Please?*'

Keziah took a sip of coffee, put down the cup, looked Leopold right in the eye and said, 'I would sooner go for a swim in the Lake of Fire.' Then she neatly unfolded her legs, stood up, swept moist muffin crumbs off her lap, and walked away.

The sun continued to shine. Leopold was scratching his eyebrow furiously. A bird cheeped.

'Oh dear,' said Leopold.

With a sky-splitting caw, a fat pterodactyl dropped from a tree onto Keziah like a brick. It had two small hands on the end of thin lizardy arms and it used these to grab Keziah by the throat. It started jabbing her head with its beak. Keziah tried to fend it off, then made to punch and scratch its eyes. 'I thought this might happen,' said Leopold, wearily.

I took my feet out of the stream and walked hesitantly over to the fight.

'Oy,' I said to the pterodactyl, who aimed a vicious peck at me. 'Ow!'

I took a step backwards. The pterodactyl lifted Keziah off the ground. It flew over the stream, circled, then dropped her. Arms flailing, Keziah landed heavily, raising some dust.

The fat pterodactyl came to earth, shrank in on itself, and re-emerged as Gaston. He was breathing heavily and flecks of spittle dotted his chin.

'When we say worship!' Gaston screamed at her, eyes popping, little moustache twitching, 'we mean it!'

Keziah had landed awkwardly. She looked dazed for a second or two, then rolled over, stood up, dusted herself off.

She ran straight at Gaston, hands reaching for his throat, insanely brave. He looked shocked. Then he elbowed her savagely in the face, shoved her backwards, and hit her to the ground with his fist.

He looked like he was trying to get his feet the right way round to give her a kicking. At which point a trumpet blew.

Gaston froze. He and Leopold looked at each other, Gaston breathing fiercely.

Gaston then said something, using what I took to be a deep corner of language reserved for feelings more intense than humans can express. 'Oh, bother' seemed to be the direction.

Leopold was looking sheepish. 'I did tell him that mid-morning would be the best time. I didn't know it would be today though.' He pulled up his white socks and started straightening his jacket.

I crossed the stream using stepping stones, walked to Keziah and helped her up.

'You all right?'

'What do you think?' she asked, shaking me off.

'I was going to help but he... pecked me on the head.'

Green eyes flicked over my face for a moment. 'He pecked you on the head,' she said.

'Sorry.'

The trumpet blew again. Not a single blast this time, but what sounded like the beginnings of a rather good jazz riff.

Leopold, frantically smoothing his hair, stepped up.

'Er—guys,' he said. He linked his fingers, then unlinked them. '*Guys.* We do have a bit of an issue. I think we might have to postpone the actual worshipping. We can revisit it on another day. Sorry about that. The thing is—' He flashed a quick look over to Gaston who was walking around in small circles. 'We... have a visitor. He's a very important spirit. He looks after us, in a way. This is a morale-booster, probably.' He looked quickly from Gaston to Keziah, and from Keziah to me. 'If I could just say this. It's quite important that we all put on a good show for him. Laying aside any temporary differences.'

Leopold's leg was jerking up and down. 'Somebody here, for example, might think, *why should I*—well... here's the thing. Our visitor is called "The Almighty Toad."'

'The "Almighty Toad?"' I asked.

'Yes, yes. He's in senior management. Knows how to use a dagger. Now if we do all behave properly...' Leopold swallowed and looked across at Gaston, who was staring at a tree and pressing his fist very hard into his open palm. 'We'll cancel the worshipping for the day. How does that sound?'

The sky rocked with another jazz riff.

Leopold was pleading.

'OK,' said Keziah, with a shrug.

'Excellent,' said Leopold. 'I want us to line up in front of the house. Oh and Keziah. Please no mushrooms, darling. Please.'

We walked hastily to the cottage I'd built. Leopold fussed around us, as if for a photo-shoot. 'Look natural,' he hissed. He tried to neaten up my shirt. Keziah was much more crumpled than I, but Leopold held back from touching her.

The sky was throbbing with a trumpet solo, which just on the point of being astounding, failed. We heard a muffled, high-pitched curse.

Leopold dashed to my side. Gaston, like someone with hemaerroids, walked stiffly to stand next to Keziah, moustache still twitching.

A palanquin was descending. It was borne by a bull, a multi-armed woman with terrible hair, a thing like a sphinx, and a large black dog. Around them flew a cloud of small furry beings. The palanquin landed gently, the beings lowered it to the ground, and the woman with all the arms and the really bad hair opened the door. Everyone bowed, except Keziah. I inclined my head a tactful few inches.

What stepped out wasn't a Toad, strictly speaking, wrong dimensions, but he was irresistibly Toad-like. Clad in a cloak and small crown, he peered myopically at the flying trumpet soloist and rasped, 'Inadequate.'

The small flapping thing sighed—'Aaah'—crumpled, fell to the floor, and lay twitching, like a fly caught under a fresh coat of paint. The other flying beasts whistled and cooed.

Calmly the Toad examined us in turn. His large eyeballs had bumpy things like warts growing on them. Then he nodded, 'Gaston, Leopold.' He had a faint voice, terribly dry.

'Your Unholy Brightness,' said Leopold, with a bow.

'Magnificence,' intoned Gaston, with a slow dip of his head.

'Jamie Valentine Smith,' wheezed the Toad. He moved across the forest floor like a tank, heavy and flat-footed. His green skin was sore and bits of it were flaking off. He put his face just a few inches from mine. His lips had fresh cuts in them.

Suddenly his tongue flicked out and probed my face, my eyes, my hair, my body. It was so quick and so disgusting, that I only had time to flinch.

He retracted the tongue.

'Sound,' he muttered to Leopold.

He trod over to Keziah and looked her up and down, flat face taut, diseased eyes greedy with lust. Keziah stood quite calm, in her sulky-teenager pose. I started to chew a knuckle. Irresistable force, unmoveable object, all that.

113

'Keziah Grace Mordant,' he wheezed, eyes searching.

'Guided tour,' he said abruptly to Gaston.

'Leopold's the chief trainer, my Lord Toad,' said Gaston in a voice with all emotion strangled out of it. 'As your Lordship knows, my role is the strategic planning and marketing.'

'Guided tour,' rasped the Toad.

'Right,' said Leopold. 'My Lord Toad I'll show you round and as we go I'll explain the things I've been teaching. Obviously, that's the true strength of the model. What they're building is one instance of our values interacting with their creative natures. Not the only permutation, but an authentic proof-of-concept.'

'Clear,' said the Toad blandly.

'Of course it is to you, my Lord Toad,' simpered Leopold.

We trailed along behind.

After quarter of an hour, we returned to the front door.

'Gaston, Leopold,' breathed the Toad, 'restrain Mordant.' They looked at each other for a moment, then each grabbed one of Keziah's arms. 'Will view her habitat. Stay.' He streaked away, leaving his cloud of flying animals.

'Why is he doing that?' Leopold asked Gaston, over Keziah's head.

'Just perversion, I expect,' said Gaston. 'Girls' bedrooms.' We stood around in silence until the Toad returned.

'Learnt,' he said, a smug look on his face.

'Do you want to look at my habitat?' I asked. I had nothing to hide. 'I did a maglev.' He looked at me a bit like he'd looked at his failed-trumpeter-insect.

'Animal shut up,' he wheezed.

'Fair enough,' I said. 'Only offered.'

'Question,' said the Toad, turning to Leopold. 'Worship practice of Smith and Mordant. Plans?'

'That's a good question, my Lord Toad,' smiled Leopold, with a quick look over to Gaston. 'I think it's probably fair to say that we are still turning over in our minds whether to adopt a gradualist approach or a more robust process for the training. It's rather nuanced.'

'Gaston?' asked the Toad, quizzically. 'Opinion.'

Gaston's face looked like he was being forced to eat egg-and-cress sandwiches at an Aunt's.

'It's evolving, Majesty,' he muttered finally.

'Need faster progress,' said the Toad, his voice hardly more than twists of dry breath. 'Can't wait. Go for Big Bang. Plunge in, sort it out early. This inspection? Satisfactory. Am taking personal charge. Daily meetings.'

'Magnificence,' gulped Leopold, 'daily meetings will leave us very little time for finishing the training.'

'Hour with me, more valuable than day with cattle. Efficiency will improve.'

'Indeed, Almighty Toad, I don't know what I was thinking of.'

'In future, think before speaking,' said the Toad. 'New Trumpeter: closing theme. Note perfect.'

'Your brightness,' asked Gaston. 'Do you know when it's going to start?'

'Negotiations ongoing,' rasped the Toad, briskly. He looked at his retinue. 'Closing theme.'

One of the furry animals started playing a tune. Gaston, Leopold, the Toad and the other furry beings all stood to attention, the furry beings flapping frantically to hover over the same spot. The Toad climbed back into his palanquin and the whole party rose languidly into the sky, leaving a little shower of crisp skin.

We watched them rise until the Toad became a fat blob surrounded by a cloud of dots against the blue sky. The Toad then sped away, a streak of light. The rest, like a shoal of mackerel, followed in a silvery flash.

Gaston and Leopold relaxed.

'That was an experience,' I said. 'You said something about "When's it going to start?" When what's going to start?'

'Oh, it's nothing to concern you,' said Leopold. 'It's a high-level thing.'

Keziah had walked over to where the furry animal was still writhing in the dust. I followed.

'What's your name?' asked Keziah kindly, crouching down to see the little beast. It was mostly a trumpet. Underneath its fur it had wings and legs like an insect, a small head, and a huge, wobbly external lung. The being was lying on its side, and it moved up and down slowly as the lung worked.

'First Trumpeter 291-3471,' the voice was high-pitched.

'That's your name?' I asked.

'I have a stage name, "Miles,"' squeaked First Trumpeter with dignity. He turned to lie on two of his little elbows, sitting up slightly to keep the throbbing lung off the floor. 'Not everyone can remember it, though. There's hundreds of First Trumpeters and they've all got wonderful stage names—*supposedly!*—so there's no way for your ordinary punter to pick the silver from the dross. In any case, I think using my reference number has a kind of funky edginess.'

'What happened to you?'

'Didn't practice enough.'

'Do you work for the Toad?' Keziah inquired.

'Did,' First Trumpeter squeaked.

'What was your job then?' I asked.

'Ceremonial entrances and exits,' said First Trumpeter, sitting up and wrapping his arms round his knees: one knee was wire-thin; the other looked like a central-heating joint. 'See, we were promised jazz riffs, not just orchestra work. That's why we all signed up. We get down here and, fair enough, you can launch your solo career.'

'And?' I asked.

'No audience,' said First Trumpeter. 'No call for it. Anyone with spare *admiration* will keep it for when they need it. Nobody's going to sit for nothing and just listen to you play. Even if you're as good as me. So you have to get commercial work, praising others.'

'How do you mean *work?*' I asked. 'Why do spirits need to work? As far I can see you don't eat, you don't die, you don't need anything.'

First Trumpeter sighed. 'Because we have massive, hypersensitive egos, forever hungering for admiration. That's what we starve of, every day.'

'You never thought of a career in law?' I said.

Leopold, who had been in urgent conference with Gaston, walked over. 'Out,' he said to First Trumpeter. 'This is private.'

'Can't,' said First Trumpeter.

'Let me stamp on your antennae for a bit,' said Leopold. 'You might find that motivational.'

'Still can't,' said First Trumpeter.

'I've just about had it with beings saying "No." You do what you're told.'

'Would if I could,' said First Trumpeter.

'Right then,' said Leopold, lifting his foot and trying to wrench it round so that it was pointing forwards. Keziah stood in the way.

'If he says he can't, he can't.'

'You know I can't,' insisted First Trumpeter. 'I'm suffering from depression. I'm a *musician*. We can only soar and fly when we feel lifted by something.'

'So cheer up and *then* move on,' said Leopold.

'What is there to be cheerful about? I've just been fired and I'm going to have to relaunch my solo career for the eighty-ninth time.'

Gaston walked over.

'Look,' said Leopold, 'I don't care what you have or have not felt cheerful about. Just get your ugly face out of my territory.'

'Mind you, you've got even less reason to be cheerful, as I observe,' said First Trumpeter.

'Meaning?' asked Leopold.

'The Toad thought we were great,' said Gaston gloomily. 'I thought of everything but I didn't think of *that*.'

'I still don't understand how that can be a problem,' said Leopold.

'Because if he likes it a bit, he'll just let it happen and extract his percentage. But if he likes it a lot, he'll take it over,' said Gaston with a sigh. 'We seem to have got ourselves a winner. So it's a loser. All that effort. All that grovelling to those Collectors. All wasted.'

'He can't just—how can he take over?' asked Leopold.

Gaston turned heavy-lidded eyes towards Leopold. 'Not difficult. He just calls intensive, daily meetings with us. Gossip will do the rest.'

'But these are our ideas, not his!'

Gaston made a cawing noise (getting in touch with his inner pterodactyl again, evidently).

'Leopold,' said Gaston, with the air of someone teaching someone how to pick their nose when the person trying to pick their nose, just isn't getting it. 'Everybody will know we had the ideas. Everybody will know the Toad stole all the credit. They will laugh at us and fear the Toad.'

'So what are we going to do?' asked Leopold.

'What can we do?' replied Gaston, moodily. 'What would anybody do? Plot. Be treacherous back.'

'Against the Toad?' asked Leopold. 'Plot against the Toad!'

'Yes,' insisted Gaston. 'Or lose everything.'

'Well,' said Leopold thoughtfully. 'Losing everything isn't that bad, is it?'

'We're still paying for it, Leopold. Do you think those Collectors will say, 'Oh, too bad, you've lost your investment, we'll let you off your debts.''

'Still,' said Leopold. 'The Toad.'

'Somehow I've got to fit it all in between worshipping the Collectors, schmoozing with senior spirits, and now meeting the Toad every day. Which of course leaves me *loads* of time for plotting to defeat the Toad which is no doubt *exactly* what the Toad wanted.'

'You know,' squeaked First Trumpeter, 'listening to you, I'm beginning to cheer up.' Wings a blur, he flew up into a tree.

Gaston watched him go. 'Oh goody,' he said, moodily. 'We're already late to worship the Collectors. What a productive morning this has been. This time, Leopold, you are going to do the melody and the words and I'm going just going to hum in the background.'

'That'll be a big change then,' said Leopold.

They were both rising into the sky.

'I carry burdens you have *no idea of*,' Gaston was insisting as they rose upwards. 'All I ask is that you cut me a little bit of slack occasionally—'

And they were gone.

'Cup of tea?' I asked Keziah.

'No,' she said.

'Sure?' I asked. 'It's just the thing for pterodactyl-related stress.'

'I'm going to work on my habitat.'

'You all right?'

'Fine.'

'Keziah,' I was exasperated now. 'Do we have to do this stupid thing of you saying you don't want to talk and me saying yes you do and you saying no you don't and me saying in a wheedling voice *you do really* when we both know—'

She spun on her heel, walked back and looked like she was going to slap me.

'What?' she said. We were almost nose-to-nose.

'We've an opportunity here,' I said, calmly, taking a step backwards. 'We can ask First Trumpeter some questions.'

'Thanks for your help back then by the way. Wringing your hands on the sidelines. That really got them worried.'

'What is the point of picking fights all the time?'

'What is the point of letting them abuse you?'

'It's for the *short term*,' I said. 'Can't you get that into your thick head?'

'That's what abusers always say,' said Keziah steadily. '"Just this once, Keziah."'

I looked at her.

She looked at me.

'Sorry,' I said.

I wasn't sure what I'd said sorry for, exactly. *Sorry-that-I've-got-my-head-screwed-on-and-you're-completely-tinpot.* 'What I thought was,' I said, 'we could have a cup of tea, invite Caroline round—she's clever, Caroline—ask First Trumpeter here to play some music. In exchange, we can see what we can learn from him.'

'All right,' said Keziah.

'I know just the place,' I said. 'I'll build it. I'll send Dumbo when it's ready. I'll only be a few minutes.'

'I never liked this place,' said Keziah sulkily.

I had rebuilt one of Cambridge's more popular out-of-town cafes, its tables scattered through an old orchard. Just at our feet (ours was a good table), the little River Cam squeezed itself between its banks, grey and oily like all the tourists of the world liquefied.

I'd fixed up a girly tea for them, cream cakes, éclairs and a roulard. Fresh strawberries. I added a pile of samosas and a bowl of salted cashews for myself. We sent Dumbo off to browse among the banana trees which I'd planted downstream. First Trumpeter 291-3471 was hovering above the river, excited.

'Right, here's the programme,' I said to Keziah and Caroline. First, we have a little chat with First Trumpeter here—'

'First Trumpeter *291-3471*, or *Miles*,' called down First Trumpeter 291-3471, from mid-air.

'Then in exchange, we enjoy an evening of jazz.'

'This is historic,' said First Trumpeter 291-3471.

'We're looking forward to it,' I said.

'The Omniverse has waited a long time for this.'

''Course, there's only the three of us,' I said. 'It's hardly the West End. Or even Cambridge Corn Exchange. There's only two of us if you don't count Caroline, who's a kind of memory.'

'Which, let me tell you, is a nightmare all its own,' said Caroline, looking disgruntled. 'Have you ever tried being what some guy thought you were? Monochromatic.'

'I'm doing my best,' I said, 'to make you a vivid, three-dimensional character.'

'Pitiful,' sniffed Caroline.

'So,' I said to First Trumpeter. 'A few questions first. You said there were hundreds of you?'

'Journeymen, most of them. Can't hold a tune, half of them.'

'Nevertheless. And spirits like Gaston, Leopold and the Toad.'

'Praise Be To Him,' said First Trumpeter.

'Sorry?' I said.

'Oops,' said First Trumpeter, 'habit.'

'All these beings. How many altogether? Where do they come from?'

'I've heard of Earth,' said First Trumpeter, 'obviously. Everywhere on earth you find life. People drill miles down, find bacteria. Look on the bottom of the ocean, find groupers. Same in the heavenlies. Spirit beings *everywhere*. Plus all the bits of spirit beings—'

'Bits?'

'—Get broken off in fights, but still have life in them. Float around until they make up some new spiritual organism. You have the spiritual equivalents of viruses and bacteria. Litter everywhere, of course, some of it alive. And other things: metaphors, for example, or memories. Some of the metaphors are huge, more like wossisnames, meta-narratives. Cover half the sky.'

'Cool,' I said. 'Where do you all come from?'

'We entered this Omniverse not long after the Moment of Creation. We were refugees from a war: a colony of artists, warriors, thinkers and leaders. We came to the Omniverse to forge a new order, based on freedom.'

'I see,' I lied.

'It's rough though. A rough colony. Radiation. You're sheltered in this habitat but it's difficult to keep the radiation out for long, really. Stings. Burns. Everyone's got a headache all the time. It makes us age. Can you imagine that? Eternal beings and we're *ageing*.

'So the Omniverse doesn't have what we need. Toad (Blessed Be His Name) dries up. Creative beings have creative block. Sensitive beings are numb. Beings with administration skills meet incompetence and frustration all the time. Sexual beings, which is all of us, can't, you know. Sociable beings are lonely. Musical geniuses can't get gigs.' He flapped his wings furiously.

'We fill up with existential angst, ready to pour it out, and no-one wants to know. Completely wasted angst. Some of us dream that somewhere, somewhere, there's an Omniverse where we belong. Over the rainbow, as it were.'

'What do most beings want?' I asked.

'Respect,' he said. 'Adoration ideally. A few of us have gifts that really deserve it, like me for example. Now look, you're spoiling the atmosphere of expectancy with this chatter. Ideally, we should have a reverent hush.'

'We think we've been captured by Gaston and Leopold,' I said. 'Why would they do that?'

'Let me see,' said First Trumpeter scornfully. 'Perhaps it might be to exploit you in some way.'

'They say they want to make us happy,' I continued. 'Not exploit us.'

'And?' inquired First Trumpeter.

'I was wondering if there would be a way they could be exploiting us, and at the same time making us happy?'

'You what?' asked First Trumpeter.

'I thought they might be aiming for a win-win situation.'

'Look, we need to get playing, but obviously if it's a win for everybody you haven't got the maximum advantage out of the situation. You can squeeze it for some more.'

'And what's all this about the Toad and power struggles and treachery?'

'Perfectly routine back-biting. Now come *on*. Let's play. I want silence. Perfect silence.'

'OK.'

'Can you dim the lights?'

'That's the June sunshine,' I said. 'I'm not dimming that. Can't you think of it as Jazz for a Summer Evening or something?'

'What you have among you,' said First Trumpeter, 'is not jazz for a *summer evening*. This is jazz forever.'

He closed his eyes. 'I need 12-bar blues on a honkey-tonk piano.'

'One moment,' I said. It took an effort of memory to recall a soundtrack, strip out the piano element, then set that piano element on a loop. 'There you go.'

'And drums,' he said.

'Bongo or snare?'

'Snare. With brushes.'

It took a few goes, but finally we had the 12-bar blues going and the drums scatting.

'We start simple,' squeaked First Trumpeter. 'Then we fly.'

He didn't warm up. He simply inflated his lung, and blew. With two wings keeping him stable in the sky, his fist clenched in the air, First Trumpeter played the most unbelievable improvisation you have ever heard.

It was a long way from perfect, and he squeaked a curse every time he missed whatever-it-was he was trying for. Still. Down it poured, a cloudburst.

First Trumpeter soared and seemed to swell inside. His grey fur became streaked with rivulets of gold and red.

Still he played.

We listened for a long time.

It was awesome.

You know, even brilliant music gets boring after a while. You start to shuffle. You look at each other. You scratch yourself. You do little mini-Pilates-stretching exercises with your fingers. I noticed Caroline, who was in a summer dress, had brought a light jacket, but the jacket didn't quite go with the dress, so she wasn't wearing it and was shivering a little.

Wouldn't mind an interlude, you think. Stretch the legs. Warm up. Maybe find the Gents'.

The long evening faded to black, and still he played. Constellations came out—the *Christmas Tree*, the *Apple Logo* and a new one I'd done, the *Complete Guide to Fielding Positions in Cricket*.

This was getting ridiculous.

I came to a decision. I glanced at Keziah and Caroline for affirmation and made a throat-slitting gesture. Then I cut the drums and the piano.

Three bars later, First Trumpeter stopped. There was a moment of what would have been silence had it not been for the slurping of the Cam against the mud, and the distant sound of Dumbo trampling the banana plantation.

First Trumpeter turned white.

'*No…!*' he screamed. He swooped down at us. 'No… That's total musical—how *can* you?'

'Er—' I said.

'You *cannot*—' First Trumpeter was flying within inches of our faces in turn, scowling, spitting.

'The thing is—' I said.

'What you've just done is *evil*,' he said. '*Sacrilegious*. I was *performing*.'

'Now hold on,' I said.

'We were at the start of a journey together! An eternal journey! Fans were going to gather! Momentum was going to build! *Thirteen point eight billion years waiting for this moment and you cut the music! You strangle it at birth!*'

As Gaston had done earlier, First Trumpeter now stepped out of the subset of language we all held in common and started on some expletive riffs of his own.

'We can always—' I said.

He started spiralling round us, climbing, but at the same time seeming to get heavier and more wobbly. His fairy-wings were throbbing with the effort of keeping him aloft.

'Maybe you can do an album or something—'

Wings whining with strain, flying an agony, he pitched sideways into the Cam with a splash. A few moments later, we heard a trumpet-like *whumping* noise and saw a dome of grey water, fringed with white, which dispersed with a chaotic, musical hiss.

The Cam has swallowed everything that twenty generations of students have dropped into it, including twenty generations of other students, and it flowed on.

'He could have gone on for ever,' said Caroline thoughtfully. 'I think he would've.'

'He would,' said Keziah.

'No wonder he found it hard to book gigs,' I pointed out.

'What did you think of the music?' asked Keziah. 'Did it—what did you think of it?'

'It was good,' I said. 'It was, yeah, it was good. Bit long.'

'Did you *feel* anything?' Keziah asked, eyes searching my face.

'No,' I said firmly. 'Look. I want to think. Caroline. Since you are a figment of my imagination, you can summarize what we know.'

With a glance to Keziah, and a sigh, Caroline adjusted her glasses.

'OK,' she said. 'What have you got going for you?

'1. You are not dead.

'2. You have been visited by a therapist who is keen to help you manage your situation.'

'Irrelevant,' I said. 'Strike that out.'

'You think,' said Keziah.

'Irrelevant to me, anyway.'

'Which is all that matters,' muttered Keziah.

Caroline looked at us over her glasses. I could see her growing into a bossy school-marm role.

'2.' She continued, 'Mushrooms.'

'Strike that out as well,' I said. 'Emotional. Not rational.'

Caroline made a face and Keziah had a look in her eye that almost suggested a giggle.

'Alright. 2.,' said Caroline, with dignity. 'You seem to be safe enough in the short-term because they need you for something—probably to do with worshipping them.

'3. Stresses are appearing among those who are managing you.'

'For example,' I said. 'Leopold's scared of you, Keziah.'

'He'd be scared of you if you stood up to him,' said Keziah. 'They all would. They're terrified.'

'4.,' said Caroline, 'However you look at it, the slightly longer term future doesn't look good.'

'What we need,' I said, 'is a plan to keep us alive until our bodies recover. Caroline, brainbox that she is, mighty mental capacity in full spate despite the power-drain of being County Assistant Librarian (Local History Archive) at such a tender age, is going to suggest a strategy. Aren't you Caroline?'

'What about escaping?' suggested Caroline.

JAMIE'S MYTH

'I don't think that's a very good idea,' I said, instinctively reaching for a samosa.

'Why not?' said Caroline. 'It might buy you extra time.'

'Practicalities,' I said firmly. 'There's all that radiation and everything. Therapists running loose. Dangerous.'

'You don't know that,' she said.

'Everybody says so,' I replied.

'You don't *know*. It could be really empty.'

'When we first left our bodies it wasn't long before we were captured, was it?'

'You're not, scared or anything?'

'Pfff,' I spluttered, which isn't a brilliant idea when you have a mouthful of samosa. 'Sorry. The crumbs'll just flick off. Really Caroline it's not about danger, it's about what's wise and what isn't.'

'Sounds quite practical to me,' said Keziah, with an unusually innocent expression on her face.

'Look,' I said, 'we don't even know where the edge of our cage is. So it's impossible.'

'The HELP system might help,' said Keziah.

'That's a novel idea,' I grumbled. 'A HELP system that actually helps you, that might catch on. Look, you're both being ridiculous.'

'I think it's good to have a bolt-hole,' said Caroline. 'At least to see if you can't find one.'

'Caroline, I think you've been helping out in the Melodramatic Thriller section again, and all this adventure's gone to your head. Escape! I mean.'

'A refill of tea, Keziah?' asked Caroline.

'Thank you Caroline,' said Keziah.

'Look,' I said. 'I don't think we can find the edge of the habitat. I've flown the space shuttle and I never got near any edge of any habitat.' I seized another samosa and killed it with a single bite.

'I've been thinking about that,' said Caroline. 'Since there's not much to do in the lighthouse apart from re-cataloguing your music collection.'

'How's that going by the way—'

'I think you make space in this habitat by imagining it. If you just rose up into the sky, not thinking about anything, you'd soon reach the edge.'

'All right, suppose for argument's sake you can find the edge. What do you do then? Just stick your head through?'

'You could try.'

'And have it bitten off by whatever's out there, or peppered with radiation, or—'

'They might just be telling you that to stop you trying to escape,' said Caroline.

'Or, alternatively, think of this,' I said. 'They might be telling us that because it's really true and really dangerous.'

'Only one way to find out,' said Keziah, examining her nails.

'So you're saying,' I said, looking from one to the other and at the now-empty plate of samosas, 'go up to the edge of the habitat, stick my head out, have a look.'

They both nodded.

'Which Gaston and Leopold will both be fine about,' I said.

'Except they're not here,' said Caroline. 'They'll be busy toadying to the Toad.'

'You *think*.'

'Peace be Upon Him,' said Caroline.

'Suppose for a moment we could get to the edge of the habitat, and suppose we could stick our heads out and have a look, where would that get us?'

'It might mean that we had somewhere to escape to, which could prolong your lives, which could give time for your bodies to recover, which could mean that you return to them,' said Caroline.

'Or get my head fried off in radiation.'

'Good job we've a man about the place,' said Caroline. 'To do some of the brave stuff.'

'I will ignore that improper statement, because the County Council hasn't organized your Diversity Training yet,' I said. 'Plus I've had a thought. You're a figment of my imagination, OK, no disrespect, I've done my best for you, but if your head was fried off, *I* could put it back on.'

'Your point?' Caroline folded her hands across the table and looked at me.

'My point? My point is that if we're being *ruthlessly* practical... Keziah, if we're being ruthlessly practical, wouldn't you say that if there's a hazardous mission,' I was faltering a little, but to my great credit, carried on, 'fraught with unknowns and dangers, that the wisest course of action, when you really need a clear head in the face of mortal peril, is to send the County Assistant Librarian (Local History Archive)? I mean who better in a crisis? Especially given that, in the unthinkable scenario that she was in any way hurt, we who stayed behind would be in an excellent position to put her head back on.'

Neither girl replied.

'You're not sure whether to look on with sorrow or anger,' said Caroline to Keziah.

'Aw all right,' I said. 'I just think it isn't that great an idea, that's all. But I will give it some thought.' I took a fistful of salted cashews from the bowl.

'The thing is,' said Caroline, after a short pause. 'It's probably one of these things better done sooner rather later.'

'No time like the present,' added Keziah.

I closed my eyes. 'I tell you what,' I said. 'I'll ask the HELP. Then I'll think about it. *Pablo!*'

After a gap of some ten seconds, Pablo the HELP system emerged from the trees. He was shuffling, using a crutch, and his nose was encased in plaster. His labrador eyes looked at us sorrowfully in turn.

'*Señorita, Señorita, Señor.*'

'Pablo,' I said. 'How are you? Did you have an accident?'

'It was an encounter with a B-2 bomber, *Señor*, if you remember.'

'Can't we fix up your leg and that nose?'

'Some things are beyond mending, *Señor*.'

'Sorry.'

'I am coming to terms with it. You wish to know about the edge of the habitat? The two *señoritas* are in most respects correct. The edge of the habitat is quite near. You can reach it so long as you do not exercise any imagination. It is a clear boundary, like the surface of water viewed from underneath, easily found. You can indeed put your head through. I am not informed what you will find, but Gaston and Leopold recommend you don't do it.'

'Will an alarm go off or anything? Warn Gaston and Leopold?' I asked.

'I think they were of the view, *Señor*,' Pablo said, 'that the sheer horror of the situation would send you back.'

'I see. Would I be able to breathe?'

'*Señor*, surely you have learnt by now that your spirit is like what your physicists called an elementary particle. Or perhaps like a complex molecule. It simply exists, oscillating with its own intrinsic energy, requiring nothing to keep it going. It can travel anywhere in the Universe. Of course it can feel extreme pain, and be dissembled into its constituent parts, but each bit of you is immortal.'

'Thank you very much Pablo,' I said. 'You're a great HELP. I'm very sorry about the limp. Would it help if I recreated you as something else?'

'No *Señor*, the damage is to my core being and would show up in whatever form you created me.'

'I see. Sorry. You couldn't get some more salted cashew nuts could you? I particularly like the jumbo ones.'

'Jamie! Get them yourself!' scolded Caroline.

'I was only asking! Perhaps on second thoughts I'll just magic up some more myself. Thank you very much for your help. I won't blow you up this time. I was a bit upset before.'

'*Señor*,' said Pablo. He nodded to Keziah and Caroline and shuffled away.

'That settles it,' I said. 'Obviously, there's no point in going. You heard the man. Very risky. You'd have to be a fool to go.'

This led to an awkward pause, and we were quiet with our thoughts, until one of the stars from *The Christmas Tree* constellation above us—a greeny white one—removed itself from the sky, dropped down in front of us, expanded, and turned into Stub.

'Are you finished?' he asked. 'I've been watching your conversation. I know this isn't a good time. I have to tell you something tonight.'

'What?' I asked, very much in a bad mood.

'I've found out what they're doing. It's the Biennale,' said Stub. 'I should have remembered.' He didn't look well, bloodied and lacerated. 'It's a thing that happens every couple of years—'

'That could be why they call it a Biennale,' I said.

'The evil spirits have broken up the old monopoly, which never really worked, and have divided themselves into purchasers and providers. (You need to know these fashions sweep through heaven and earth from time to time.) The Almighty Toad heads up one producer group. He's a kind of business leader or warlord. Gaston's a manager and Leopold's a designer. They're putting together a package—that is, you're the package—for the Biennale. Which is attended by the purchasing groups.'

'You're not being *massively* clear at the moment,' I said.

'The clamour for new movements, sir, is constant,' said Stub, glancing over his shoulder. 'Everyone wants the latest spiritual fashions. Gaston and Leopold seek to re-introduce spirit worship into postmodern culture. Some postmoderns long for the certainties that their grandparents had (jobs, marriages, families). Gaston and Leopold want spirit-worship and spirit guides to be the route to that imagined happiness. So they're gambling that their mixture of pop-philosophy, cynicism, physics and spiritual experiences will become a new movement among postmoderns in the West.

'You guys are the pilot. You're the working model. They're going to show you off at the Biennale. If all goes well, their ideas get taken up by the purchasers. Gaston, Leopold and the whole of the Toad's working group get a massive increase in power and prestige. *That's* why they fought so hard for you.'

'When does this Biennale take place?'

'When the pre-conference haggling is over.'

'How long will that be?'

'Are you aware, sir, that time moves at a different speed the further away you travel from the world of matter?'

'Er, no,' I said.

'Up here time moves at about twice the speed of earth-time—T2, we call it. Two days at T2 are one day on earth. It's actually about T2.1 here. I am normally based at T12 because it gives us more time to sort things out. If we have some emergency decisions to make, we can go as high as T30 or T40. The Biennale is a bit closer to Earth, about T1.8. Obviously, the districts where time passes most slowly are the more desirable. From where you are, I should think the main events of the Biennale start in a couple of days. It's a tight deadline for Gaston and Leopold.'

'So that's why they've been filling our heads with pop ideology and trying to get us to build Paradise together?' I said.

'Exactly, sir.'

'What happens after the Biennale's over?' I asked.

'Well, sir, if they win the contract, they'll probably hang onto you for a bit, do some more experiments. If they lose, they're in big trouble. You've probably noticed that caring for you goes completely against the grain for them. So I imagine they'll dispose of you in some entertaining way, sooner or later. They might sell you to the highest bidder, recover their investment. Or invite people round for a party and torture you publicly.'

'Fabulous.'

'I am trying to give you objective advice, sir.'

'Do you know how they're doing down at the hospital?'

'No sir. It was, if I may say so, stressful enough to find out what I did. I haven't had time to visit earth recently.'

'So your advice is?'

'You? I give in.'

'That's helpful.'

'I will stay nearby. I had hoped to return to my colleagues, but I think this is an emergency.'

He flew off. Keziah and I glanced at each other.

'It doesn't look like we have long, after all,' I said.

I was badly needing some me time by now so I left Keziah and Caroline. I had been practising the high-speed streaking that Gaston and Leopold did and managed to shoot myself back to the lighthouse almost at the speed of light. (I had to slow to go round corners.) The lounge was dank and chilly, the fire not lit, and no-one had put out any nibbles.

I found Caroline, Mel and Annie sitting around the kitchen table, eating cream cakes. They ignored me. The only thing on the stove for tea (I poked it with a wooden spoon) was Lancashire hot-pot made from some gristly bits of dead cow.

I looked at them.

'What?' I said.

'The girls and I have been chatting,' said Caroline.

'But you were up in the tea-garden a second ago.'

'You forget I can move at the speed of thought,' said Caroline. 'Which even in the case of your thoughts, gives me plenty of time.'

'Can't we light a fire?' I asked, 'I'm freezing.'

'I had a headache,' said Annie, whose job it was. Then blushed deeply with the shame of uttering an entire sentence that people actually listened to.

'What's this for tea?'

'It was your turn to cook,' said Caroline. 'But out of the goodness of our hearts we made something.'

'You've been having too much salt and saturated fat,' added Mel, with the confidence of someone who got a C in Nutrition Studies, alongside her A in Sports Studies, thus proving she was an academic all-rounder.

'Caroline…'

'Unreasonable people,' said Caroline prissily, 'do not get our cooperation. Do they girls?'

Annie shook her head and Mel nodded.

'Right,' I said. 'Never mind, I'll light the fires—*woof! There!*—I will fix myself a meal. In the meantime, Caroline, I would be grateful if you could collect everything I've ever read about fusion power, and some maps of the East Coast.'

She looked at me mulishly.

'I'm not cooperating,' she said, and gripped the table. Her cheeks went slightly pink.

'Caroline…' I reminded her, 'There is still in this world, as I know you know, such a thing as Duty.'

'You are a piece of pond scum.'

'Duty, Caroline.'

137

She gave a little squeaky *hmph*, then stood up, strode over to the door and yanked it open. 'I'm only doing this because I'm a Librarian,' she said proudly. 'Not because I want to.'

Despite the fires, it remained chilly in the kitchen. Caroline was ages but did finally return with a stack of paper which she dropped heavily on the table in front of me. Then she went for a lie-down.

'I think I'll read these in the lounge,' I said.

An hour later, I got a call on the blow tube.

'Sorry to disturb your important researches,' Caroline said sweetly. 'Gaston and Leopold are back and they have summoned you and Keziah to meet them.'

'But it's really late!'

'I can tell them "no," if you like.'

'You could,' I said airily. 'I suppose I can fit them in.'

The sun shone at the same angle through the woodland as when we'd left earlier in the day, which I thought was a bit sloppy on Leopold's part. As I wandered towards the clearing, I had the feeling that I was walking in on an argument.

Gaston was looking away from Leopold, who was sitting with legs crossed and was leaning back in a completely artificial manner, as if trying to say, 'I'm not bothered what you think, I'm completely relaxed.' Leopold was dressed in a tracksuit, Gaston in a business suit.

Keziah arrived next to me in overalls splattered with oil and dirt. She was wearing her hair up, held in place by one of those savage hinged combs that girls leave lying around sometimes like bear-traps.

'Still working on your model?' I asked.

'Finally getting somewhere, I think,' said Keziah.

'Looks messy.'

'Yes,' she said.

'Why aren't they here already?' snapped Gaston to Leopold as we walked into the clearing. 'Why do *we* have to wait for *them?*'

'They're here now,' said Leopold.

'This is their last chance to get this right,' said Gaston.

Leopold coughed. 'Jamie, Keziah,' he said brightly. 'Do pull up a tree trunk.' He gave a nervous laugh. 'I know you've been enjoying our little sessions together. I think we've been having some memorable times—'

I put my hand up.

'Just suppose,' I said, 'for argument's sake, we weren't actually dead? We'd just left our bodies for a bit?'

'What makes you think that?' asked Gaston.

'I keep dreaming I'm in hospital.'

'I've told him,' said Leopold to Gaston, 'that these things happen to people who are recently dead. Nothing to worry about. In any case, it's irrelevant. The Universe is the Universe. Eternity is Eternity. We're here. You have to deal with that whether you're in your bodies or out of them. What we're teaching works in both cases.'

I kept my hand up.

'If we're dead,' I asked, 'where's everyone else?'

Leopold looked over at Gaston for a moment, then said, irritated, 'You're getting your perspective wrong again. Imagine you had a pet hamster. How many other hamsters would your hamster see in a day? Not many? Yet there are thousands of hamsters in your country. You forget that the heavenlies are vastly bigger than the earth. The whole human population could be here and you'd hardly ever see anyone else. The cute idea that all the humans are gathered in one little place called heaven or Valhalla is another of your human-centred fantasies. *The Universe is not about you* and little bags of skin and water like yourselves have to find your way as best you can.'

'Does that mean all the other dead humans have been captured by spirits?' I asked.

'Only the very lucky ones,' said Leopold. 'The rest are splattered by radiation, or just randomly preyed upon. Whereas with us,' he added smoothly, 'you two have found the Promised Land and two beings who care for you and have a wonderful plan for your ongoing deaths.'

'Provided you learn to worship us,' put in Gaston.

'Which we have agreed,' said Leopold, firmly, glancing at Gaston, and with a little tremble in his voice, 'is something you will grasp *naturally* and *without being forced* so long as you have a full understanding of who you really are and who we really are.'

'And provided you do it soon,' Gaston muttered.

'*Which you will* because you are grasping things very well and you know what's good for you,' insisted Leopold, through his teeth. '*Anyway*,' he added hurriedly, 'we haven't got long this evening—'

Gaston snorted. Leopold looked at him furiously and then carried on. 'We wanted to look at this worshipping idea from another angle. You see, some people find making and worshipping their own idol, well, not entirely to their taste, wouldn't you agree?

'That's a reasonable scruple. Why would eternal spiritual beings want to be worshipped by their pets? It's ridiculous!

'Unfortunately, the research shows, it works for you. Dogs need a pack leader; humans need a god. You don't need to believe in the god, or like the god, but there's something in the rituals that works for you. Like keep-fit.'

'Oh what's the point,' groaned Gaston suddenly. 'Even if they grasp this. Even if they get it into their *thick heads*, the Toad'll still take all the credit.'

'One bridge at a time, Gaston, dear,' hissed Leopold to Gaston. He looked at us conspiratorially. 'He's not had the best of days, the Lord Gaston. You might think it's wonderful to be an eternal, superintelligent being but actually there are downsides.

'So: what does this mean for you?'

I tried to look suitably thoughtful. Keziah, as girls do when they're not listening, let her hair down, put her man-eating comb in her mouth, gathered up her hair in her hands, twisted it together, folded it over and jammed the comb back in. I always enjoyed watching people do that, and even scrawny Keziah did it with effortless grace, like all girls do, the product of years of practice on *My Little Ponys*, I imagined, or maybe just some gender-specific predisposition to hairstyling, dating back to when female australopithecines deloused each other on the herbaceous plains near the Great Rift Valley.

'Mystery!' said Leopold, snapping me back to attention. 'Nobody knows the point of worship.

'Nevertheless our research shows it does work, so we go the extra mile and accept it, a bit like parents admiring a child's painting even though, by any standards of Art, it's rubbish.

'Now since worshipping us is essentially meaningless (as you may agree), you can do it with a clear conscience. You can worship us, knowing in your heart that it's all really an act, and it doesn't matter.

'This kind of performance has sustained humans for centuries. It works! It's harmless! It doesn't matter! We don't know why! It's all mystery and paradox! So let's do it anyway! A bit of harmless worship!' Leopold was slavering again.

'That makes sense to me,' I said, meaning it for once. I can be quite comfortable with insincerity. 'What about you, Keziah?'

Keziah sighed.

'I think,' I said, 'Keziah and me need time to think about this, don't we Keziah?'

Keziah opened her mouth.

'—Yep, Keziah thinks so too,' I said hurriedly.

'Good,' said Leopold equally hurriedly. 'Very good. I'm sure mature reflection will lead you in the right direction. Now unfortunately it's coming round to a busy time for the Overlord and I. Neither of us will be around tomorrow, or the day after that. What I would like you to do is think all this through, get your worship structures organized, and continue building your world—maybe a park around the house?—then when we get back it'll be great. We can really move on. Gaston, are you ready?'

Gaston sighed loudly.

'After you,' he said.

Leopold climbed into the sky. Gaston looked Keziah in the eye for a long moment. 'We will win you know,' he said slowly to her. 'Nice or nasty, we'll win.'

Keziah stared him down. She was magnificent sometimes. Stupid, but magnificent. Gaston twitched his fingers as if they were already around Keziah's neck.

'You have no idea,' he said, 'what I can do to you.'

'But you're afraid,' said Keziah.

Gaston looked at her for another long moment, and streaked away.

'I thought it was better not to have another fight,' I said to Keziah.

'Did you.'

'Yes, and I was right. I mean what would it achieve?'

'We don't know what it would achieve, because you always chicken out.'

'What it would achieve is another beating up, or maybe they'd throw us out, or maybe all sorts of things.'

'Which you think is worse than what we have now?'

'Look,' I said. 'All they're asking is that we pay them a bit of respect, and give them honour and worship, and they even *said* it doesn't matter if you mean it. You just have to do it.'

'Like prostitution really.'

'No, like survival. Like politeness. Like many things. Keziah, it's only you that's making this a problem.'

'So long as we do it.'

'So long as we *appear* to do it. That's all. Suppose we were dogs and they said, "I won't give you your food until you sit." We might think that's terrible, a breach of doggy rights but in the end, you sit and they feed you. They're happy, you're happy, end of problem.'

'Except you're still a dog.'

'Keziah, compared with Gaston and Leopold we might be a lot less than a dog.'

'*You* might.'

'Nevertheless I think I might make them a small god to keep them happy.'

'I think I won't.'

I looked at her. 'Can I change the subject? It looks like we've got two days off. What do you want to do?'

'I'm going to work on my habitat and eat mushrooms.'

''Cos I thought, I might try flying to the edge of the habitat.'

'You?'

'Yes. They're not going to be there, are they, Gaston and Leopold? So now's as good a time as any.'

'You're going on a dangerous trip to the edge of the habitat?'

'Don't rub it in. I hope it isn't *that* dangerous.'

'Would you like me to come?'

'Er.' I hadn't thought of this. Then, I thought, *Keziah, why don't you go instead of me? You're OK with pain and danger in a losing cause.* Then I thought about a man having to do what a man has to do, and what a stupid idea that is, and all the problems that's caused over the centuries. I thought of Caroline, Mel and Annie on strike back at the lighthouse, and I sighed and said, 'That's very kind but I think I'd better just go myself. Otherwise I'm in danger of being locked out of my own lighthouse.'

Keziah smiled. No, really. It didn't exactly take over her face, but it was there.

'There was a bit of steam coming out of Caroline's ears.'

'You don't know the half.'

'They say, "raging is caring".'

'Do they. Anyway, no, I think I must go alone but I might ask you to look me over when I return. Have you ever dealt with radiation sickness and mortal wounds?'

'I don't do blood, sorry.'

'First I'm going to have dinner and a film. Then in the morning I'll see if it's true that a condemned man eats a hearty breakfast.'

Maybe I went to sleep thinking too much about my trip to the edge of the habitat. Maybe my subconscious was looking for the Caroline-who-won't-come-in-the-Dome. Either way, in my sleep, I thought I might have a look outside the Dome. I pushed my way out and padlocked the door behind me.

Ghost-like, I drifted over the mounds of rubbish, close enough to see rats scurrying around. The people I glimpsed seemed to be avoiding me. They were wrapped up against the cold and were shuffling around, heads down in the rain.

Lorries were winding up a road and unloading at an ugly brick building attached to the Dome. Rubbish flowed from the building down a chute, adding to the piles of garbage all around. Smoke from the building's chimney filled the sky.

The rubbish slowly grew less as I glided away from the Dome, towards a bleak city. I passed derelict factories, pot-holed roads, charity shops. The streets were empty of tax-paying normal people and dotted instead with old ladies, single mums, shaven-headed men. Litter was being blown into piles like snowdrifts. I peeked through the locked gates of a great, but now trashed, park.

In my dreamlike movement I passed beyond the city and on to a mountain range, then on between peaks and clouds until at last the hills fell away suddenly into steep slopes and a cliff face. Below was a churning blue sea, with a wake stretching to the horizon—as if the whole Dome-landscape was a boat and I was looking out over the stern. I could see nothing beyond the horizon but the blue of the sea. Rainclouds blocked my view of the sky.

I turned and glided back to the Dome. On the way in, I noticed a sign above the entrance, in cheap lights, like the entrance to a funfair:

JAMIE'S MYTH

Then in smaller painted letters
A creation of Jamie Smith fantasy productions.

I looked over the landscape, the piles of rubbish, the sick and unpleasant people outside, the rain falling, the gloom, the poverty. Someone spoke in my ear, and I jumped.

'How can you not see, sir?'

'Stub?'

'Yessir.'

'Where are you?'

'Here, sir.'

'Have you been watching me dream?'

'Yessir.'

'Go away.'

'I would urge you to look around yourself sir. Take ownership. Stop hiding. It's all *you*.'

'This trip was your idea, wasn't it?'

'I may have helped it hatch, sir.'

I wrestled with my bunch of keys and pulled the Dome entrance open, luxuriating in the warmth, in the smell of the swimming pool and in the jungle noises of people having fun.

'Stub. Not today.' I quickly walked in.

'I have tried, sir. I don't know what else to try.'

'Perhaps you just shouldn't try. I'm OK.'

'You're not.'

I locked everything up, leaving the ghoul outside.

The next morning I breakfasted alone on the lighthouse balcony, having arranged a calm sea with a turquoise-and-orange sunrise, a light breeze and some wheeling seabirds. My white tablecloth swished in the morning breeze like a girl's summer skirt. I worked resolutely through roti prata, curry sauce and hot sweet coffee. It's good to have variety in your fats and carbs. Caroline popped her head round the door.

'Still planning your flight?' she asked.

'It's no use trying to persuade me now,' I said. 'I'm adamant. I know the risks are terrible, but it must be hazarded.'

I'd created a suitably legendary aeroplane for my flight, a World War II Spitfire. I thought I looked rather good in my leather boots, flying jacket and helmet. Caroline, Annie and Mel joined me on the runway.

I climbed into the Spitfire.

'I'm about to depart on a dangerous mission, hazarding all, though I do expect to be back for lunch. You may take out your handkerchiefs and wave them sorrowfully if you wish... I will attempt to maintain radio contact. Chocks away!'

Mel pulled on the wedges and I steered the plane down the runway and into the sky.

My plan was to concentrate on keeping the Spitfire spiralling slowly upwards. I mustn't imagine any sky above me, otherwise I wasn't going to get anywhere except further into the folds of my own imagination.

'Are you there Caroline?' I asked, 'Over.'

'Where do you expect me to be?' said Caroline, a little irritatedly, over the radio.

'You're supposed to say, "Over",' I said. 'Over.'
'Why?'
'Because that's what they do,' I said. 'Over.'
'Stupid,' said Caroline.

'Anyway,' I said, 'this is to report that I'm at 5000 feet and still climbing. Over.'

Still I climbed. The whole habitat stretched below me: my part, the part created by Leopold, and in the far distance, the hazy outlines of Keziah's place, which I had never visited since that first time.

Was it getting colder? I kept the Spitfire in its gentle upward corkscrew, keeping my eye on the instruments. Round and round, up and up.

I could feel a weight in the bottom of my stomach. Not the *roti prata*: anxiety. Was the engine straining? Up and up.

'You all right?' asked a crackly Caroline.

'I'm fine,' I said. 'Over.' I could feel fear spreading up my body and down my legs. It was paralyzing. I recognized the feeling: a similar wave of dread had washed over me just before my spirit was captured by the Collectors.

I was, I noticed, clenching my teeth. I took my eyes briefly off the instrument panel and looked up, taking care not to think about what I should see. The blue sky had straggly, fleecy elements, like bits of sheep wool caught on a barbed wire fence.

Another half turn and when I looked up again the sky had a graininess about it, and a direction of flow: pieces of blue sky, different shades, rolling slowly like boulders over my head, interspersed with white and grey fleecy bits.

148

I was terrified, unable to move the joystick, which stayed jammed in turn-and-climb. It was like being frozen in the moment before Keziah hit me.

With a loud hiss, we were suddenly among all the blue boulders that used to be the sky, the plane being jostled and swept along like a boat in white-water rapids. The engines died, the dials zeroed, the radio light went out. I looked around. I was surrounded by house-sized pieces of blue sky. Everything was out of control. It was the most mind-numbingly terrifying moment of my life, and my jaws opened but I couldn't scream.

It felt the plane was going to be broken into pieces and I was going to be crushed. Again.

Above the boulders were grey clouds. A yellowish rain, evil and fat and sticky, was splattering onto my cockpit.

Jostled by boulders, the plane swung round giving me a different view of the sky-above-the-sky. No clouds here: it fizzed with colour.

A small blue boulder clattered over the plane. For a moment I thought I saw something flutter through the sky, from right to left. I wondered if I could glimpse ropes stretching back from this thing. I would have followed this up but my eyes were determined that I looked to the right instead.

Something enormous, like a giant iceberg, massively higher than the boulders, was churning its way toward me. It wasn't pointed, like a supertanker: it was more like a broad cliff-front pushing through the rubble. Like an icebreaking ship, or a bulldozer, it was piling up pieces of blue sky and grey-white rubbish in front of it. I couldn't see the top, but I thought I glimpsed some hills, maybe a building at the edge of the cliff.

This massive hunk of cliff was going to crush me.

A blue boulder must have become trapped under the aeroplane wing, because I could feel the Spitfire beginning to tip. I was swept along for a few seconds, then my whole world turned as with a lurch, the plane capsized. I wasn't strapped in, so I fell out of my seat and my head and shoulders hit the canopy. I heard the hinges creak, something tore, and I tumbled headfirst out of the plane, back towards the habitat.

Funnily enough, it became less scary as I fell out of the sky. It was such a relief not to be surrounded by all that jostling blue.

'Parachute,' I thought, and felt its wonderful, reassuring tug on my shoulders. I tried to slow my breathing down.

Below me was the central part of the habitat—I must have been swept that way by the sky-boulders. I could make out the woodland and the clearing, and next to it the *Splendide* and its swimming pool. Keziah's habitat was in the distance, and had something big and grey looming out of it, a range of hills, perhaps.

Craning my neck, I could see my own habitat on the other side. With a little thought, I created a rocket pack on my back thinking to fire myself over to Edwards and land elegantly on two feet. Not a brilliant idea, however: I got tangled in the parachute and briefly zoomed around the sky with it wrapped round my head. So I mentally erased both the rocket pack and the parachute and thought, 'Dumbo!'

The cartoon elephant materialized below me. He was too wide to ride like a horse, so I sat cross-legged on the back of his neck, holding each flapping ear where it joined the head.

'Take me home,' I told him.

EVERY SPIRIT'S GUIDE TO KEEPING HUMANS AS PETS

'What happened?' asked Caroline after Dumbo and I had pulled up on the runway at Edwards. I was still breathing quickly and trying to unclench my fists, which were gripping folds of the elephant's cartoon skin.

'Nothing,' I muttered.

'What happened to your plane?' asked Caroline.

'Smashed.'

'Did you find an escape route?'

'There isn't one.'

'Do you want a cup of tea?'

'No. No. I want to go to Lord's Cricket Ground to rewrite the 2006-7 Ashes series. All afternoon. On my own.'

Things had looked up when I rowed back to the lighthouse in the evening. The lights were on. I tied the boat at the jetty, climbed over the rocky path, unlatched the wooden door. I was trying to forget the terrors of the morning and was feeling invigorated from the cricket.

I had tweaked things from the strict historic record to include a series-winning batting, bowling, fielding and captaincy performance from that outstanding England player, J. V. Smith, a man who amazingly had been playing for a pub team just a few months earlier, and who led his side to five improbable victories. The breakup of the Australian team and their descent into alcoholism and madness followed soon after.

Caroline put her book down when I opened the door.

'Hello Jamie,' she said pleasantly. 'Good cricket match?'

'Fantastic,' I said.

'I'm cooking suckling pig,' said Caroline. 'Possibly against my better judgement.'

'Oh,' I said, surprised. 'Thank you.'

I dated all our relationship problems to the last time Caroline and I had eaten suckling pig. A bunch of us had gone out to a village pub that specialized in it. Afterwards, Caroline and I had driven back to my house. Lizzie, who shared my house, was away at a nightclub. We'd been cuddling on my sofa next to my fire. I was full of the pig and contented, and I'd happened to mention to her, 'Do you know, Caroline, I'd rather be here with you than anywhere else in the world, or with anyone else in the world.'

It had popped into my head and I'd said it. I didn't think much of it: I could've said the same words to the suckling pig itself an hour earlier.

The effect on Caroline had been alarming.

Two people can be sitting on a sofa and they could be anywhere on the following scale:

1.0 Hardly bear the sight each other
2.0 Be quietly contented with each other's company
3.0 Be hardly able to keep their hands off each other.

Caroline had flipped from a comfortable 2.3 on this scale to a supercritical 3.9, without any kind of warning. She'd gone all floppy and her eyes were intense. This had not happened before to the amusing, sharp-tongued, offhand Caroline, not in eighteen months. Her previous record was probably a 2.8 during our June walking trip in the Lake District.

I panicked.

I can't remember what I said but I must have given the impression that I was reversing fast back up the scale past 2 and heading north to 1. I was probably at about 1.3 when I drove her home. By then Caroline had morphed again, this time into the Ice Queen of the North.

Things weren't the same after that. The next time we'd met, I'd been back at my good old reliable 2.2 or 2.3 but Caroline was somewhere around the arctic regions of 0.7 or worse.

We'd stumbled along for a few more weeks, during which time Caroline had occasionally thawed to 1.5 or so but had also initiated consultations with her mother and a wide-ranging panel of girlfriends.

Finally she'd initiated a disciplinary hearing ('we need to talk'), issued two sorrowful final warnings, then given me the sack. Trust a librarian to do it by the book.

I still wasn't sure what I'd done wrong.

Anyhow. Suckling pig was back on the menu. Perhaps the librarian was offering me a renewal.

'That's very kind of you,' I said. 'Do I know how to cook suckling pig?'

'You read a recipe in a Sunday supplement one wet November afternoon.'

'I didn't think you liked suckling pig.'

'Pigs can surprise you,' she sniffed, ambiguously. 'Mel said she'd eat some. I'm doing stuffed peppers for Annie and me. We've invited Keziah round and she said Stub might turn up too.'

153

'I can't believe I've got a memory of a recipe for stuffed peppers.'

'Dentists' waiting room,' she said. '*East Anglian Country Lifestyle*. Your alternatives were *Hello* magazine or a short film about cosmetic dentistry.'

'Fair enough.'

'I'm just going to text Keziah and tell her you're here.'

We had quite an enjoyable meal, which helped muss over the sad fact that three of those round the table were reconstructed figments of my imagination, one was a neurotic demon therapist and the only other human was Keziah, who has yet to win the Little Miss Sunshine Award for being good company at parties.

The trick with suckling pig, as you may know, is to keep drinking Chinese tea. Like a good tour guide, it slips into your stomach and makes arrangements so that the next half-kilo of pork has somewhere to go.

Stub, looking quite dapper in a collar and tie, wasn't eating, just taking occasional sips of water. He'd turned up with Keziah; they had been working on Keziah's model together for the past hour. Stub seemed even more on edge than usual, his welt-splattered neck chafing against his collar. He kept looking around with sudden paranoid jerks, and he couldn't keep his fingers still.

I was quiet too. The girls were telling unsavoury stories about me that Keziah seemed to be enjoying. Keziah herself was tackling the meat with surprising relish, as was Mel.

'So what's the edge of the habitat made of?' I asked Stub. 'All I could see were these blue blocks.' We were an hour into the meal and, soothed by the pig-meat, I was OK about talking a little bit about my trip to the edge.

'Pixellated Fear, sir,' said Stub. 'It is used as a fencing material.' He looked around, as if there were someone behind him.

'How do you mean?'

'All those blocks of fear, sir, they're spirits in their own right. They have a schooling instinct. Your habitat's surrounded by a shoal of them. The nearer you get to them, the more frightened you feel—it's governed by an inverse square law, sir, like gravitation or light—so they make an ideal material for borders and edgings. You can get them in any colour: Leopold must have picked blue ones to look like sky.'

'So how do you get through them?'

'I'm afraid, sir, it's a question of capacity. A human can stride over a fence that would be an impossible barrier for a rabbit. We spirits drink more deeply of terror than humans do. So, sir, a small layer of Pixellated Fear that would stop the bravest human isn't a barrier to us at all.' He took a nervous sip of water.

'The bravest human?'

'A shoal of Pixellated Fear that thick would paralyse the heart of even the bravest unaided human, sir,' confirmed Stub. 'According to Building Regulations, anyway.'

'Thought so,' I said, relieved. I helped myself to yet another piece of pork, feeling much better. 'Hey girls,' I said. 'Stub here said I was brave.'

The figments and Keziah stopped their conversation, looked at me, then went back to their plates and glasses.

'I just mention it,' I said. 'It happened to come up in conversation. I mean it's nothing really. Another question,' I said to Stub, deciding to change the subject. 'I still don't understand how you get inside my head at night? I have to say I wish you wouldn't.'

Stub did not appear to be listening. I repeated the question.

'Sorry, sir. I was a bit distracted. The fact is we don't get inside your head. Your memories are stored elsewhere in the heavenlies.'

'The HELP system told us that.'

'Indeed. So anyone in the heavenlies willing to risk the radiation can climb in and root around and stir things up. That's what I've been doing.'

'You mean to say that anyone can climb in and riffle through my memories?'

'Yessir. Few do though. For one thing, they have to brave all the radiation. For another, forgive me for saying so, but most people's minds are rather tedious. It's like looking through a near-infinite slideshow of someone else's photos, sir.'

He was tapping his finger on the table again.

'Or wedding videos,' I added.

'Precisely.'

'I like wedding videos,' said Mel, who, like the other girls, was now listening in on our conversation. 'I think they should have a TV programme of them, like they do with car chases.'

Annie looked like she was going to agree, but when Annie opens her mouth all kinds of warnings and fears about making a fool of herself kick in and they did so this time, so her mouth closed again.

'In the British Museum,' said Caroline, who had finished her stuffed pepper, 'they still have boxes of clay tablets that were dug up a century ago. Thousands of years old and no-one's ever got round to reading them.'

'An apposite example, miss,' added Stub. He was rubbing his hands together, as if drying them. They weren't wet.

'So if I can't get past the Pixellated Fear, how come I can recall my memories?' I asked Stub. 'Caroline, who is a figment of my imagination, fetched an article from *East Anglian Country Lifestyle* magazine earlier on and she didn't leave the habitat.'

'Your spirit and your memories are entangled together, sir,' said Stub. 'Just as your spirit and your body are. It shouldn't surprise you that they can act on each other at a distance.'

'I think I follow,' I said.

'It's even more complicated than that,' said Stub. 'In "reality" everything is tangled up in an extremely complicated way. The view I am describing—with your body on earth, your spirit here, and your memory storage further out in the heavenlies—is true in one sense but in another sense is also a convenient oversimplification that helps us find our way around, sir.'

'But we left our bodies,' said Keziah.

'That's what makes you unusual, miss,' said Stub. 'When you and Jamie entered your comas, your spirits did what spirits do when the body dies—they left. That's actually an irreversible reaction, like being born, or breaking an egg. You're changed forever.'

'Does that mean we can't go back?' I asked.

'No it doesn't, sir,' said Stub. 'It just means that if you did go back, it wouldn't be the same. Your spirit will be able to leave your body at will, sir—after some practice anyway.'

'Handy for boring meetings,' I said.

I filled everyone's glasses with Chinese tea, before offering fifth helpings. So much wonderful cooked flesh.

'OK,' I said to Stub, feeling expansive after all this luscious meat. 'The therapy thing, then. How does that work? Not that I want any, you understand.'

157

Stub put his glass down, looked round, and tapped his finger on the table rapidly.

'Sir,' he said, 'among other things my colleagues and I search in people's memories trying to find something that will make them less dysfunctional. When we find it, we can send it to their spirit—remind them of that memory.

'Sometimes, on earth, sir, you might be struck with a thought that offers a fresh perspective. That might be our work. Of course, you might just have summoned the thought yourself.'

'That's what you have been trying to do to me, in my dreams.'

'Yessir.'

'But because my spirit has left my body, I can *see* you working on my memory storage.'

'Some of the time, sir. There is a random element. Your attention wanders. I guess Leopold has visited to dig up memories and you didn't even notice, possibly because your attention was elsewhere, sir.'

'Do you do this therapy with everyone? With people on earth?'

'In principle, sir, yes, but we're a very small team. We have to make an assessment before each intervention.'

'Don't tell me you've been poking around in my head for years?'

'No sir,' said Stub. 'You would have been one of the thousands we looked at and decided we could do nothing with.'

'Because I was healthy.'

'Because you believed you were healthy, sir.' Stub looked around again. What *was* he looking for? 'Of course in your altered situation, we thought we might try again.'

'You've been working on me, haven't you?' asked Keziah, putting her fork down.

Stub looked at her carefully, his head in its humble-old-retainer stoop, eyes still fearful.

'You were on our books Miss Mordant,' he said.

'Suicidal thoughts put you up the list?' she asked, with a little wry smile. 'Self harm?'

'No, miss,' said Stub. 'Too common. The cry of the brokenhearted: that's like a fire alarm in the heavenlies.'

Keziah stared at him for a moment.

'I *knew*. But you were only stirring up more muck.'

'That's a risk, miss.'

'I need a glass of wine,' said Keziah.

'It doesn't work up here,' I reminded her, 'and you've given it up.'

'Never mind,' she said. 'Just to hold it and gulp will help.'

I provided something and she poured it out greedily and kept the bottle.

'So how many of you are there, these therapists?' I asked Stub.

'Only three for Cambridge City,' said Stub.

'Three! What use is that with 18,000 neurotic students?'

'Plus another 70,000 people in the city itself. My colleagues are extremely able.'

'Wow, we must be somewhere up the priority list, for you to be spending all this time with us.'

'You were an emergency, sir.'

'So you came out to rescue us,' I said. 'Braving the radiation.'

'Yessir. I do not know that it was especially brave. It was clearly the correct thing to do. Neither of my colleagues could do this job.'

'Why not?'

'Sir, they are human like you. Unlike pure spirits, they are unable to change shape and are thus unsuited for undercover work. They would find it hard to evade the defences set up by the Toad on behalf of Gaston and Leopold.'

'Human?' I was temporarily at a loss, not knowing which question to ask out of the many that were suddenly clamouring to be picked. 'You mean human like us?'

'Yessir. They have bodies on earth, but they work in the heavenlies. As therapists.'

'They *commute*?'

'In a manner of speaking, sir, yes.'

'How does that work then?'

'Sir, in the case of my colleague Miss Corrie Bright, she is an old lady who lives alone in her small apartment. So long as her carers are not around, she can leave her body whenever she wishes, sir. Nobody notices an old person having a quiet doze.'

'Good grief.'

'Our senior colleague is one who's name you may recognize. His body lies deep in a tomb in Mosul in Iraq —the site of the former Nineveh. As is sometimes noted in saints of the Eastern Church, his body has not yet decayed. While that remains true, he can technically return to it at any time. He has in fact been resident in the heavenlies for many centuries. His name is Jonah— the prophet Jonah.'

'As in the whale? That Jonah?'

'It was a fish,' said Keziah. 'Not a whale.'

'He's based in *Cambridge?*'

'Hardly surprising, sir, when you think about it.'

'Oh completely obvious. I'm surprised you mentioned it.'

'He has something of a track record for changing the destiny of the whole world by working in a strategic city, sir.'

'After this fish sicked him up,' pointed out Keziah, helpfully, 'he went to Nineveh, which was the centre of the greatest empire on earth.'

'In every essence correct, miss,' said Stub.

'However much you try to forget Sunday School, it still comes out.' Keziah finished another glass of wine.

'You should visit the British Museum,' added Caroline, to me. 'They've got a large Assyrian section. They dug Nineveh up and put it there.'

'So what's he doing in Cambridge?' I resumed. 'Changing the world?'

'Some think, far too much,' said Stub.

'Hang on a second.' I was thinking. 'We used to play this in the pub. Cambridge: where Isaac Newton wrote *Principia Mathematica*, which has been called the single greatest achievement of the human mind. Cambridge: where the electron was discovered, most fundamental of all fundamental particles. Closely followed by the neutron. Cambridge: where DNA was figured out. Later, just down the road, the human genome. The neutron star was discovered here. Cambridge: where the jet engine was invented, transforming the world. Cambridge: where, even today, the chips for every mobile gadget on the planet are designed, transforming the world again. Cambridge: where dwarf wheat was developed, transforming agriculture. Cambridge: no city on earth has more Nobel Prizes per square mile. The hospital I do a contract for—the hospital right now where my body is lying—houses a research centre that claims a stake in *eight* Nobel Prizes. Near my bike park. That's only science. Cambridge: breeding ground for world leaders and politicians. Cambridge: possibly the only city where an Italian language student can meet an Indian university student in a restaurant and forty years later be offered the job of Prime Minister of India (which Sonia Gandhi then turned down).

'Modern culture? Cambridge: home of Pink Floyd and *Monty Python*. Cambridge: where the first game of soccer according to modern rules was played, shortly before—you've guessed it—it transformed the world. Stub you might have a point.'

'You have ignored the religious dimension sir, Cambridge: one of the intellectual homes of the English Reformation.'

'Is that a good thing?'

'It is, sir.'

'I'll believe you. We used to think it was because Cambridge is a kind of funnel into which you siphon all the brightest and best at the most creative time of their lives.'

'No sir,' said Stub. 'I'm afraid that's just a recipe for a more energetic and imaginative class of dissolution.'

'So Jonah—'

'And Miss Bright, and in a very small way myself. Unearth creative thinking. Jolly things along. Yessir.'

'What, you drag bits of memory into people's consciousness—'

'Help them make connections. Yessir.'

'It's not just advancing human thought and civilisation, diverting though that no doubt is, but it's also helping people overcome their problems and live their lives?'

'It's all of a piece, sir. Mending souls changes the world eventually, and that is our main focus,' said Stub. 'Transforming the sum of human knowledge is more of a rewarding sideline, sir. Part of the total job, but the kind of thing you do on Friday afternoons.'

'Gee, I hope you being here hasn't dammed up too much of the creative flow of Cambridge intellectual life.'

'It's true we are rather short-staffed,' said Stub. 'I'm sure my colleagues will have it in hand, sir.'

'So who do you all work for?' I asked.

'Who do we work for?' repeated Stub. 'Who do we *work for?*' His face suddenly contorted, as if he'd been shot. 'Who do you think we work for? Well I think that could be said to be a *sore point.* I am in something of a dispute with my employer.'

'Oh really?'

'And it is impossible,' he whispered, not to me, to himself, going rigid, eyes staring at something I couldn't see, face working. '*It is impossible.* I am doing the right thing, in the right way, at the right time, but I am doomed to fail. And still it is demanded. Because the one we work for demands it.' Alarmingly, he started swaying in his seat. 'He demands it,' he whispered. Then he wrapped his long arms around his head and fell off his chair. The chair also toppled over.

A long noise came from him, like a death wail. Curling himself into a ball, he screamed. It wasn't high pitched, like a girl's scream: it was the full-blooded honk of male anguish, a sound you almost never hear.

'I have tried!' he wailed. 'Like waves breaking against a rock. Broken! Broken! Broken! I cannot die!'

Keziah glared at me and pushed her way over to him, knocking over chair and wine-bottle. Stub rolled around the floor, cursing and bellowing. He was foaming at the mouth.

At first it was simple angst, like that Norwegian painter, you know the man. *The Scream.* Could have been Stub just then.

Soon it developed into a stream-of-consciousness thing. Graphic. I heard swearwords I hadn't heard in years. All the time Keziah knelt next to him, trying to take hold of him.

Then his cursing started at me, on the theme of 'stubborn, thick-skinned, stupid.' He rolled onto his back, still curled up. Fresh wounds seemed to be erupting in his skin. I could smell smoke. Then with one of those little tricks they do, he shrank away and transformed into the light green snake again (this too was bloodied and smouldering), turned his head to us with pure malice, opened his mouth, hissed, flicked his tongue, and slid under the lighthouse door.

Keziah's wine was dripping onto the floor, so I got up and turned the glass the right way up.

'What was all that?' I asked Keziah. She stood up.

'If he was human,' said Keziah, 'I would say he had a personality disorder, bordering on madness. He just flipped.'

'Really,' I said drily. 'That's perceptive.'

'It's a clinical diagnosis,' she said testily. 'Some of my clients have it. Something snaps and they're gone. It's an *illness*.'

'So the self-appointed therapist is a deluded nutter,' I said. 'How very surprising.'

'Jamie,' said Keziah, wearily, looking at me. 'Oh never mind.' She walked out.

I looked round at Caroline, Mel and Annie, who were looking at me the way girls do when they think you have done a very wrong thing. Quiet and severe.

'What?' I said. 'What?'

I went to bed, slept and drifted to the Dome.

What Stub had said (before he cracked up) made sense. Outside the Dome was where I kept all the bad memories; inside it were all the good ones. That's how it was going to stay.

Tearing my gaze away from the beach volleyball game, which was replaying, I felt I ought to make an inspection of the Dome walls.

I carefully walked round the perimeter checking for leaks and glancing up at the rubbish. Outside, *Zlotcwicvic Enngerrgrunden Transportowicz, Krakow* was revving its engine and driving up and down the piles of rubbish, perhaps looking for a way to ram the Dome. But my concrete was strong. I kept walking and scanning the rubbish dump outside, hard though it was to see in the yellow-tinged greyness of the rain.

It wasn't long before I saw a familiar, light-green snake slithering over the top of a hill of rubbish. There was a jerky, frantic air to his movements, like a movie being played slightly too fast. Fixing his eyes on the Dome, he wrapped himself around a large lump of steel, a piece of derelict car engine.

With a flick like the lash of a whip, he hurled the piece of metal at the Dome.

It hit with a crack and left a white mark on the transparent skin of the Dome. Head darting to the left and right, the snake burrowed into the rubbish pile. He emerged near another piece of metal, a section of railing.

Again he threw, and again a crack echoed through the Dome.

Right, I thought. I was pretty sure my Dome was strong enough to resist even this onslaught. But I could do better.

I casually whistled up my old friend the B-2 bomber. It glided silently into view over the Dome. The air-to-ground missile hit Stub just as he was lining up for a third shot. *I'm sorry*, I thought, *no hard feelings, but I have to defend my own.*

Back to the beach volleyball. I could settle down and enjoy myself for however long the dream lasted... Bikini-clad girls walked past. Glasses clinked. I let the dream run. Good to know that even after your spirit has broken free of your body, you're still allowed to dream. It was a happy, lazy afternoon in my dream-time.

A long time later, Lizzie waded across to me, with a serious expression on her face.

'Jamie,' she said. '*I don't know if you can hear me.*'

'Lizzie?' I said. 'Lizzie?'

'*Jamie. I hope you're listening.*' Now the dream was slipping away.

'Jamie,' Lizzie continued, a voice in the dark now. '*I wanted to say that they're a little tiny bit worried about you. I don't think it's anything really, but there's this little thing called a haema-something.*

'*They've decided to operate on the haema-thingy and drain the fluid from your head. They had been hoping that they wouldn't need to do it. They think that'll help you get better.*'

With a feeling like an electric shock I felt her fingers entwine with mine in the dark. Actual fingers. Then she kissed my hand, which was as limp and lifeless as if it were lying on the meat counter in a cannibal supermarket.

'You've got to be strong Jamie. You've got to really fight. I mean really, really fight.' Her voice was breaking up.

I am fighting, I thought. *Lizzie I'm fighting as hard as I can.*

I felt something warm and wet drip onto my hand. Tears? Mascara? Possibly snot. An upset Lizzie tended to be a bit of a cocktail.

But she was crying *for me*, and I think she was sober.

'*Just get through this*,' she whispered. '*Jamie you've got to get through this.*'

More fluid dripping on the hand. She's crying for me. Oh dear God.

When I woke up again in my lighthouse, I lay there for a little bit, watching the fire play against the walls while the daylight returned outside. I listened as the sea heaved itself around the place like a fat person and the gulls shrieked.

All my hopes for not being dead presumably now rested in a couple of surgeons on earth. Probably, they had only just scraped through their finals. Surgeons become surgeons because they reject as too boring jobs as test pilots, bullfighters, professional gamblers, parachute testers or cavalry officers in the Light Brigade. They probably juggle with their scalpels before an operation and lay bets as to whether my blood will hit the ceiling or not. I expect when I'm anesthetized they do ventriloquist's dummy things with my mouth, one handed, while operating with the other hand. They probably make brain-surgery jokes: 'I know, let's turn his brain around in his head and see if he walks out backwards.'

It was quiet again over breakfast. (I decided to have the all-you-can-eat hotel breakfast again, eggs cooked by a Selection of Female Jazz Artistes from the Modern Era.) No sign of Caroline or the other figments spontaneously popping in for a friendly chat.

Suitably fortified, I wandered to the woodland in the centre of the habitat and started building a god.

Once you get into it, making your own god is a lot of fun. I started thinking up symbols of things that I really loved.

I love my house, which is within cycling distance of everything: railway station, city centre, Botanical Gardens and some funky restaurants. It's shaded by a giant tree. My bike is tied up in the tiny front yard. So I added a bike to the pile, and my door-knocker and some horse-chestnut leaves.

I am very fond of girls: as with cricket, devoted but lacking basic talent. The Internet. Private space travel. Gadgets and solar power. Algebra's in there somewhere, as are cryptic crosswords, with their elegance-without-redundancy. Fresh bread. Apple computers. Sunshine through mist in cold forests. The Lake District in North-West England, host to our walking holidays. I added symbol after symbol to my pile.

How to make a god of all of these? I looked at them, symbols piled around me.

I picked them up and held them in my hands. Hair straighteners, my symbol of all things feminine. My door knocker. An Apple laptop. My bike. My seasonal pass to the Botanical Gardens. An apple from the apple tree in the Botanical Gardens that is a descendant of the tree that Isaac Newton was watching when he thought up gravity, thus becoming the first one after God to entertain this ruse. A model punt, memory of lazy flirtatious summer days on the Cam. Some Afghan murtabak bread and curry sauce. They were beautiful things; my jewels. I stared at them.

Gaston and Leopold are not having them, I suddenly thought. *I refuse to be honest about the things I really love.* Like a child who hides treasures in the back of a drawer, I didn't want to broadcast intimate things to two spirits whom (I knew really) weren't gods at all. Just bullies and exploiters, part of a great web of exploiters and deceivers, all trying to carve a living from me.

On the other hand, these evil spirits were bigger than me and had me in their power.

Time to lie then.

Now what would Gaston and Leopold think I loved? What would make them think they were really getting somewhere?

After a couple of hours my patchwork god was coming on beautifully and I was taking a breather. Leopold walked in through the woodland, and announced himself with a little cough. He was wearing a very short kilt, white socks, a white shirt with a ruffle, and a jacket. The kilt had a slit in it to reveal still more brown wrinkled leg. I swallowed, mostly to keep down the vomit.

'Leopold!' I said. 'I thought you weren't coming until tomorrow.'

'Thanks to the Almighty Toad,' said Leopold, 'our negotiations finished early and satisfactorily.'

'Where's the Overlord Gaston?' I asked.

'He's gone to bring Keziah,' said Leopold. 'Well,' Leopold was almost shy. 'We have some news! I can't give you the details but we've been in negotiations—the Almighty Toad has been helping—and it seems that the way we are looking after you has made the leading powers of the Omniverse look up!

'Think of it, Jamie! Here's Gaston and I, caring for you in our little way, roughly throwing in a few ideas, just acting in what we saw as the best interests of our dear little human spirit-pets. Suddenly, we might be celebrities. People might use what we do as a model! Right across the Omniverse! The Toad seems to think we're practically writing the manual—*Every Spirit's Guide to Keeping Humans as Pets*.

'Those things we've been teaching you about happiness and about following the spirits' advice, and about building your patchwork god, the Almighty Toad —praise be to him—thinks it could be a whole pattern for how we spirits interact with humans. We're the next big thing!

'He's been really selling our case and it seems that in three days, we're going to put on a reception. Hundreds of other spirits are going to see a presentation about you two.'

So they'd got a booking in the *Biennale*. I tried to act surprised. What I was really thinking was, *only three days! I need longer than that for my body to heal.*

'That's amazing,' I said. 'I don't know anything about these things. It seems very sudden. I wouldn't have thought we were quite ready.'

A cloud seemed to pass across Leopold's tanned face.

'I know, I know,' said Leopold. 'It was the Almighty Toad (*p.b.t.h.*) who was hurrying all this along. I said I didn't think we'd be ready. He said, "Every confidence in you." You've got to back his judgement. The Toad, praise be to him, seems to think I have a special gift with creating environments and worldviews for humans... He also said he really liked my fashion sense, by the way.'

'I've always thought it was unique,' I replied. 'Takes courage to wear what you wear.'

'So did taking you two on. It was a gamble, you know. Still is.'

'I still think a better time for a demonstration might be when both Keziah and I had built our patchwork gods and were worshipping, and had got Paradise a little more sorted. Maybe even done some of the breeding you wanted. You know, quite a lot later.'

'Yes, well I don't think the timing's ideal,' he said. 'Gaston and the Almighty Toad, praise be to him, both seem to think we can pull it off.'

I scratched my head.

'What exactly,' I said tactfully, 'will you do about Keziah?'

'Do you think I hadn't thought of that?' Leopold snapped. 'I mean do you really think I hadn't thought of that?'

'I expect you've got a plan,' I said soothingly.

'The Overlord Gaston and His Brightness the Almighty Toad, praise be to him, seem to have confidence that my work with Ms Mordant will swiftly move on from this incipient phase.'

'*Incipient phase*,' I said. 'Leopold, she will stand fearless against the host of heaven and completely refuse to bend. She won't give an inch. In metric, she won't give a millimetre.'

'Do you think I don't know that!' he hissed, in such agitation that he dropped onto all fours and momentarily seemed to be mutating into a Komodo dragon. With an effort of will he fought his body back into humanoid form and staggered to his feet. 'Do you think I'm not worrying about that day and night?'

We heard a crashing noise, and we looked round. Gaston was pulling Keziah through the forest, one knobbly hand gripping a thick bunch of her black hair. She came calmly enough. In his other hand he held Stub. I noticed Stub had a particularly large scorch-mark halfway down his body.

'O Leopold,' he said slowly. 'O Leopold look what I have found!'

He shoved Keziah in front of him, very near to where Leopold and I were standing. He kept a grip on Stub's throat. Given the dust and cuts on Gaston's face, I wondered if there'd been a fight.

'You stay there!' he snapped at Keziah. 'I'm going to deal with the worm first.'

Keziah tossed her head to straighten her hair and stood next to me, eyes blazing. She was breathing quickly.

'Hello Jamie,' she said, without exchanging a glance.

'Hey,' I said.

'Gaston,' said Leopold, 'What's happening? What are you doing?'

'Leopold,' he said, still breathing heavily. 'Look at this. We have an intruder.' He shook Stub violently, and then, overcome with rage, took hold of Stub with both hands, held him horizontally in front of his mouth, and bit into him, right into the burnt skin. Stub squealed and hissed and tried to get free. 'You, snake,' he said. 'What's your name and who do you work for and what are you doing?'

'My name is Stub,' said the snake, wearily. 'Like you, I'm going to the Lake of Fire. Who cares what happens between now and then.'

'Did you work for the Toad?'

'No.'

Leopold murmured 'Praise be to his name' under his breath.

'Don't lie to me.' Gaston sank his teeth into Stub again. 'You can't get past the Toad's guards unless the Toad lets you in. You *must* work for the Toad.'

'I don't work for the Toad,' said Stub. 'I have been trying to undermine the work of the Toad and of you and of Leopold.'

'If I can say something...' said Keziah.

Gaston looked at her as if he were about to metamorphose into a pterodactyl and rip her head off.

'What?' he spat.

'He's got a personality disorder, and he's flipped. If he was helping me, he isn't going to any more. You can let him go.'

'Thank you for that helpful advice which I will choose not to take,' said Gaston. 'Leopold, we've got to think.'

He looked at Stub again. 'If you don't work for the Toad, how did you get past the Toad's defences?'

Stub gave him a look of undiluted hate. 'All we spirits can metamorphose, am I right? We can't adopt every shape, but we can choose from a set of shapes that all reflect who we really are. Mostly, we spend our days either being reptiles or trying to stop turning into reptiles.'

'Thank you for the lesson in Angelology 101,' said Gaston. 'Do you want me to bite you again?'

'Of course we can add extra limbs or special tools, or similarly we can divest ourselves of almost everything until we are just stripped down to our essence.'

'I think I will bite you again,' said Gaston, and did.

It was a little while before Stub spoke again, but when he did, it was with a mulish air of I've-started-so-I'll-finish.

'The Toad's guards are trained to look for those things that we always possess, whatever shape we are. Our essence. Which given the variety of shapes we can adopt comes down just to one thing.'

'Pride,' said Leopold, mostly to me. 'We all have our pride. Differing in glory, but we all have it. It's our badge. The mark of the Free. That's who we are.'

'Not me,' said Stub. 'I have an unmeasurably low self-esteem. I have no pride.'

Gaston and Leopold looked at him with a new level of disgust, almost of horror. Even Gaston seemed short of words.

'O you filth. O you filthy filth,' he finally said. He was squeezing Stub so tightly now that I thought something was going to squirt out of Stub one end or the other. 'You filthy, treacherous *slågönomic €mnigrrvient! Ng! Ng!*

'Leopold,' said Gaston, making strenuous efforts to calm down. 'He's been working to undermine us all.'

'What's unusual about that? Every spirit does that.'

'You don't understand. He wants to go back. He wants to betray us all, everything we've fought for. He wants to go back into bondage.' He looked at Stub again. 'That's right, isn't it?'

'I don't know any more,' said Stub.

'But you've failed, haven't you? God won't take you back. I could've told you that. God won't take you back.

174

He won't take any of us back. You work for him but he doesn't pay.'

'Shut up,' said Stub.

'You've worked and worked and you have succeeded sometimes but often you've failed and you know God won't take you back. You're not good enough. You thought you could work on these two but it hasn't happened, has it? Jamie wouldn't listen to you. *We* have Jamie. So you concentrate on her, the woman, the weak one.'

Keziah? I thought weakly. *Keziah the weak one?* Gaston, you need to go on a course or something. 'So it's you who have been behind the stubbornness of our scrawny friend here.'

'I told you,' insisted Keziah. 'I would be stubborn anyway.'

'She has a point,' I added, but Gaston shot me a look of such murder I thought I'd maintain a tactful silence from now on.

'This evil creature,' continued Gaston, shaking Stub violently, 'has been at the root of the Mordant girl's stubbornness.'

'You mean Keziah,' said Leopold. 'We're on first-name terms with our subjects, remember. It's part of the training regime.'

'Leopold. This is important.'

Leopold looked angry. Meanwhile from the expression on Stub's face—eyes bulging, forked tongue lolling—I thought his head was about to squirt off into the forest like a lemon pip.

'Oh charming! Oh charming! I work for you night and day! Who does the mucking out?' snapped Leopold.

'Leopold! Not now!'

'Who goes out in the radiation and gets the welts sorting through their memories to build that habitat?'

'*Leopold! Not now!*'

'Oh,' sneered Leopold, 'it's always "not now!" It's never "now" is it? It's always, some other time, Leopold. It's always, Leopold I'll trample all over your thoughts and wisdom—'

'Leopold—'

'I don't think you realize how much I'm adding to this partnership! It's supposed to be a *partnership* Gaston! You're not my employer. We're in this together.'

'Leopold! Shut! It!'

Leopold looked mutinous but shutted it.

'What we have here,' said Gaston, fighting to control his breathing, 'is the reason Mordant is so stubborn. Do you know what else? *The Toad doesn't know.* Leopold, the Toad doesn't know.'

'I expect you'll tell him,' said Leopold sulkily. 'Since you take the rest of his advice.'

'No,' said Gaston slowly. 'This is a weapon in our hands. Against the Toad. If only I knew how.'

PRIDE AND TREACHERY

'Gaston,' said Leopold, 'you can try all you like, but you need to know something. If we go on as we're doing, I think our demonstration is going to be a disaster. I'm serious. I can't see how it's going to work.'

Gaston looked at him for a long moment, idly twisting Stub into a corkscrew shape. 'I know that you and the Toad both think we can accelerate the training,' Leopold continued. 'I've spent time with these animals and I just don't know what to do with Keziah. I've wanted to say this for a long time. We're not getting anywhere with Keziah.'

Both spirits turned to look at Keziah.

'What is it exactly you want her to do?' I asked. 'You might be able to help, might you Keziah? If we found out the minimum requirements?'

'Jamie—' said Keziah.

'No, we may as well find out,' I said. 'If it's impossible, it's impossible. I understand that.'

Leopold said, 'Gaston?'

Gaston thought, wrapping Stub absently round his arm. 'There has to be some sort of domestic bliss. You know, so we can say it's the basis of a new society. They'll want some worship. You'll have to give them some worship.'

'Both of us?' I asked.

Gaston sighed. 'It has to look that way.' He coiled Stub the other way around his arm.

'So,' I said, 'just to be clear, you have to have the convincing appearance that both of us are worshipping you?'

'Yes,' said Gaston.

'Suppose just I did it and Keziah was, I don't know, at home being supportive?' I carefully avoided Keziah's gaze.

'No,' said Leopold. 'They'll be asking all kinds of rigorous questions afterwards. They'll want to see Keziah worship. They won't take any spiritual system that doesn't tap into the sacred feminine.'

'It doesn't even have to be genuine, does it?' I asked. 'Doesn't it just have to look authentic? Am I right in thinking you don't have to mean it?'

Leopold brightened. 'No of course you don't have to mean it. Where would we be in all this Omniverse if you had to mean things?'

'I don't know why I'm even listening to this,' said Keziah.

A thoughtful silence fell.

'You're right,' I said to her. 'I'm sorry.'

'But you're all missing something,' she continued. 'The Toad obviously wants you to fail.'

'What?' said Leopold. 'The Toad, praise be to him, has been doing everything in his power to make us *succeed*. He's put personal prestige into the project. He's fixed up the meeting. He's invited half the powers of heaven. He's going to introduce us.'

Keziah sighed. 'You're not thinking like a lawyer,' she said. 'Look. You're the Toad, OK. You agree to sponsor Gaston and Leopold's idea. Fair enough—

you've got to keep on being innovative. It's a reasonable experiment.

'When you inspect it, you go straight to the core—you look at Jamie's and my personalities. You immediately conclude it isn't going to work. It's like giving obedience training to a cat. It isn't going to happen.'

'But—' said Leopold.

'I haven't finished,' said Keziah. 'So now you, The Toad, are in a fix. Disaster looms. Questions will be asked about your judgement. You have to shift the blame onto someone else. So you review your options and it's a no-brainer. What can you always rely on evil spirits to be? Always?'

'Proud,' said Leopold, not without a tinge of pride. 'That's our hallmark. That's what we'll fight to the death for. Except we can't die, but you know what I mean. We are The Free Spirits of the Omniverse!'

'Right,' said Keziah. 'The Toad is going to get out of this by tapping into your endless resources of pride and treachery. So now it's easy. He takes you under his wing —'

'More like an armpit, really,' I said. 'Snug in the Almighty Armpit.' Keziah gave me a look. Directly behind me, I imagine, a tree withered.

'—He starts giving you advice. He works out which of you is giving the worst advice, and he emphasises that. Day after day the Toad forces this rotten counsel on you and what happens? The resentment builds. It builds between you, and it builds against the Toad. A dreadful sense of doom and failure creeps over you. You fight it off, it keeps coming back.'

Everyone was silent now. Even Stub, I think, was listening. 'The Toad hasn't finished,' said Keziah. 'He piles on the pressure some more. He absolutely guarantees your failure by setting an impossible deadline. There's now no way you're going to get this project ready in time. Deep down you both know you're going to fail. You are facing total ruin. What do you do?'

'You fight,' said Gaston, unwrapping Stub from his arm and thoughtfully pulling him taut.

'You do,' said Keziah. 'Because your pride tells you to. Every cliché you ever learnt tells you to. *Back yourself. Give it your best shot. Get out there and prove him wrong. Even if the odds are desperate. At least go down fighting. Do not go softly into this good night but rage against the dying of the light.*'

Another silence fell. 'He *knows* you will rise up against him. He knows you'll make some desperate effort to make this project succeed. You'll reject his advice, do it your way, and then stand up to him, probably not long before the performance so that he can't fight back. You'll make sure it's a very public break. He retreats, saying, "They refused to listen to me, they're on their own." You do your performance. If the Toad has calculated right, you fail, you are lost and everyone admires the cunning and treachery of the Toad.'

'What if the Toad has calculated wrong?' asked Gaston.

'That's easy. You triumph and the Toad is humiliated in front of all the powers of heaven.'

Gaston and Leopold appeared to savour the warmth of that thought for a happy moment.

'So what do you suggest we do?' asked Leopold.

'Don't fall into his trap,' said Keziah. 'Limit the damage. Do the opposite of what he expects. You've got to manoeuvre so that he—'

'No,' said Gaston. 'No, no, no.'

180

We all turned to look. Gaston was smiling, and Stub was being twisted.

'You know she's right,' said Gaston. 'I'll tell you why. It puzzled me why everyone was coming. Leopold, how many of the Biennale people have you spoken to?'

'Not many obviously. I've been busy here. And— you don't always pass the party invitations on.'

'I've been talking to many of them. Loads of them are coming. Senior spirits are coming. Our rivals are coming. They're clearing their schedules to come. Leopold, *why* are they coming? It's not like we are, you know, the most popular designers in the Omniverse with a massive porfolio.'

'Speak for yourself. I invented Scottishness!'

'Which affects what, a minor tribe of five million people? Come on Leopold. They're talking about strategies for the whole of Europe, rolled out to the entire world.'

Leopold looked exasperated. 'Look, our achievements with Scottishness were well thought of. That's the sort of thing that *should* be rolled out across Europe. The Americans love it. Tanker-loads of Scotch whisky leave for Asia. It was groundbreaking.'

'Leopold. What would our rivals and the warlords do if what we were doing was truly groundbreaking?'

'Adopt it all through the Omniverse?'

'No Leopold. *Pride and treachery.* They are not coming to admire us. They are coming because they're expecting a disaster. They have had a whisper, from the Toad himself probably, that it's all going to fall apart and to be sure not to miss it. Oh, the humiliation he's lining up for us Leopold! Smith and Mordant aren't the show. *We're* the show. We're the *nngyrting* show. We're the entertainment at the beginning of the Biennale!'

Leopold wiped a hand over his face. 'But Leopold, you've forgotten something. Even Miss clever-clogs know-it-all *Mordant* has forgotten something. Leopold, O my kilted kitten Leopold, he doesn't know about the snake.'

'Why does the snake make any difference?'

'The snake has been helping her to be strong. The snake has been helping her sort her mind out. The snake has been undermining the good work we've been doing.'

Leopold thought for a while. 'Do you know, that makes sense? I thought I was more persuasive than that. I couldn't see how I wasn't getting through to her.'

'Can I just say something?' asked Keziah. 'I can despise you two all on my own without any help from a snake.'

'So Leopold, what do you suggest we do?'

Leopold brightened. 'You want my advice?'

'Leopold, my darling Leopold, I want your advice. I am going to listen to your advice on animal training.'

'We've got to go back to basics. First, get rid of the snake. Then—we've still got three days. Everybody has a breaking point. We've got to torture her until she breaks. Coercion isn't as good as seduction but it will do nearly as well. Especially since we've already got Jamie in the bag.'

'You can do that in three days?' asked Gaston.

'When she came here, she was already cracking up,' said Leopold. 'And that's just the damage she did to herself. Wait till I start to work on her. Three days? Simple.'

It was at this point I should have stood up and said,

'Look here. If you're going to torture Keziah, you have to torture me first.' There could have been mention of things being done over my dead body, for example.

The thing is, I would have liked a night and a day to think about that, weigh everything up, perhaps talk it through with Caroline. I'm confident I'd've eventually come down on the right side. I just felt a bit rushed. All I did say was, 'Er—'

Gaston spat at me: 'What?'

'Nothing.'

'So what do we do?' asked Gaston.

'Adamantine,' replied Leopold. 'Adamantine chains for the worm. I'll find some,' and he walked off, with a little shimmy of his slitted kilt.

'Adamantine chains,' said Gaston wolfishly to us both, 'are the business.'

A silence fell. As if to break it, Gaston, renewing his grip on Stub's neck, started talking to me. 'Smith,' he said. 'You've seen more sense than this Mordant woman.'

I didn't want to reply. 'Well?' he insisted.

'I've built a patchwork god if that's what you mean,' I said. 'I'll show you it. It's only over there. Of course, it isn't finished yet. This is the proof of concept. I can build on this.'

'Come on, Mordant.' Gaston reached for Keziah's hair again. She slapped his hand and glared at him.

'I can walk on my own.'

'You're going to be tortured,' replied Gaston. 'I will enjoy that.'

'Here it is.' We reached the space in the clearing where my patchwork god stood. It was a work-in-progress, various bits of symbol still lying around. 'I worship Intellect,' I said. 'Hence the pumpkin, like a big fat head, brimming with ideas. Can't stand thick people. Shouldn't be allowed to breed. And sordid sex, of course —because *I* should be allowed to breed—that's the pile of lads' mags here. Money. I love money. Hence this money fountain. You can just stick your head under it, like this,'—I demonstrated—'oh, and you just feel money, money, pouring around your ears, it's wonderful.

'When I sat down and thought, you know I really like cruelty. Not the big stuff. The petty, mindless acts of malice. So I have here a brick and a jellyfish. The jellyfish can shuffle along the ground, but not fast enough. Watch.'

I picked up a brick. 'O little jellyfish! See this? It's called a brick.' There was a terrified *squeak, squeak, squeak.* 'Look! It does this!' I dropped the brick. You could hear a bursting noise and a little wimper from the jellyfish. 'Is that fun or not? Of course the jellyfish reconstitutes itself automatically, so you can go round again.

'This is only the beginning. I can build more. Now, for your actual act of worship—I'm still working on the ritual, but I'm tentatively suggesting you do it seven times a day, once for each mealtime: breakfast, snack, lunch, snack, tea, supper, raid-the-fridge. That's workable in my schedule.

'So you prostrate yourself against the pumpkin and tap your head on it, worshipping sheer cleverness and craftiness. Obviously, I'm thinking of you as the god behind all this.

'You finger the lads' mags, like this, making grunting noises. Then you get up, jump in the money fountain, wash in it, drink it, then jump out invigorated.

'Finally you pick up the brick, and taking as much or as little time as you like—obviously some parts of the day you have more leisure than others—and watch the jellyfish scuttle. Wait until it starts squeaking with terror and then…

'Release the brick!

'So what do you think, O my Overlord?'

Gaston was slavering. 'I am surprised Smith,' he said calmly, 'and quite pleased. Do it again.'

'In time, in time, my Overlord Gaston.' I said. 'I wanted to see if I was on the right lines. We can tweak.'

I still hadn't looked at Keziah. She was standing nearby, and I felt that she had relaxed a little.

Gaston was thinking. 'So how did you come to make that god?'

'I followed your instructions—I mean Leopold's really. But I know who is the intellectual force behind them. "Jamie," I said to myself, "just be true to what you really feel. Let your creativity go."'

'Do you think other people would respond the same way?' asked Gaston. He was trying to keep the excitement out of his voice, like a dealmaker who is oh-so-close to a bargain.

'On earth? Oh I expect so,' I said airily. 'The trick is to feel. Not think. Follow your basic instincts. So freeing. And you know what else? I feel it made me closer to you. You've rescued us and you look after us, and we don't have ways to show our gratitude.'

'You say you'd repeat this ritual, what, seven times a day?' said Gaston with an air of casualness.

'Why not?' I asked.

Gaston was seemingly doing a calculation.

'Hmm,' he said.

We heard the clank of chains.

'Adamantine chains,' said Leopold enthusiastically, dragging them through the trees. 'I knew I had some.'

'Leopold,' said Gaston, 'have you seen this one's patchwork god?'

'No, not yet,' replied Leopold.

185

'It's good,' said Gaston. I felt a surge of pride. 'It means that when we win, we win big. Now, can you help me with the snake?'

Gaston folded Stub roughly in half while Leopold wrapped a chain round him, finally tying the chain back onto itself. They lowered the chained bundle onto the ground. The bundle twitched.

'Excellent,' said Gaston. 'Leave him there while we deal with Mordant.'

'Why doesn't he just change shape and escape?' I asked.

'Adamantine,' said Gaston, 'is quality.' He turned to Keziah. 'Mordant,' he said. 'I have had to look after you for what feels like a long time. I have not enjoyed this. Now that we are moving on to simple torture, I think we will find that I start enjoying it.'

I again felt I should say something at this point, but I couldn't think what. It all seemed so depressingly inevitable.

'Leopold,' said Gaston. 'Would you be kind enough to advise how exactly we should torture Mordant?'

'Easy,' said Leopold. 'Take her back to her side of the habitat—we need the room here to get ready for the Biennale. Then I go to her memory storage and dig up all the most painful memories. I send them to her spirit. Memory after memory rains down on her, a bombardment that never ends.'

'Can't she fight them off?' asked Gaston.

'Not if we send them fast enough. They're terrible sticky things, evil memories. They overwhelm you.

'Then we leave her. Evil memories splashing onto her like the Golden Rain itself. Herself, twisting and turning under them. Day and a half of that, two days

186

maximum, and over she goes. Begging for mercy. Begging for it to stop.'

I'd like to point out that in the next sentence I was quite brave and cunning. I only mention this as there are people who say I was chicken-hearted throughout the story.

'Excuse me,' I said. 'My Lord Gaston, you don't think I could make one more attempt to talk to Keziah? Now that she's seen my patchwork god, she might want to change her mind. What do you think Keziah?'

'No,' said Keziah, shaking her head slowly.

'I could show you how—'

'He's been useless so far,' said Gaston. 'Despite all our help. I think he's useless with women.'

'I see what you're trying to do Jamie,' said Keziah, honest green eyes flicking onto me for a half-second. 'Don't worry about it.'

'Are you OK with that?' I asked. 'Being tortured and everything?'

'I fight memories every day, Jamie. But on earth I can't lay my hands on them.'

Gaston and Leopold looked at each other.

'This *is* going to work,' said Gaston. 'Isn't it?'

Leopold smiled.

'She's got memories like you wouldn't believe. Abuse. Betrayal. Revenge. Self-hate. Oh! Our Father Below! She'll never have faced anything like what I'm going to drop on her!' Leopold was dribbling a little. 'Two days, she'll be begging like a dog. On all fours, if you like.'

'O Leopold,' said Gaston, with a groan. 'Do it, do it, do it.'

'You really think we are going to defeat the Toad?' asked Leopold.

Gaston put his hands on Leopold's shoulders and gripped him tightly.

'Leopold!' he said. 'Don't you remember when we first got together? You'd been through all those jobs and not really found your feet—'

'I thought I'd—'

'Oh you'd shown glimpses of genius, Leopold. You understand how these humans work. I looked at you and I thought, *this spirit can go far.* Then I looked at me and thought I probably don't have his sheer artistry with humans, but I can hustle and I have a bit of ability in selling and banging heads together. I can make things happen. I knew then, Leopold, I knew *then* we had the makings of something very special. You create, I sell.'

'Yes—but I'm not just an artisan—'

'Absolutely not! Of course not!—'

'It's not just about you going the parties and me doing the mucking out—'

'No, of course not. Of course not,' said Gaston hurriedly. 'No. What I was going to say was, I thought to myself,' Gaston seemed to swallow something, 'what a team we'd be. What a partnership. Gaston and Leopold. *I want to spend the rest of eternity with that being.*' He coughed.

Leopold said, 'Did you really? Is that what you really thought?'

'Yes. Yes. Of course it is. You know that. Thick and thin. We're together.' He coughed again. 'Forever. You and I.'

Leopold hugged him. They held the hug, cheek to cheek. 'We need to have faith! Two of us, both exceptionally gifted, we can beat the Toad.'

'I'm frightened,' said Leopold.

'When we got together,' said Gaston, 'didn't I say, "It will be quite a ride?" Isn't it?'

'But the Toad.'

'We've outsmarted him so far. We have. We can do this Leopold. Together.'

They relaxed the hug, Gaston leaving first.

'I still don't like it all that much,' said Leopold grudgingly.

'You should let the snake go,' said Keziah unexpectedly. 'He isn't going to do you any harm, or me any good. He's flipped.'

We all looked at her. 'You could see the signs,' shrugged Keziah. 'Anxiety. Paranoia. Repetitive movements. If he was human and doing that in my office I'd have him sectioned—I'd've phoned the people in white coats. You can chain him or unchain him as you like. He's got so many chains in his head it won't make any difference.'

'No,' said Gaston cheerfully. 'Leopold, just put the snake somewhere out of the way, in a bit of woodland or something. Take Mordant to her habitat. Then, dear Leopold, I'm going to have to ask you to brave the Golden Rain again and dig up all those wonderful memories from Mordant's storage. Don't hold back. Give her everything. You don't mind me going to the Biennale meetings again? I think I ought to do some more.'

'No, I don't mind,' said Leopold. 'No pain, no gain.'

'What?' asked Gaston.

'On earth,' said Leopold. 'It's a thing they say.'

'Ridiculous. What's pain got to do with gain?... Leopold, you're still worried aren't you?' Gaston's tone was earnest.

'I just don't think we can beat the Toad,' said Leopold glumly. 'I think it's Fate.'

'The thing with Fate,' replied Gaston, tapping him on the arm, 'is you never know until you try.'

They made their exits—Stub tied to a tree not far away. Keziah led off with Leopold. Gaston going to schmooze with the Great and the Bad. I was just about to leave when I heard Stub calling, slightly muffled by the Adamantine chains.

'Hell,' said Stub to me, in a dangerous monotone.

'I'm sorry?' I said.

'Hell. Do you know the secret about it?'

'I don't. I'm sure you're going to tell me.'

'Many spirits jump in.'

'Sorry?'

'The entrance isn't chained off. It's called the Lake of Fire. Any of us can go there and jump in.'

'I suppose it's a bit of a tourist attraction. Mouth of Hell. I can imagine the postcards.'

'Have you ever been?'

'Could you imagine it? "Dear Mum, am at the Mouth of Hell. Wish you were here."'

'If you'd been, you wouldn't joke about it.'

'Well I haven't.'

'Your time will come.'

'Thank you for that cheery word.'

'The point is,' Stub continued, 'many spirits jump in. Nobody pushes them. They volunteer.'

'Really.'

'You can't get out, once in you're in, but still they jump.'

'I see.'

'Aren't you going to ask me why?'

The mad. I hate the mad. They should shoot them all. I was still standing some way from Stub, not wanting to have a conversation.

'Why.'

'Depression. They figure, "That's where I'm going to end up. I'm a failure. My life is a disaster. Why not jump in and get it over with?"'

I was silent. 'If it wasn't for these Adamantine chains,' resumed Stub, 'that's where I'd be now. Standing on the edge.'

'Really.'

'But the problem is, we're eternal beings. I know you're not engaging with me, Jamie Valentine Smith, but I'm going to continue anyway because I am having a psychotic breakdown and beings who are having psychotic breakdowns break conversational conventions. So if it wasn't for these Adamantine chains I would be taking hold of your arm and putting my face right in yours.'

'Look—'

'And don't say, "I'd better be going" or "is that the time?" because I *know* that you have nowhere to go, not really, and no-one to see. So as I was saying: Eternity. That's the problem. You might say, "I'm depressed, may as well jump in the Lake of Fire, get it over with." Then think: *Eternity*. Eternal changelessness. You, the eternally changeable being are throwing yourself into that lake of eternal changelessness and pain. So you say to yourself, "Do I or don't I jump in?"'

'Do you.'

'Yes, you do. Then you realize that standing mentally on the edge of the Lake of Fire, saying "Shall I or shan't I?" is almost as bad as being *in* the Lake of Fire.'

191

'I see.'

'You work out—it isn't difficult—that you don't need to be standing at the Mouth of Hell to have those thoughts. You can have them anywhere. Anywhere you like, you can have the Mouth of Hell experience. Here. Now. Today.'

'Which is what you're having?'

'Durr... Hence the psychotic breakdown.'

'Well, good to talk to you—'

'It's the sheer impossibility of getting back out, you see. I might as well jump into Hell because morally, logically, I'm already in. Since I'm logically in, why not just jump in anyway? Get it over with. But then you ask yourself: suppose my logic is wrong? Then I mustn't jump in. It would be awful to endure Eternity in the Lake of Fire because of a bit of sloppy thinking.'

'You've never sought help about this?'

The little pile of Adamantine chains shuddered and clanked.

'Help! Who is there to help? Climb an unclimbable mountain. Oh yes, many people will be able to help me there. Bridge an unbridgeable chasm. Expect I'll get a kit from a do-it-yourself shop.'

'I mean psychological help. You might be deluded.'

'Do you not think I've asked that question sometime in the past 13.8 billion years?'

'Don't you have pills and things? You're the therapist. You should know.'

The bundle that was Stub cast a dark eye on me from his mass of Adamantine.

'You may have a point,' he said. 'I don't need pills exactly but Jonah and Miss Bright tell me that I should go to the *Diner* as often as possible. I haven't done that for days—spent too long with you people.'

192

'What's the *Diner*?'

'The department we work for,' said Stub impatiently. 'We have staff recreation facilities. Since our offices got taken over, that's all we have. Jonah and Miss Bright tell me that I have to spend time in the *Diner* every day if I can. It has a pool. I can wash off the psychological crud. Helps stop me getting into these psychotic cycles, and they can keep an eye on me. Of course none of this answers the fundamentals.'

'In my world,' I said, 'fundamentals are a bad idea. Totally sorting something out is a bad idea. If it works for now, it works.'

'Ridiculous.'

'You should become a web programmer. I always tell my clients, never try to sort things out once and for all. Building a website isn't like building a house. Just go for things that are OK for today. Then tomorrow, for something that's OK tomorrow. It turns out in web programming that the "final solution" is an endless succession of provisional solutions. So if you've got a provisional solution, like your work with these two other therapists, why worry?'

'Why worry?' The little pile of chains was trying to hop up and down. 'Why worry because I'm one psychotic breakdown away from jumping down the throat of Hell, that's "why worry."'

'You've managed since the beginning of the universe, haven't you?'

'Barely,' said Stub. 'Barely hanging on.'

'There you are then.'

'Thirteen point eight billion years is *nothing* compared with Eternity. One breakdown and *poof*, I'm gone. Do you know why I'm having this current breakdown?' asked Stub. 'You.'

'Me?'

'You. Stubborn heart. Blocked up ears. Blind eyes. Thick head. I don't mind the pain, you know. In my state you expect pain. You carry it around with you. There's always pain. I don't mind the *fresh* pain, that I get from going out into your memory to smash up the Dome. Every drop of the Golden Rain a fresh tear in my being, a fresh wound. I don't mind having to call you "sir" all the time. *Sir.*

'When I go through all this and try to make your thick head understand what do I get? Hostility and insults and threats!'

'And air-to-ground missiles,' I pointed out.

'It didn't hurt,' he said. 'It's nothing compared to the wounds I already carry for you. I ask myself, "Why can't he see? Why doesn't he get it? Is it my fault? What am I doing wrong?

'"Is it Jonah and Miss Bright? Is it their fault? Sending me. Do they hate me? Why do they send me on a mission that must fail?"

'Then I think, "No, they don't hate me." They care for me. I know they do.

'So who hates me? Who dooms me to fail? Who gives me impossible jobs? I can't bear it!'

I felt it best to leave, so I stepped out, leaving Stub ranting and rolling around in his Adamantine chains.

You save things for moments like this. I knew what I needed. I had had it up to here with people, evil spirits, figments of my imagination, psychotic breakdown, self-analysis and the rest.

I streaked to Osama's. I got Louis Armstrong and his Hot Fives wound up and playing. The Giant Surly Bread Chef moved into high gear, which is one murtabak every 90 seconds. (Which is actually the same as low gear. Never mess with the Giant Surly Bread Chef.) Gregory Peck and Jimmy Stewart put together several of the formica tables, spread a cloth, and placed all Osama's offerings on them: the six different curries that bubbled behind the Giant Surly Bread Chef, the bhajis and samosas that were stored in glass shelves on the counter, the pots of rice: plain, basmati, pulau and Special, and the pickles. I took a bowl and a fresh murtabak and walked right along, helping myself to everything, piling the plate up. I set it on my favourite table.

I magicked up *Total Javascript*. I tucked in my napkin, opened the book and read, and ate messily, and didn't think and didn't care, while Osama looked on, eager to please.

It was very late when I staggered back to the lighthouse, and I was waddling tenderly home, not wanting to set off heart palpitations. The bottom of my throat, a usually uncomplaining part of my body, was burning. I hadn't felt like this in years, not since the epic bhaji challenges of my student days. (Fourteen, since you ask, and I didn't even vomit.)

I had trained *Total Javascript* to fly next to me and it swooped along like a vulture, great downward sweeps of its pages hauling it into the sky, followed by a long glide.

I opened the lighthouse door-latch, told *Total Javascript* to play with the seagulls, and stepped in. The kitchen fire was low, and the lights out. The figments in bed. I climbed the stairs to my own bed, magicked a change of clothes, and settled to sleep, my stomach happily gurgling and digesting like a slurry-tank on a farm.

Slept and dreamt. Went to the Dome. Getting good at this now. Wished I hadn't. Everyone was asleep. Some were floating unconscious on little rafts. The bartenders dozed. No fountains played. The wave machine was switched off. All through my coma the Dome had still throbbed with life until now.

Like everyone had been gassed or something.

I fixed my own breakfast in the morning, a simple fruit smoothie, a gentle start to the day, and I sipped it looking out over the lighthouse railings onto a calm sea. *Total Javascript* was perched on the railings nearby.

Caroline strode in and sat neatly down on the slatted bench next to me.

'Morning Jamie,' she said briskly.

'*Eeeeuuuurgh,*' I replied.

'Disgusting,' she said.

'Ate a bit too much last night.'

'Serves you right.'

'Worth it though.'

'Jamie,' she said. 'We've got some news from Leopold. Gaston and the Toad have had a big argument. It was at one of the parties last night. Very public. It started with a dispute about the methods they were using to train you and Keziah. Blazing row. Ended with the Toad completely disowning them. So at the exhibition—day after tomorrow—it's going to be just Gaston and Leopold.'

'So it's started then.'

'Yes, and it's done wonders for the numbers coming. It's going to be packed.'

'How does Leopold feel about it?'

'I think he's a little bit on edge. He's been phoning us every five minutes to get us to hurry you along.'

'Have you heard anything from Keziah?'

'She's not returning our texts. I think you should go and see her, Jamie.'

I wiped my face with my hand.

'I'd rather be reading that,' I said, pointing to *Total Javascript*.

'I think it's time you thought of others,' said Caroline.

'Thank you for the lesson on moral improvement. It is much appreciated.'

'It would be easier to keep quiet,' said Caroline, going a little pink, and strode out.

NOPE

Leopold was pacing up and down the habitat and pulling on a cigarette when I turned up.

'Where've you been?'

'I just had breakfast and then I came over.'

'Didn't the girls pass on my message?'

'Yes, so I thought I'd better have a specially relaxing and calm breakfast.'

'What about your morning worship?'

'Oh that. Sorry. Forgot.'

'Fantastic. Marvellous. I'm getting ready for my biggest day for 200 years and people are strolling in at half-past ten in the morning.' He had one cigarette in his mouth but started lighting another. 'I just don't know how we're going to do it. Gaston says, "no, no, it'll all be fine" but *Gaston* isn't at the coal face. *Gaston* is busy at all the parties.'

'How's Keziah?'

'I've been digging up memories all yesterday and all night. Nothing. She's filing them. The cow. Twice I've had to go and dig up some more and I'm going to have to go again.'

'What will you do if she doesn't, you know, yield?'

'She's bound to. Nobody can take that kind of pounding. Simple mathematics.'

'The Toad might have thought differently,' I said.

'Look,' said Leopold, with such venom that his Komodo-dragon forked tongue sprang out of his mouth and his chin went scaly. He twitched like one garrotted, then fixed his eye on me. This eye turned from grey to yellow and back to grey again. 'Animal training is what I do. Extensive research shows that everyone has a breaking point, somewhere between 1.9 and 2.6 days.'

'Including Keziah?'

'Now we've got rid of the snake. Yes. Simple laws of the Omniverse.'

'Where is the snake by the way?'

'Same place he was. Muttering to himself. Screaming occasionally. No, Keziah will break easily enough. It's a kind of physical law, like digging up a tree root. It just takes time and effort. *My* time and effort. Which I haven't got much of.' Leopold threw both cigarettes on the floor, stamped them out, looked at them, sighed, and lit two more. 'Now. Oh Jamie, we've got such a list of things to do. We can't possibly get through them all. I don't know how we're going to be ready.'

'Tell me your list,' I said.

'Build up your patchwork god,' said Leopold. 'Get it to a final form. Add to, and tidy this part of the habitat. Get Keziah to build her patchwork god—that'll have to wait, obviously. Figure out exactly what you and Keziah will be doing in your performance in front of all these Powers. Hold a dress rehearsal. Rehearse some model answers for the question session afterwards. Tell them about the Three Spiritual Laws, how they make sense for you and provide a framework for all of life.'

'Leopold,' I said. 'If we cooperate and come through this, what will happen to us?'

'As far as we're concerned,'—Leopold puffed on his cigarettes and avoided my gaze—'it's an ongoing experiment, which means we should keep your paradise going.'

'What if it fails?'

'Mockery and humiliation. Then the accountants move in, and find that our liabilities are enormous and assets are a joke. So that's the end of my career, and the end of my home. We sell ourselves in slavery to one of our creditors. Or flee somewhere so horrible that even debt-collectors won't follow us. All of that is assuming the Toad is in an unusually good mood. If he isn't, we'll enjoy some torture and corrective punishment first.'

'No, I mean Keziah and me?'

'You two? Oh, it'll be entertaining for a while, I suppose. Some variation on being fought over, toyed with, mocked and dismembered.'

'Blast the doctors!' I said suddenly. 'Blast and curse all doctors! Why can't they get their act together? Don't they know I could die up here?'

'You're still hoping you can get back to your body? Jamie, I wouldn't.'

'You haven't seen my body,' I said. 'Greek gods would fight over it.'

'Greek gods will fight over anything. That's how they lost their empire. That and the sex-with-mortals fiasco.'

'The point is, Leopold, I want to go home.'

Leopold looked over at me, ceasing his manic pacing as if struck by a fresh thought. 'You don't get it, do you? Suppose it's true. Suppose you do go back to your body. What then? A few decades, then it's over. And you're back with us, Jamie.'

'Either way I come to you?'

'Or to my kind. Yes, and they devour you.'

'How does anybody cope with this? How do you cope? How do we stop going mad like Stub over there?' The pile of Adamantine that encased the snake was just visible in the woodland, moving up and down jerkily.

Leopold looked at me oddly, as if we weren't quite two separate species, the master and his dog. Just two lost souls. 'You have to manage as best you can, don't you? Keep on the fairground and hope the music doesn't stop.'

I blew some air out of my cheeks. 'What do you want me to do first?'

'Finish off your patchwork god. Then at least we've got one done. I've got to go back again to Keziah's memory.'

'Her memories,' I said. 'What are they?'

'Oh, they're good,' said Leopold with relish. 'She's a garden of delights, that girl. A Paradise. Her mother's the presiding genius, so murderous, so cold. Her dad's depression makes her almost like an orphan. The abuse at school sets it all alight. Her rejection of her sister marinates everything in self-hate. Cook that for years in a boiling temper... she's a culinary masterpiece. You can go down there and completely forget yourself. Which would be fine except I have *so much else to do*.'

'While Gaston parties.'

'He is not *partying*. He is engaged in extremely important high-level strategic networking.'

'Why don't you get help?'

Leopold sighed. 'Because everyone wants their cut,' he said. 'Or they're spies for someone else... So anyway, see what mental torture you've avoided by being compliant. Now go and finish your god and at least that'll be one thing done.'

It wasn't hard to finish off my god, practice the worship routine, tidy the habitat. I did that and still Leopold wasn't back. So I thought I'd try an experiment.

I sat on the woodland floor, my back to a tree trunk, my eyes closed. I tried to relax. This Miss Bright and Jonah commute, apparently. Why can't I?

I thought of myself tumbling from the habitat to my body. *Don't imagine it*, I said to myself. *Just do it. Just go. You're tangled up with your body still. Lizzie's voice has called you back. Now just go back.*

Nothing.

Even that view, I thought to myself, *of body in one place, spirit in another, memory-landscape in a third, is a simplification. Everything is tangled together. I'm one. I'm still one.*

Come on. Oh, come on.

A whooshing sound in my ears. I jerked into a different position, lying flat on my back, eyes closed. Good grief.

Then I drifted out again.

Come on. Get back in. Come on. Do what you just did.

Whoosh. Another moment in my body: I trapped in a spider's web of tubes and wires. My breathing was gentle and shallow, a susurration. A slight nasal honk also.

I sensed people around me; the heat of a lamp in my face; tension in the air. I felt something scratching at my head.

I heard a single word, irritated: 'Nope.'

Nope, I thought. *What you do mean, nope? Try harder. What are you paid for? You weren't put on this earth to say 'Nope'.* But I lost concentration and out

203

drifted my spirit again, up and out. The whooshing sound (my blood in my ears?) disappeared.

Again I concentrated hard, squeezing and forcing my spirit back into my body. Again there was the flapping, pushing, the sudden falling into place, the whooshing noise (I'd forgotten how noisy bodies were), the sense of being back. More digging and scratching at my head.

As I soon as I lifted my concentration for a single moment, out I popped again. It was like trying to hold down a float in the swimming pool: one tiny movement, out I flopped.

'It won't work,' sneered Gaston, making me jump.

I opened my eyes onto his fat face and his rat's-tail moustache. He was wearing jodhpurs and carrying a whip.

'I could see what you were trying to do because your spirit was fading out and back in front of my eyes. Your head's too smashed up. It's like trying to pour a liquid back into a broken bottle. You won't get out that way, Smith.'

'What do you suggest, O my Overlord Gaston?'

'You've always had the right idea, Smith. Same as we all do. Cut the best bargains you can with the exploiters around you. Exploit all those below you. Best key to long-term survival.'

He coughed, looked around.

'Look, I've just popped back for a minute. I thought it might be in all our interests if you went to see the Mordant woman and had a little chat. Does she really know that all she has to do is pretend? It's like acting. She doesn't have to mean it. We could make it worth her while.'

'What do you mean, "worth her while?" I thought you were going to keep us in Paradise indefinitely? "Follow the spirits, find happiness."'

'Oh absolutely,' Gaston harrumphed. 'Absolutely. No question. But this would completely secure it going forward.'

'I'll go over if you like,' I said. 'Is Leopold—'

'The Lord Leopold is at Mordant's memory storage. He's having to excavate quite deep. You probably won't need to mention this little trip to him. He doesn't always like me helping him out in his particular bit of the work.'

He flew away, giving himself a little smack with the whip to go faster.

I considered for a moment. It would be good to see Keziah. Better take a peace offering though. I could walk through the forest and pick some mushrooms on the way. Yes. With a little thought I created Keziah's trug.

The trug had quite a collection of mushrooms by the time I reached the entrance marked GIRLS in the wall of the *Hotel Splendide's* swimming pool. For good measure I magicked up a large bunch of flowers and an ebony slab of dark chocolate, 70% proof, and put those in the trug as well.

I phoned her up.

'Jamie,' she said, briskly. She sounded quite busy.

'Hello Keziah, can I come in? I'm just outside. I won't if it isn't convenient.'

'Hang on a second. I've just got to—'

There was a long pause before she came back to the phone. 'Just push the door,' she said. I turned the wrought-iron door handle, and opened the door onto Keziah's world.

The wind was whipping rain into my face. I was standing on a mountain plateau. Down a gentle slope from me, volcanoes were erupting. Keziah herself was standing perhaps half a kilometre away, between me and the volcanoes. It was bleak. She gave me a hasty wave and I started walking towards her.

All around was rocks, rubble and ash. Small rivers ran off to either side, and another stream ran over my path down towards Keziah and beyond that to the volcanoes. Behind me, I was vaguely aware of some buildings.

Keziah was looking upward and as I walked, I saw a blob like a giant fish-egg falling gently out of the grey sky. It was the size of a small house. Inside its shiny surface I could make out giant figures arguing. It dropped lugubriously right onto Keziah's head, and enveloped her.

I kept walking, a protective arm over the trug to stop the flowers and mushrooms being battered by the elements. The fish-egg sat on the scree, completely hiding the little lawyer. Suddenly, she burst out, back first, wiping slime off her body. A kind of goo started oozing out of the hole she'd made. This goo fizzed when it met the rocks. The fish-egg, like a tent being taken down, started to lose its shape.

As I watched, I saw Keziah kicking and pushing and half-rolling the collapsing fish-egg down the gentle slope. Goo was bubbling and pouring out now, sinking into the scree.

By the time I got within range of Keziah the fish-egg had drained itself among the rocks and stones. Keziah looked like someone in big need of a shower.

I added a hot towel to the pile of things I was carrying, plus some girly handkerchiefs.

'You might need these,' I yelled above the wind as I reached her. Her hair was matted. She was fighting for breath.

'Get behind the rock!' she shouted, cupping her hands to be heard over the howling wind. 'When that stuff from the bubble seeps into the earth, the volcanoes explode and the earth moves.' She wiped her dripping face with the towel.

'Oh right,' I said. 'Thanks for the—'

I didn't finish the sentence because of the explosion. It had two parts, a crack and a boom. The *crack* lifted everything, including many of the rocks, two feet into the air. The *boom* gave you time to land.

'That was the first one,' she said. 'There'll be a couple more. Then watch out for flying rocks and dust.'

'This is—' I started, but was silenced by the kind of explosion that knocks out birds in flight. Barely had that finished echoing between the mountains than another joined it.

'Just be ready to jump if a big rock falls,' she said, looking up. A patter of dust and small pebbles fell on us.

'Ow,' I said.

'They don't count as big unless they make a dent in your head.' She scanned the sky again. 'Good. Now we've got another couple of minutes till the next one. They're coming a bit slower. I think they're running out of the best memories.'

'Leopold's gone to fetch some more,' I said.

'For all the good it'll do him.'

I looked at Keziah. She had a happy intensity about her—full of life.

'I brought you some presents, though they're a bit of a disaster.' I pulled out the sorry-looking bunch of flowers.

'Mushrooms,' she said, rummaging in the trug. 'Wonderful.' She popped a handful in, and resting her back against the rock next to mine, closed her eyes. I watched her.

'You've been crying,' I said.

'Yeah, well, have a lifetime of your worst memories pass in front of you and you'd cry. It's OK though.'

'They don't seem to be winning, Gaston and Leopold.'

'No,' she said, eyes still closed, 'they're not.' She recovered more breath and looked at me. 'This landscape. It's what I've been seeing in my dreams. It absorbs the memories. I hardly have to remodel it now at all.'

'And?'

'The landscape is *me*. I've never seen it all before, laid out like this. It's horrible, but it's me, and I can see it all.'

'That's a comfort?'

'Better than crying in the darkness. So it's OK. What about you?'

'Well, I've built my god and everything's ready. Gaston and Leopold are panicking at the lack of you.'

'Tough,' said Keziah.

'Gaston's sent me to persuade you to come over. He doesn't trust Leopold. Meanwhile Leopold's taken to smoking two ciggies at once. And I've been trying to get back to my body. I can get in, but I can't stay in.'

'I've got to keep an eye on that memory,' Keziah said, looking up. 'When it falls, jump out of the way.' She took another mushroom. 'These are great. Thank you.'

'In the hospital, they're operating on my brain. Right now. Some kind of last-ditch thing. I don't think it's going well. I heard one of the surgeons say, "Nope".'

'It's just about to fall,' said Keziah. 'Can you make sure the trug is OK? I don't want to lose the mushrooms.' I did as asked, and moved to safety while Keziah dealt with another falling memory. After it too had rolled down the slope, fizzing and collapsing, she returned to the shelter of the rock. The rock was now dripping with the slime from the burst memory.

We paused while the volcanoes exploded.

'Big volcanoes,' I said.

'The scree is the damage done to me,' said Keziah. 'The volcanoes are what I do to myself.'

I stiffened. Touchy-feely.

'I thought I could ask them to stop torturing you,' I said. 'I could say, "If you give her a night's rest, I might be able to persuade her in the morning." It would at least give you some respite.'

'That's kind,' she said. 'I'm OK though.'

'I'm not,' I said. 'Not when I'm having brain surgery evidently and the surgeon is saying "nope" all the time. Why can't he be saying, "Yo!"? Why can't he be high-fiving the nurses? Why can't he be saying, "O Yes!"?'

'It could be all sorts of reasons. A nurse could have asked him, "Would you like a cup of tea?"'

'It wasn't that kind of "nope". It was the it's-all-going-pear-shaped sort of "nope". It was a tomorrow-I-quit-brain-surgery "nope". Anyway,' I continued bleakly, 'I think it's going to finish for all of us tomorrow.'

'Good,' said Keziah.

We paused and I moved while Keziah dealt with another memory. 'What you are you planning to do?' she asked when she returned, shaking goo from her hands.

'Oh, I don't know,' I said. 'Perform on my own, I suppose. Spin everything out. Hope against hope.'

'Yes,' said Keziah.

'You've never gone back to your body, have you? Not even in your dreams.'

'Never,' said Keziah.

'Don't you want to?'

'Not really. So much going on in my head all the time. I was sick of fighting it.'

'Sad.'

'Yes. There is one thing I would like to do, though,' she continued, dropping another small handful of mushrooms in her mouth. 'Before it all ends. You won't like it. I'd like to show you around.'

'Me?'

'You're all there is,' said Keziah, with a little smile. 'I don't ask you to understand this Jamie but it's empowering to explain this landscape to someone. Even you. Perhaps especially you.'

I scratched my eyebrow. Here was something I could do, at least.

'I could come tomorrow morning,' I said. 'I could tell them that I would make one last attempt to persuade you.'

'I would like that.'

'I'm assuming that you *won't* be coming to perform... I figured you wouldn't.'

'Do you mind?' she asked.

'No. I feel bad that I didn't defend you or anything. I meant to. Sorry.'

'I have a bit of debt to you as well,' said Keziah.

That's true, I thought.

'Can I bring you anything tomorrow?' I asked. 'Mushrooms on toast? I could bring a breakfast tray.'

Above us, another fat memory wobbled down from the sky.

I walked back through the forest and collected another basket of mushrooms, ready for the next day. I called up *Total Javascript,* gave it a head and a beak, and got it to carry the trug to the lighthouse. Then I returned to the clearing. Leopold was back and was eager to know where I'd been. I explained, omitting the part about Gaston sending me.

'Do you think she might come over?' he asked.

'You never know. I might have one last effort at persuading her tomorrow. Another night of torture might soften her up.'

'Our exhibition doesn't start until the afternoon,' mused Leopold. 'You know how quickly things can get done here. Even if she isn't at breaking point until tomorrow morning, there's still time for her to assemble a patchwork god, and for you and she to put together a simple performance, and for all the Powers to be astonished by our ideas. Just.'

'I think I'm ready,' I said. 'I've completed my patchwork god, I've tidied up the habitat, I've practiced a worship routine.'

'Excellent,' said Leopold. 'What we'll do on the day is, Gaston'll be narrating. He'll introduce me and I'll get you and Keziah each to do your worship routines. Just be simple and slow and steady. No need to be nervous.

'Then, you can cook and Keziah can do the garden while I describe your life together. You and Keziah can have a happy meal outside, where everyone can see. No time for much more than the house and the worship now, but I still think it'll be OK. We can tell them we were rushed.

211

'Finally there'll be a question time. What you've got to get across is just a few main points. First, that you're just an ordinary person, typical of millions. Second, that though your life was materially full, it was spiritually empty. Third, the teaching that you had a spiritual component as well as a material was a real revelation as well as making a huge amount of sense. Fourth, following your spirit guides and making a patchwork god was a perfect combination of art, relaxation, spirituality, and rediscovery of meaning. It gave you an edge in the quest for happiness. You could see it becoming a lifestyle choice for millions. You got all that?'

'I'll work on it.'

'Do... and Jamie—'

'What?'

'I like to think we've got closer over the time we've been working together. You know, not so much pet and owner as friends.'

'Definitely,' I lied.

'Whatever happens,' he said. 'I've enjoyed working with you.' He squeezed my shoulder; I tried not to shudder.

'Thank you,' I replied.

Time for a party at the lighthouse for the figments and me. Bob Dylan as DJ. Really loud music. I encouraged Bob to dig up some of the most pained Blues ever written: Elmore James, Billie at her lowest. Loads of high-fat, high salt, high MSG, high-everything party snacks. Fire banked up; lighthouse pulsing with agonized music and the beam of light sending erratic messages in Morse to any passing ships: *woke up this mornin'... decided to sink... get down to the bottom... that's what I think.* Of course there weren't any passing ships. No time now to create the *Titanic* or the *Lusitania*, fun though it would have been.

The party ended with Annie having excused herself and gone to bed, Bob Dylan having packed up his kit and gone home ('it's late, man'), and Mel asleep on the sofa, face down, occasionally twitching with kick-boxing moves or shouting 'penalty corner, steady girls'.

Caroline and I were sitting on the floor, backs to my wonderful gross white leather male-ish reclining armchair, next to the dying fire. Caroline was resting her head on my shoulder. She was slightly too tall for this to be entirely comfortable, but I was enduring the pressure of her boney head with manly fortitude.

I was feeling like Lizzie does when she's allowed people to put gin in her cocktails: so mellow I was putrifying. The end of all things was coming.

'Do you know what I fancy?' I asked Caroline, 'a fry-up.'

Caroline opened a sleepy eye.

'Ugh,' she said.

'I fancy some of those mushrooms,' I said. 'I fancy wickedly and rebelliously eating some mushrooms.'

'Umm.'

'Obviously, if you're having a fry-up, no point in having half a fry-up. That's against the whole fry-up religion. You've got to invite the whole fridge. Tomatoes. Onion, eggs, they've got to come. Spot of pepperoni. Old potatoes. The odd sausage, maybe. I could be persuaded. OK, you've persuaded me.'

'*Hngrgh*,' said Caroline, yawning and tucking herself against me. The ideal girl for tucking herself against people would be a foot smaller than Caroline and a little more generous in the upholstered sections. Watching Caroline tuck herself against me was like watching

213

someone trying to get flat-pack furniture back in the box, but still.

'... Obviously, a spot of Worcester sauce and a dash of hot pepper sauce. You know the kind of thing... I'm happy to go do it myself, of course, but someone has to watch the fire go down.'

Caroline was asleep.

I sighed and gently moved myself away, still letting Caroline's head rest against my arm. With a moment's thought, I created a giant sleeping gorilla and carefully swapped places with it. Caroline snuggled herself against the hairy form and they both grunted happily.

I trod down the stairs into the kitchen, set some oil sizzling in the wok, threw in various things from the vegetable store and fridge. The mushrooms were on the table. With a slightly naughty thrill, I took a handful, brushed off the dirt, sliced them, and dropped them in the wok.

All the partying had left me hungry so when the fry-up was done I tipped the whole thing into a baguette. Then I wrapped the baguette in a napkin, tucked it under my arm, climbed the stairs past the sleeping girls and the sleeping gorilla, up to the lighthouse balcony. It was cold. The skies were clear and growing pale. As an extra touch I posted bright Venus and tiny Mercury so that they flickered above the horizon, waiting for the sun.

Perhaps this was my last night either on earth or in the heavenlies.

I unwrapped the baguette and examined it: magic psychedelic mushrooms. They didn't seem to have harmed Keziah—quite the opposite. I took a bite. Nothing happened. Nothing except a soft note of sadness sounded distantly in my heart, like the church bells of a long-drowned village.

A scatter of seagulls flew cawing round the lighthouse and out of my sight. *Total Javascript*, I noticed, had joined the flock. It looked damp, scuffed and happy. I took another thoughtful bite while the sky turned into that light emerald that you see when it's shaping towards another dawn.

Slowly, quietly, I felt sadness creeping over my heart. It widened, steady and deep, over a few moments, like a tide filling a bay. It was so gentle and so relentless it became almost unbearable.

I stopped eating the sandwich.

It wasn't a bitter sadness. It was soft and kindly. There was just so much of it, and it was so desperately sad, and it kept oozing in. All the friends I'd never see again, the family I'd never visit again. The bread I'd never make again, for goodness' sake. Everything rolled in. All the Christmases of childhood that had promised so much and never quite delivered and had gone again. Childhood itself. *This is getting schlocky*, I thought desperately. It didn't stop. All the delighted teasing looks of gorgeous girls, gone forever. All the crisp winter's days, crackling fires—*stop it! Stop it at once!*

It was, I suddenly understood, like I was in the shade of a blazing happiness, in the negative field of sweet sadness that always surrounds the happiness to make the universe equal. The sadness was the taste of a near miss with Joy.

It slowly ebbed away.

So much for Leopold's theories. Happiness isn't rare. We're just not at the right party.

I threw the rest of the sandwich over the railings and blew my nose and wiped my face and went to bed.

In my sleep, I tried to get back to the Dome, and I think I managed it, but all was quiet and the lights were off.

KEZIAH-LAND

A gentle knocking woke me. 'It's me, Caroline,' said a voice through the door.

'Hello Caroline,' I said.

'Don't expect this every morning,' she said, pushing the door open and carrying a tea-tray. 'I brought you an apple for your breakfast. Seeing the mess in the kitchen I can't imagine you're hungry.'

'What time is it?'

'Eight o'clock. Leopold said he wanted you in the forest clearing by 8:30.'

'Ugh.'

'Quite.'

'Caroline. Could you round up Mel and Annie before I go? I want to say goodbye to you all. And could you make sure Dumbo is ready outside?'

'OK. Oh, Jamie,' she added lightly. 'Is it OK if we keep the gorilla?'

'Is that a trace of pink I see on your cheeks?'

'That's because I've just climbed the stairs,' said Caroline primly. 'It's called vasodilation.' With a trim swirl of modest calf-length skirt she was gone.

My brain rebelled against this day. Surely there was some way to escape, or wake up, or be told everything had been cancelled, or for the U.S. cavalry to appear over the hill. Surely there was something other than this sense of, yet again, being strapped in a car facing a headlong collision.

I sipped the tea and ate the apple and arrived in the lighthouse kitchen. The gorilla had his arm round Caroline's shoulder. She was feeding him grapes.

'He's very friendly,' said Caroline, by way of explanation.

'Guys,' I said. 'I hope you don't mind but I'm going to have to send you back to the memory storage.'

There were murmurs of protest.

'I know, I know,' I said. 'But I don't know what's going to happen to me. I can always call you back if things work out.'

'Jamie,' said Mel. 'I've put in hours in the gym and lost loads of weight. I hope you're not going to lose the weight I've lost.'

'I'll make a mental note,' I said.

'What about the gorilla?' said Annie, then blushed furiously.

'I'll send him too,' I said. 'If you like, I can make one each for you when we come back.'

The girls weighed this in an approving way.

'In some ways it'll be a relief,' said Caroline. 'It's such a strain being what you think I am all the time.'

'*I* thought I was being clever to make you think that way,' I said.

'An obvious literary device,' sniffed Caroline.

'Well, *I've* enjoyed your company, girls,' I said. 'Thank you.'

I gave Mel and Annie a hug each. Caroline didn't extract herself from the gorilla's arms but offered her face for a kiss, which I obliged, keeping one eye on the seven-foot primate. Then with a little twist of thought, like in a dream, I sent them all back to the deeps of my memory.

I stepped out of the empty lighthouse kitchen and trod carefully over the wet rocks to where Dumbo was standing, the foam splashing around his legs. He hoisted me onto his back, and we soared into the air.

My habitat looked good from the sky: the lighthouse washed by the sea, Osama's on the coastline, the hotel next to it, Lord's Cricket Ground, the beach with the ruins of Pablo's bar, the maglev. Further inland was the Cam and Edwards' Air Force Base, with the shuttle neatly parked up.

I wheeled Dumbo round and we flew towards the central habitat. As we neared the woodland clearing we flew over the walls of a giant rainbow-coloured oval stadium that had sprung up in the night.

Dumbo lowered us down into the centre of the stadium, which rose high all around us. Each tier was a different colour, and the whole thing flickered slightly. The tiers were wide and deep, built for something far other than a human span. They were completely empty. I felt a whiff of fear. I caught a glimpse of Leopold pushing a kind of trolley across the ground.

Dumbo lifted me off his back and I patted his leathery skin. 'I'd better send you away too. I don't want you run into the ground by joyriders.' He put his trunk on my shoulders by way of goodbye, and was gone.

Leopold was walking towards me. He was in full Scottish gear with, thankfully, a longer kilt than yesterday.

'Morning!' I called. 'How are you?'

'Terrible,' he said. 'Migraine. Caused by digging half the night through Mordant's memories.'

'Is she—'

'No,' he said. 'No, unless you can do something we have to demonstrate our new human society with just one examplar. You.'

'Do you think—'

'Disaster,' he said, rubbing his forehead as if trying to squash the migraine against his skull. 'Utter disaster. Gaston spent some time last night trying to persuade her to come over. Nothing. He threatened to bring her over by force. She *laughed* at him. The cow. He warned her about being thrown out of the habitat to the mercies of the radiation and the marauding evil spirits.'

'Why didn't he just do it right then?'

'Because we still hoped that one more night of torture might push her over the edge.'

'But it hasn't.'

'She said nothing outside her head can frighten her as much as what's inside her head, and she's not frightened of that any more.'

'Did he try bribery?'

'Of course he tried bribery. There's nothing left but you, Jamie. That's how desperate it is.'

'Me?'

'She said she wanted to talk to you again. Privately.'

I scratched my neck.

'What are you going to do if I can't persuade her?'

Leopold looked uncomfortable.

'I don't know. We may say she's shy.'

I whistled.

'We may say she's shy and very traumatized by the whole experience. We may say that we haven't had long to get everything ready, but in principle it will all work.'

'You expect them to believe that?'

Leopold gave me a bitter look. 'What do you think? I can tell you what *Gaston* thinks. After *Gaston* left

Keziah last night, he went to see the Toad. He pleaded for mercy. He offered all our assets and our servitude to the Toad if the Toad would just get us out of this mess.'

'Gaston didn't think I was going to persuade Keziah then?'

'There was some talk of the Lake of Fire freezing over first.'

'I see. What did the Toad say?'

'The Toad didn't say much. Gaston's memory is more of the Toad's feet jumping on his face.'

'Where is he now?'

'Gaston? Working off his feelings on the snake.' Now he mentioned it, I did hear, over the birdsong and the rustling wind, a distant sound that could be a snake, wrapped in chains, being kicked and whipped.

'Well, that's all wonderful,' I said bleakly. 'So what do you want me to do first?'

Leopold sighed. 'OK, I've got to finish stacking up the amphitheatre with supplies, so why don't you get everything absolutely ready for the dress rehearsal? Then we can go through the whole thing and practice your questions and answers. We'll get all that done before the guests start arriving. Then you can go and see Keziah.'

'And if I persuade her to come?'

'It's going to be too late to build her patchwork god, but we can probably get away with that. Perhaps she could lean lovingly on your arm while you do your worship routine.'

'Nothing difficult then. Hey, I just thought. Couldn't we use one of my memories? Instead of Keziah? I did create Caroline, my ex-girlfriend, and I've really worked hard on making her realistic.'

'Jamie, the difference between a real girl and your mere impressions of a girl wouldn't fool—'

221

'Fair enough. Just a thought. So what are you doing with the trolley?'

'Refreshments,' said Leopold. 'We've built the whole stadium out of the Seven Deadly Sins, pixellated, which our guests will enjoy standing on. I'm just laying these snacks around to provide variety: a pile of Malice on the Lust tier of the stadium, for example. These pixellated sins, like Pixellated Fear, glow with a gentle ambience that the spirits find restful. Not that any of it's going to do us any good.'

We went to our work.

Gaston briefly returned, red-faced and blowing after giving Stub what he described as a 'therapeutic beating'.

He was dressed in a ceremonial Army uniform, but his eyes were bloodshot. After checking up brusquely on the preparations he left to welcome the guests. Things did not seem too affectionate between the Lord and the Overlord.

We were still working on our questions and answers when the first of the crowd waddled in, two fat four-legged reptiles with small heads and vast bodies, not unlike what older children's books used to call brontosauri. (You remember this species had a long existence in dinosaur books until it was realised they were a paleontological error. Thus the poor brontosaurus is not merely extinct, it never existed in the first place. Say what you like, however, these two definitely looked like brontosauri to me.)

'Why do they look like dinosaurs?' I asked Leopold quietly as we watched the two brontosauri making themselves comfortable on the Greed tier of the terraces.

'Not all of them will,' said Leopold, waving at them with a grin that fell off his face as soon as he turned to me. 'They're dressing down. Not a good sign. They're treating it as an afternoon out rather than a proper networking opportunity.'

'Why do they look like dinosaurs at all?'

'It was a complete mess-up,' said Leopold. 'Our Research Department had Earth in its targets for a long time. They watched a couple of mass-extinctions, saw some promising developments and then told us to move in. We had a full-on invasion.

'It was all a terrible mistake. They hadn't done their research properly and millions of us ended up stuck in the bodies of dinosaurs. Absolute tragedy, no idea how it happened. So for 100 million years we were beleaguered on earth wandering around marshes and eating ferns and each other.

'Disgusting, dear boy. You died but then came back as another one. Did you know what that world smelt like? The mud and the parasites and the predators and... you don't want to know about the sex. It was awful. Worse than not having sex.

'Anyway. Rumour went around that we weren't going to get out until the seas had laid up enough oil and gas for the beings that were due to emerge after the *next* mass extinction. They needed a *lot*. So it proved.

'The world did finally end again, not a moment too soon, and we were free to travel through the Omniverse. But it left scars. We spirit beings still default to reptile-shapes unless we constantly work on our appearances.

'Now, you'd better get over to Keziah. I'll be waiting for you in the house.' He put his hand on my shoulder. 'Don't fail us Jamie.'

'OK,' I said.

'Jamie,' Leopold said, taking hold of both my arms with surprising force. 'You've got about an hour.'

'OK,' I said.

'I know there isn't any hope, not really. But just *imagine* beating the Toad. *Imagine* being a celebrity and superstar. Imagine being a fashion icon all through the Omniverse.'

'OK,' I said.

'Instead of, you know, just being a nearly person. Someone who never quite made it.'

'I'll do my best,' I said.

'It's sad really,' said Leopold. 'I can't help wishing… never mind.'

'I'll do my best,' I said again.

'Sometimes I wonder if really just living a quiet life would be better. Than all this ambition and glitz and, let's be honest, slight sense of almost *failure* at times. Oh, I don't know. Too late now.'

Finally, he let me go. I streaked out of his sight, but veered back to my habitat where I entered the lighthouse, grilled the mushrooms quickly, made toast and tea, arranged a breakfast tray. Then I streaked over to Keziah's door, and phoned her.

'Is it OK if I come over now?'

'I was wondering if you were still coming,' she said.

'I said I would.' I was a little piqued.

'It's open,' she said, 'just push.'

It was still teeming with rain in Keziah-land. Keziah was sitting on the grass, with her back to a rough stone wall, brooding.

She stood up quickly when I pushed through the door, and for a second looked slightly empty-handed and awkward. A kiss, clearly, was too intimate a way of saying hello but a handshake too formal and in any case I was holding a tray. In Jane Austen's day a small bow and a little bob-like curtsey would have done the business, but this was the graceless twenty-first century and we were its clueless inhabitants.

'Thank you for coming,' she said, offering a hesitant moment of eye-contact by way of welcome. She tucked a sodden strand of hair back behind her ear.

'I brought some more mushrooms,' I said. 'And toast. I don't know if there's anywhere to eat them.'

'I've got a little dining room in the cottage,' she said.

I saw now that the door through which I'd come was the entrance to an outside privy. Next to the privy stood a small cottage, at just about the highest point of the mountain plateau. The cottage had thick walls, a slate roof, small windows—built to survive the weather.

The cottage door opened directly into a small living room which was minimally furnished and covered with piles of paper. Keziah had, however, laid up for a meal at one end.

We busied ourselves sorting everything out to eat.

'How much time have we got?' Keziah asked.

'Leopold told me to be back in an hour. They've built a stadium around our Dream House and it's slowly filling up with dinosaurs. It's a long story. They're all reptiles at heart, it seems.'

'An hour should be enough.'

Keziah started neatly cutting her way through two slices of mushrooms on toast. The atmosphere was strained: being pleasant to each other wasn't easy.

'I finally followed your example and ate some mushrooms last night,' I told her.

'What did you think?' she asked. 'These mushrooms are fantastic, by the way.'

'I didn't much like them, to be honest,' I said. 'It was like, big sad emotions.'

'That basketful you sent me kept me going last night. They made me think, *I don't have to take this.*'

'You did beat them, you know.'

'I know,' she said, with a sudden shy grin. 'It's the next bit that's more tricky.'

'What, facing whatever happens at the end of today?'

'Not that so much,' she said. 'Showing *you* around. That's terrifying. Come on. There's a raincoat if you want it.'

I took an oilskin from the coat-stand and she led me out of the cottage towards the volcanoes. The rain tumbled down and was being picked up and flung at us by the wind.

'You aren't going to laugh or make stupid jokes,' she told me, a requirement, not a question. 'I'm expecting a large amount of not being able to cope on your part. But you *will* cope so long as you don't try to give me any advice or counsel. Just by listening you're helping. Is that clear?'

'Right,' I said. 'Remind me why you're doing this?'

'To explain myself before I die,' said Keziah.

'Fair enough,' I said. 'I knew there was a reason.'

'This scree here,' said Keziah as we tramped, 'is like a great scar. It runs almost the whole length of my landscape. Can you see how it's all gouged up? You can often see insects and crows poking in the mess that's been brought to the surface.'

'Glaciation,' I said. 'We did that in geography.'

'My mother,' said Keziah. 'Her hardness into my softness. She ploughed my heart.'

I shut up. Keziah stopped and looked over the great scar. Half of the landscape was scar, ripped-up earth, uprooted trees, and slimy moulds and underneath (no doubt) were squirmy orange things with too many legs. 'Then all the abuse got in as well. Right into the wound. Like a canker, made sure it never healed. Look at it. My life.'

She gazed out over it, then snapped: 'I'm not crying. These are angry tears.'

If we were being pedantic here, Keziah, I thought, *that wasn't logical. The emotional source of the tears is irrelevant. Excessive moisture from eyes equals tears.* I'm glad to say I kept this thought to myself. Caroline accuses me of being insensitive! Hah! If she could see me now. Jamie. The Listener. The Wise Counsellor.

'The volcanoes,' Keziah continued, blinking, starting to walk towards them. 'That's my response.'

'They stink,' I said.

'Yes.'

'Sulphur dioxide,' I added. 'Rotten eggs.'

'And smoke, and poisonous gas, and lava, and rocks. See how the lava and rocks ruined the landscape far beyond the scree.'

We clambered through the rocks that led to a high pass between two of the volcanoes. Still the rain fell.

Keziah's words were as brisk and steady as our walk. 'The volcanoes try to fill in the damage caused by the scree. All they really do is trash the landscape and the sky. Look how barren the land is. Look how foul the air is. Look how ugly it all is. Look how all the rain gets in, despite all my efforts.'

'Why do you want to stop the rain getting in?'

'All this is just a crust,' said Keziah, nodding her head to the smoking rockscape. 'The whole mountain is hollow. I spend a lot of time fixing stream-beds and blocking up holes to stop the water getting inside. Come on.'

We climbed to the top of the pass—a volcano on each side—and looked over. A further rumpled slope fell away in front of us.

'Now some other relationships,' she said. The path zig-zagged down the stony mountainside, with the two volcanoes slowly diminishing behind us. We kept glimpsing a wide, grey lake, to which, with a final turn, the path led.

Nothing grew at the lakeside. 'See all these ruins? There used to be trees here and grass and a beach. There's even a deserted boathouse over there. It was like our own private loch in the mountains. I was a princess here. Can you see all the appropriate technology gadgets?' I did notice some curious pieces of rusty metal. 'That's a plough. That's a solar cooker. Next to it is a solar dryer. That over there is a micro-hydro electricity generator... But then a frost killed the plants, dust from the desert stopped the gadgets working and the volcano poured lava and rocks into it. Do you see what this is?'

I felt her green eyes searching me. They searched the top of my head, since I was looking at my feet. 'This is the space in my heart for my dad. He was depressed,' continued Keziah. 'When I really needed him to be not depressed. The attacks started when I was five. Come on.'

Perhaps there are worse things even than death, I thought desperately. *The secrets of a woman's heart, for one. But it's only an hour. Surely I can spare her an hour.*

'You can hardly see this,' she was continuing, pointing at a stone-filled slope. 'That was a park. There was an enormous dolls' house, storybook characters, wardrobes full of clothes. African friends. Every stone you see I personally fired out from my volcanoes until I buried everything. My sister Jemima's buried under there. It took a long time to bury her, and she was crying all the time. If you ever get back to your body and see her, I know you won't, but if you do, perhaps you could tell her I'm sorry. I couldn't stop myself. I hated her so much.'

After this slope, the landscape flattened out and some patches of green appeared, battling the scree. We crossed several streams. Still the rain poured down.

Keziah led me over a stile into a rock-strewn field. Here and there among the rocks, we could see ceramic pots. Some were very large. Some had been smashed by falling rocks. Most had plants in them, a few of which were in flower. Each pot, I noticed, was labelled in what I assumed was Keziah's handwriting.

'This is where I keep all my other relationships,' said Keziah. 'All these plants are invasive. I keep them in pots, I tell myself, for their protection. I don't want them growing up towards the volcano and getting poisoned. But that's a lie.'

'Hey, that's me,' I said. In the same way you can hear your name across a crowded room, I'd spotted a notice penned with the words JAMIE SMITH. It was a four-inch terracotta pot containing a young, rather round and leafy plant, with funny little dark flowers and no fruit. 'It's not very big,' I pointed out.

'It's not you,' she said. 'It's my relationship with you.'

'Still,' I grumbled. 'Looks like a geranium cutting that didn't take.'

'Come on,' she said. 'There's a path round the volcano and then back up to the cottage.'

We turned and started off round the volcano.

'Does it ever stop raining here?' I called out to her.

'It hasn't yet.'

229

Rounding the volcano we saw below us was what looked like a film-set: a street made of shabby housefronts, interspersed with the facades of motels and nightclubs. A back alley or two snaked away. All of it was falling apart in the rain, dissolving like cardboard. Several buildings had fallen down.

'I won't take you down there,' said Keziah. 'Do you remember that artist who once put up a tent and inscribed it with all the names of the people she'd had sex with?'

'I try to forget all I hear about modern art,' I said.

'That's my tent down there. Guys and girls. All different encounters. Not one I cared about. I built all those houses myself and I made them out of rubbish to do rubbish things in them with rubbish people. I didn't need to destroy them. They just fall apart of their own accord.'

'Especially in the rain,' I muttered.

'Yes.'

I looked at the shabby street of housefronts and I hated it. This was miserable for someone who in another world could be being loved and cherished and be teaching toddlers to ride bikes. For example. Or, of course, holding down an important and professional career. You know what I mean. Whatever Keziah was for it wasn't for this—empty encounters in the night.

We trudged on. *This is terrible*, I thought, *worse than performing in front of Gaston and Leopold and a stadium-full of evil reptiles. Which is also on the agenda for the day.* I stopped for a moment and lifted my face to the skies, hoping the rain would wash everything off.

'Hey,' I said, 'this rain doesn't taste bad.' It reminded me of something. I couldn't think what.

'Come on,' she said, pulling her sodden cotton hood over her ears. 'I want to do this right to the end.'

I like hill-walking, but Keziah was lithe as a whippet and as determined as a falling boulder. It wasn't that easy to keep up. I cupped my hands and took another surreptitious drink of the falling rain. It was good stuff, sweet and warm, with deep notes of things I didn't have time to savour.

The path wound back to the cottage. Keziah was waiting there while I laboured up the hill.

She was looking out at her landscape.

'There's hardly anything that isn't trashed,' she said. 'What's trashed it? I've trashed it. *I've* trashed *me*.'

'It didn't start well,' I said sympathetically.

'It could have finished better,' said Keziah.

I said, 'So what happens at the edges of this landscape?'

'It's an island. I try to send the water over the edge. The landscape is shaped like a letter A—the cottage here is at the highest point and the sharpest point.'

'A delta wing,' I said. 'A pity you just send the water off the edge like that. It's good stuff. You could use it for hydro or something.'

'You won't think that when you see the inside. Come on.'

'Is there much more of this?'

'Lots, but it won't take long.'

'You're sure this is doing you good? Because I definitely wouldn't be doing this if it wasn't helping.'

'It's helping,' she said. 'Especially if you stop moaning.'

She opened the door and led me into the cottage again. 'I want to show you the downstairs.' She walked me through a door at the end of the room, which led to a stone spiral staircase, which seemed to burrow straight down for a very long way.

'It goes right through the mountain,' said Keziah, slightly echoey, her black hood bobbing out of sight.

'I can see what you mean about the water,' I said. The stone sides of the staircase were dripping and moss grew.

We stopped at the first landing, where a dank corridor led off into the gloom. 'It's mostly a warehouse,' said Keziah. 'This whole landscape is a honeycomb. When the memories fall, they seep through the land and get stored here. So if you walk down this corridor, you can see row after row of them.

'They're quite animated. Some are dangerous. You don't invite them out of their cages.

'There are corridors like this all the way down. Not all are for memories. There's a whole section for vengeful thoughts, for example. Another for self-hate. One of the things Stub taught me was to keep all these filed things in order. Not to keep breaking in and fishing them out. You don't deny them but you do file them. Simple really.

'Then, there's all kinds of other things walking around in these caves and I'm not really sure what they are.'

'You could probably pay some analysts,' I said. 'They'd give you suggestions.'

'Yes, I think that's right,' she said. 'And the landscape itself moves and breathes. I've never got down to the bottom. Very hot. It's often shaking and sliding around.'

'And water everywhere?'

'Yes. Making everything more treacherous.' We turned another half circle on the spiral stairs. 'This is on the other side from the corridors. It looks out over the front.'

We had climbed down to a plywood inner door, with some frosted glass for a window and a plaque outside that read:

MORDANT & CO.
Solicitors

'Your office,' I said. 'Who's the "& co."?'

'Nobody,' said Keziah. 'It's just the way you have to do it.'

'So strictly speaking,' I said, '"Solicitors" should read, "Solicitor".'

'I might expand,' she said defiantly. 'Anyway, come in. This is home.' She leaned against the door and pushed it open.

It was a high-ceilinged room, with full-length picture windows at the far end. Keziah seemed to have a taste for heavy furniture—a big walnut desk covered with papers, a black leather chair, a sofa and two unmatched armchairs surrounding a coffee table and a rug.

On the wall hung dozens of portraits of the kind of people you see in Wanted posters. Several sets of metal filing cabinets, bookshelves and a set of kitchen units lined one wall: survival tools for workaholics. I could imagine Keziah extracting a scalding ciabatta from the microwave and pouring coffee as the moon rose outside and she flipped her way through witness statements and tape transcripts.

'This office is a copy of the one I had on earth. The whole lot was donated from one of those communities that takes ex-prisoners and does furniture restoration,' she told me. 'When they heard I was starting up on my own, they moved everything in a single weekend.'

'I see what you mean about the water, though,' I said. Water was dripping through the ceiling in various places. 'You know, I'd put that little watering can under one drip and catch something for your houseplants. I'd put your kettle under another drip for your coffee, and I'd put your water-cooler under that other drip. Save on water meter costs and stop your floor flooding.'

'This is the place I'll be tonight. This is the thing I'll be saddest to leave. The one place I did some good perhaps. Felt like it, anyway. Come on. One last stop.'

We left the office and trod down the stairs again.

'This is nearly the end of the tour,' said Keziah.

'Where are we going?'

'My bedroom,' said Keziah. 'The quiet space at the centre of me. Or as you will see'—we'd gone round two full turns and were now directly below the office as she pushed open the door—'not.'

She had to give the door a fierce shove to get it completely open, and she led me in.

It was a narrow, dark room, with a single bed, and you could hardly move for the junk. The sedimentary layers of a girl's life: teddy bears, books, models of horses. On top of that, complicated girly make-up things and the crazy clothes that pre-teens try, green tights and strident lipstick and blobby mascara. Next layer: drug equipment and contraceptives and tattoo needles and razor blades and the black clothes, some of them ripped. And chaos everywhere. Bongo drums. African cloth wall hangings that had fallen down. An overflowing laundry basket. Half-opened packets of chocolate biscuits and a whole taxonomy of chocolate-wrappers. In the corner, I noticed, Keziah had tied a well-made hangman's noose to a hook in the ceiling.

'Keziah, what's that?'

'The logical conclusion,' she said. 'Isn't it? I just never had the courage to be logical.'

Water was dripping through the ceiling, splashing onto everything.

'I can understand the whole metaphor,' said Keziah, angry, like she'd had this conversation with herself many times. 'It's not rocket science. I don't need telling that I'm complete mess here, right deep inside, and need nothing but a complete sort out. Here's where the chaos starts and the anger and everything else. But how can I even *begin* to fix it when there's all this *stuff* pouring in all the time that I can't control?'

She sat on the bed and looked down, as if exhausted. A fresh irruption of water started dripping onto her head. She let it fall.

I was standing in the doorway, for the excellent reason that moving anywhere would have involved ploughing a furrow through mountains of girly detritus. In my house on earth I have grown used to treading carefully in case of used leg-waxing strips or hot hair-straighteners. But this was something else. Can a room get so untidy that it passes a critical point and can never be sorted out again? Beyond the capacity of all the cupboard space and bin bags in the world?

'Look, water's even falling into that glass you have next to your bed. I'd drink it.'

'I wish you'd shut up about the water,' she snapped. The room rocked with her flaring of anger. More water started dripping through the ceiling.

'Suit yourself,' I said, stung.

She looked at me furiously. 'All right, I will try some of this wonderful water since it's so fantastic.'

'It doesn't matter now.'

'Never mind the fact that water is causing all the mess.'

'I said it doesn't matter.'

She picked up the glass and drunk.

She held the empty glass against her lips for a long time, with her eyes closed.

'You all right?' I asked. 'I didn't really mean, drink it. It was just a... comment.'

When she removed the glass from her face, her eyes were staring into the middle distance and slowly, tears started to drip.

She swore.

She carefully took the jug (which was being refilled by drips from the ceiling) and looked at it. Then she poured out and downed another glass.

Her face wore a betrayed look. She swore again.

'Look for things you can't see the point of,' she said, quietly.

She drank a third glass. Then a fourth. Carefully she put the glass and the jug at her feet. Sobs started shaking her body. Another rumble rattled the room. The ceiling cracked and water started pouring in. This was rapidly becoming like a scene from *Titanic*. Pools were gathering on the floor.

I was standing by the door, paralyzed. A river was now gushing through the roof, down the walls. The junk in the room was being unsettled by the rising water, which was now covering my ankles. It was, I noticed, nicely warm, unlike in *Titanic*.

She looked up at the trashed ceiling.

I had absolutely no idea what to say or do. Put an arm round her? Offer to make a cup of tea? Run away?

'Are you all right?' I asked.

She answered with a single word, in the shocked whisper of someone betrayed:

'*Abba!*'

'What?' I said.

Then the ceiling fell in.

THE PATCHWORK GOD

'Look. We've got to go. You're going to drown.'

'Good.' She climbed down from the bed and sat on the floor. Using one cupped hand, she was sloshing water into her mouth and over her head.

I wondered if I should come over all manly and pull her away. *Oh help*. I took a deep breath, kicked my way through the junk and took hold of her arm.

'Get off me,' she spluttered.

OK, so that was a bad idea.

'You're going to drown!'

'I want to!'

'No, you don't!' I pulled at her and managed to drag her half up. 'We've got to *go*!'

She stood up, brushed away my arm with surprising force. She wasn't looking at me. She didn't seem to be looking at anything.

'Daddy,' she said. 'O Daddy.'

The water was round my knees now, warm as a bath.

I looked at her for a long moment.

'Bye,' I said.

As I turned to climb the stairs, I saw her standing under the waterfall that was now tumbling from the ceiling, drinking the warm water in, letting it all fall over her face and neck, while her childhood junk sloshed around her feet. The dark room was glistening.

I sprinted up the stairs, stumbling more than once; it was more like Angel Falls than a staircase. Water was fountaining out of the stone sides. Up and past the office, up to the top, through the dining room—itself, ankle-deep in water—out through the open door. A monsoon blowing. Turn left. Wrench open the privy door, step in. On the other side, not a privy, the wall marked GIRLS in the *Hotel Splendide* swimming pool. The sun shining.

Catch my breath, enjoying the warmth of the *Splendide*. Somewhere, I knew, an ugly mob of guilty emotions was battering on the doors of my mind. They had words to say about how you should rescue people, be there for people, not leave them in their hour of need. I took a breath, took aim, then streaked back to the stadium, to the Dream House, and through the half-open kitchen door.

Leopold was pacing up and down.

'Jamie,' he said. 'Well?'

I shook my head.

'*Gnõrink-llyeyuñgo*,' said Leopold, with the air of one who's been saving that curse for many years and has decided to cash it in now. He walked over to the stainless-steel kitchen-scraps bin and kicked it as hard as he could across the room.

'She's having some kind of breakdown,' I said. 'But not what you'd hope.'

'She's not coming?'

'She's definitely not coming.'

Leopold motioned me to the kitchen window, which had a view of the stadium.

'Look out there.'

I whistled. 'All seven layers full,' continued Leopold. 'They've come from everywhere.' It was a stirring sight. And the colours! No-one could have guessed that the Jurassic skins were quite those shades of red, orange, yellow and shocking pink.

Others in the crowd didn't look like dinosaurs at all. Some looked like angels, hovering in the sky. Others were sinuey, Asiatic, female and many-limbed, like one of the Toad's bearers. A small group actually looked like demons, bright red with horns and tails and cloven hooves.

('What are they?' I pointed them out to Leopold.

'Fancy dress,' he said, bitterly. 'They're all having a good day out.')

Many others looked more like machines—flying engineering work-benches with vices and saws and pincers. Near the top I picked out a crowd of many-armed beings in roll-necked Arran pullovers.

'Are they Collectors?' I asked.

'That's why they're in the cheap seats,' replied Leopold.

'And that's a Royal Box?' I pointed at a section of the stadium halfway up that jutted out from the rest and was wreathed in purple and olive green.

'Yup. The Toad's in there.' He turned abruptly from the window and paced slowly up and down the kitchen, breathing deeply. 'You know what marks the true professional? Style. Even when the cause is lost. How do I look?'

He stood in front of me, leathery orange face, dark jacket, shirt with ruffled collar and ruffled sleeves, sporran, kilt, stick-thin legs, white socks, squeaky-clean shoes with shiny buckles.

241

'You look good,' I said.

'I know,' he said. 'However far we fall, and however long it takes to get back, style always returns to the top. Circumstances are temporary. Class is eternal. I spent a hundred million years as a close relative of the Komodo dragon half choking on winged-reptile bones but I fought back. Do I need lipstick, do you think?'

'I wouldn't.'

'Bit of rouge?'

'That's up to you.'

'I think yes.' He took a make-up box from his sporran and applied some. 'Well,' said Leopold, clicking the compact shut and putting it away. 'No point in keeping them waiting any longer. Are you ready?'

'No,' I said.

'You know you rot down.'

'I'm sorry?'

'You humans. You rot down. After death. They may kick you around and pull bits off you but it's not forever. You decay.'

'So we're not eternal?'

'This is where I get confused. You see, you are eternal. You're also eternally diminishing. So your capacity for suffering is decreasing, along with everything else. If an eternal something is eternally diminishing does it ever cease? I could never figure that out. Anyway, for practical purposes it means that fewer and fewer beings are interested in you as time passes... that's a comfort, I think.'

'That's a comfort?' I asked.

'You should try the alternative. You should try being eternal and *not* diminishing. You feel the pain of old age with all the vigour of youth. Then you comfort yourself with the thought that it's only ever going to get worse. Wait here.'

Leopold left the kitchen momentarily and returned with a cage. Stomping around inside was a trumpet with two ill-fitting wings, sparrow legs, giant mouse ears and a dangling, smelly external lung. I looked at it.

'First Trumpeter?' I said.

'First Trumpeter *271-3041*,' said First Trumpeter tetchily. 'Fitted with these disgusting bits of debris. Not even half a body.' He lifted his feet. 'Look at these. Moorhen feet. Ridiculous. No wonder their last owner got rid of them. But I'm not talking to you.'

'He was all we could get,' said Leopold. 'We asked around for a trumpeter but there weren't any takers. So we had to recycle this one that we found when I was cleaning out the habitat.'

'You know what, Leopold,' said First Trumpeter 271-3041. 'I'm the only thing with *any* class in this whole performance.'

'Well now's your moment,' said Leopold. 'You know what to do.'

'I know my job,' said First Trumpeter 271-3041.

'Do it then,' said Leopold, and he opened the cage. First Trumpeter wobbled on the perch for a moment, then dived out of the cage. His humming-bird wings started to whine gently. He hovered in front of Leopold.

'These wings are rubbish,' said First Trumpeter. 'This whining sets my teeth on edge.'

'Just go,' said Leopold. First Trumpeter flew out of the kitchen.

'Where's he going?' I asked.

'Up the chimney, then out,' said Leopold. 'Which is Gaston's signal. And then we wait for our cue.'

Outside, the hum and snort and bellowing of the crowd quietened as, presumably, the assembled beings saw First Trumpeter 271-3041 emerge from the chimney, stagger slightly on his little legs, steady himself, then rise into the sky, wings whining. When he was level with the Royal Box, First Trumpeter blew.

He may have been a vain, embittered grump, but First Trumpeter 271-3041 could do a fanfare. He blew a single note that slowly rose in pitch. The sound filled the stadium, hushing it. The tiniest of pauses, then he was onto a quick, jazz riff. We looked out of the window and saw him flying straight for the Royal Box.

Still playing, he buzzed the Toad, before banking steeply and climbing, heading out of the stadium. As he banked, he emptied the contents of his stomach over the Toad and disappeared over the rim of the stadium.

'That wasn't in the script,' said Leopold, brightening momentarily. 'Good fun though.'

We watched some shouting and stamping in the Royal Box. Three attendants rose up on wings and gave chase. Another courtier lifted a slug-like being from a bag and placed it on the Toad's head. Blindly groping, it started sucking up the mess.

Meanwhile, Gaston—still recognizably himself but with his petrodactyl wings flapping in great downward beats—had risen from the front row of the auditorium. With his leathery wings holding himself level with the Royal Box, he started to speak.

'Esteemed princely beings,' he boomed. 'Onward marches the glorious reign of the free spirits of the Omniverse!'

('Standard greeting,' hissed Leopold to me.)

'Today we have come to show you a giant leap forward in the way we spirits can dominate and exploit humans! Many of us—while not for a moment wanting to criticise the advances of Modernism, which were high-level strategic decisions for the good of the whole realm —remember something of what's been lost! We remember how comfortable it was when humans just worshipped us.

'What I have the pleasure of announcing this afternoon is how recent developments in design and in post-modernism can be used to produce a renaissance in our dearest and simplest activities.

'Esteemed colleagues, we will restore spirit worship when many thought it had been discarded forever!

'Spirit worship—as you will know, colleagues—has been restricted in the West to a batty minority of tree-huggers and crystal-wearers. Where are the young guys? Where are the right-wingers? Where are the materialists? Where are the multinational corporations? Where is the media buzz? Where is the mainstream?

'Colleagues! They're coming back to the fold. With the tools we provide, you will be able to bend them and twist them whichever way you please…

'I should warn you, fellow beings, that we are just showing the bare outlines today. We have been rushing to meet a deadline. When we are granted the contract, we will in the coming months unveil a complete Developers' Kit, with full information: draft metanarratives, slogan ideas, fashion accessories, suggestions for celebrity endorsements, a press pack—everything that this movement needs to take off on earth; and all thoroughly tested in our demonstration lab here in the heavenlies.

'The total package—and coming at a surprisingly reasonable cost—will enable millions of spirit guides to receive worship and devotion direct from people on earth! Fellow beings! You are going to be *gods* again!'

245

The crowd cheered though I (who have some experience of these things) thought it was a boozy, stag-night cheer, the sort you give the groom in a pub once he's made a speech about what good mates you are. Then you kidnap him, take him on a flight to Latvia, yank his clothes off, tie him to a lamppost and spray him with Ralgex.

'Isn't he thrilling?' said Leopold, breathlessly. 'Isn't he magnificent? He's wasted on all these.'

'So without any hype or exaggeration, let me introduce my colleague Leopold, whose design triumphs include the invention of Scottishness—something, you remember, that infected a whole nation, right down to the present day. He is working with the human male Jamie Valentine Smith, a brilliant young man, highly representative of our intended market.'

'"A brilliant young man",' I said.

'He has to say that,' said Leopold. 'Come on. We're on.'

Leopold pushed the kitchen door back dramatically, and to huge—and I feared, ironic—cheers, walked out. Then he turned to face the kitchen door, and waved me to emerge.

The roar was enormous.

Over the hubbub, Gaston was still commentating.

'Notice the house and gardens,' he said. 'Notice how it is *mainstream*—the kind of thing that millions have— and yet it is *aspirational*. It's idyllic, a dream house. Our new religion will fall squarely into the middle-class aspirational market.'

As Leopold tried to direct me with eye-movements, I stepped out of the honeysuckled door and closed it behind me, pausing theatrically to admire the beauty of the cottage.

'Where's the girl?' someone shouted. 'Where's the girl?' A little wave of laughter and conversation rippled round the stadium.

Gaston ignored him. 'He believes that the reason he has the beautiful house and life is his own work and luck, plus the help of the spirits...'

I stroked my chin, as if thinking, 'Now, how have I managed to earn this beautiful house and lifestyle?'

'What about the sacred feminine?' someone shouted again, and there was laughter.

'So how *did* we make spirits trendy again in his life?' Gaston went on, apparently oblivious to the mockery. 'Obviously, you can't go for the traditional idols because everyone sees those as backward and superstitious. Our insight is to talk about *happiness*. We target his capacity for happiness.

'It turns out,' Gaston continued, echoing across the stadium, which was becoming quieter, 'that all humans feel that pure happiness is just somewhere out of their reach—that's a universal human feeling. So we develop a theology that spirituality is the key to happiness— following the spirits.'

I tried to make like a light had just dawned on me. 'Aha!' I mimicked.

'We also teach them that true happiness is rare. That means, they have to strive for it. And *that* means, given time, we can get them to dance to any tune we like.'

The crowd roared. 'Bring out the girl!' cried someone.

Behind the stadium, I glimpsed black clouds spiralling around Keziah's habitat. The girl, I thought, is drowning in a storm. With her integrity intact. Unlike some of us.

Gaston ploughed on. 'Now, how do we give form to these vague ideas? We've got to get him worshipping us, needing us, depending on us.

'This is our wonderful insight. Get him to pile up all the things he really loves and make them into a work of Art. Then bow down to it. Worship the spirit behind it. Which our model will now demonstrate. Beautiful, brilliant, brazen. You watch.'

As Leopold gestured, I tried to saunter towards my patchwork god, which was a little way from the house.

The cry was being taken up all around the stadium now:

'We want the girl! We want the girl!'

'See how this checks so many 21st-century boxes!' Gaston continued as if not hearing them. 'Materialism. Good design. A spiritual dimension to life. The pursuit of pleasure. Individual expression. As he worships his "patchwork god" I want you to imagine what it will be like when every home and garden has one!'

He's a market trader, I thought. Selling, selling. Going down fighting.

'... when worship to the spirits is being offered by everyone, everywhere. When there are festivals of patchwork gods, websites, magazines and specialist producers. In this way, they open themselves to us and we can direct them. And every spirit, again, can keep humans as pets!'

I prostrated myself before my patchwork god.

'Oh spirits,' I called, caressing the pumpkin, and jumping slightly to hear my voice amplified across the stadium. 'Make my mind as rich and fruity as this pumpkin! Lead me not into stupid, dense, thick-headed people. Give me a sharpness of mind.'

The hubbub fell away, replaced by a quiet sibilance as 80,000 dinosaurs and other spiritual beings started to salivate. Even the cries of 'Give us the girl!' had temporarily stopped.

I moved onto the lads' mags and held them like a votive offering.

'Teach me all the sexual arts!' I cried. 'Lead me into temptation! Make me a sexual artist!'

Leopold was dribbling. Behind me, I even heard one or two agonized breathy groans from the crowd. Picking up on this, Gaston continued to broadcast from his position high above us.

'Many of you came to mock. We know this. We know we still have work to do on our model. Before we can indeed, bring you the girl. *But look at the power we're already achieving.*' Glancing up, I saw Leopold casting an adoring look on Gaston.

I moved onto the money fountain. I was getting quite pumped up by now.

'Money!' I cried. 'Dear sweet money! I can pretend no longer! Source of my well-being! I love you!' I stuck my head in the money fountain, dunking myself into a cascade of clinking coins and rustling notes. When I brought my head out, Gaston was still speaking.

'This can be yours! Nobody believed in the power of this.'

'Money!' I yelled, and dipped my head in the fountain again. 'Oh! This is so liberating! I've wanted to say this all my life!' I wondered if I was overdoing this, but no, they were slavering.

'There's more!' cried Gaston. 'Hold yourselves, free spirits of the Omniverse, there's more.'

'Petty cruelty,' I said, picking up the brick thoughtfully, and turning it over in my hands.

'Just look at this!' urged Gaston. 'Watch! Don't miss it!'

Leopold was smiling.

The jellyfish scooted out from its little garage in the patchwork god and slid across the ground. I followed it with easy strides, walking alongside.

'Notice how he's taking his time,' said Gaston. 'He's obviously not in a hurry today.'

The jellyfish started zig-zagging, and I followed.

'You see,' said Gaston, 'he believes that this routine will set him up perfectly for his day's work. A little light cruelty at the beginning of the day.'

I could sense the excitement all around me. Looking up momentarily, I saw a storm and darkness had settled over Keziah's habitat. I fingered the brick, ready to drop it on the hapless, fleeing jellyfish.

'Hold yourselves in, beings!' cried Gaston. 'Hold yourselves in... and remember he does *this several times a day!*'

I stole a glance at the Royal Box. The Toad was standing very still, with the slug nibbling the top of his head.

'And he is one of millions!' cried Gaston. 'See what new vistas are opening up today!'

I find it hard to recall exactly what happened next. One moment I was poised to drop a brick on a fleeing jellyfish, watched closely by 80,000 closely-packed salivating demonic spirits in a multi-coloured amphitheatre.

The next moment, I saw a large part of the amphitheatre flying towards me, as if kicked by a giant boot. I dropped the brick in shock, missing the jellyfish. A moment later, a blast wave hit me and knocked me off my feet. A moment after that, I heard the most enormous explosion. The rumble that followed the initial crack was so loud that you just wanted to lie down and cover your head until it was over.

When I did get up after some twenty seconds, it was to a scene of devastation. The amphitheatre was retreating elastically, snapping back to its original oval state, but it was spilling evil spirits as it went back, scattering them over the ground. Gaston had been blown out of the sky. Leopold had transformed into a Komodo dragon and was bellowing. Nobody was looking at me. Everyone was looking beyond the amphitheatre to Keziah's habitat, where the supersonic bang had come from.

Keziah's habitat was shining with a bright light. I couldn't see the source since it was hidden by the amphitheatre, but I could see the glow. Fireworks were being let off. We heard a *whump* and a sizzle and then a multi-coloured umbrella of fire and light opened over us. Sparks fell into the amphitheatre, sending panic among the evil spirits.

Another firework exploded over us and another after that, firework after firework. The stands were emptying. Spirits pushed and fought their way off the terraces and into the centre. Many flew into the air. All cursed and screamed as sparks fell. They started fighting each other.

Overhead, I saw some kind of aircraft passing silently by. It was in two parts, one part pulling the other and it was dripping with silvery fire. It flew fast and jerkily over our heads. Ignoring the carnage below, it rattled out of sight over the stadium, heading for Keziah's habitat.

I couldn't see Leopold any more for the pile of monsters that now covered him, snapping, biting, tails thrashing, eyes red, fighting each other to get a better grip on him. More fireworks lit the sky, and more sparks fell.

Something sharp and flapping attached itself to my neck. I turned, as far as I could, and saw a large scaly bird digging away at me with its beak. It had little black piggy eyes. I battered at it with my hands, and it flew just out of range, cawing and going *yark!* A second bird fastened itself to my neck. I turned to flap at this one and then they were both on me.

I tried to create a machine gun, but panic disabled me. So I just fought them, waving my hands and keeping my eyes out of the way of their pecks.

I ran towards the house but stopped when I saw that it too was covered with monsters, who were ripping great pieces out of it and looting it with enthusiasm.

A second flying machine appeared over the stadium. This was dripping fire like the first, but it was circling. It was intensely bright, like burning magnesium.

It was spiraling down towards me.

The two scaly birds flew away, put off, I'm sure, mostly by my fierce arm-flapping and perhaps a little bit by this silent flying machine that was about to make an untroubled landing on the lawn.

All around me, monsters were looking up from their fighting and looting and moving away, the way you imagine animals clear from a waterhole when a lion steps up for a drink. Once out of danger, they resumed battle.

The machine came to a halt on the lawn. Close up, I could see it was something not entirely unlike a horse and cart. Though the 'horse' (the size of pony) was more like a penguin and the 'cart' (which was the size and shape of an open-topped railway freight wagon) had four balloon tyres which turned out to be living creatures themselves, complete with eyes and wings. They all had their own internal shining like an LED and they were sweating fire.

Someone let go the reins, climbed out and walked busily over. He was smaller than I (would have been bigger than Keziah, but not by a lot), and his dark glasses, hooked nose and mottled olive skin made him look like a member of the Syrian Secret Service. His suit was all wrong: its sharp lines and shiny black cloth looked like it was yearning to wrap itself round a young double-glazing salesman, but he was old. A member of the Syrian Secret Service who had been passed over for promotion, perhaps? Thick grey hair was cut unfashionably below his ears. He was slightly bow-legged.

'The famous Jamie Smith,' he said, with an Arabic accent, sizing me up and offering his hand for me to shake, which I took. 'Jonah. Minor prophet. It was a fish, not a whale.'

'Right,' I said, dazed. 'Stub told us about you.'

'Good. Where is he?'

'Stub? He's just over here. He's—'

'Cracked up? Yes. We went to the Lake of Fire first, but we couldn't find him.' We walked over to the woodland to where Stub was tied up. A couple of stegosauri were sniffing at his Adamantine chains, but they moved away.

The fireworks were still going off overhead.

'I'm here Stub,' said Jonah, kneeling and gently unwinding the Adamantine. 'This Adamantine,' he said conversationally to me. 'Older than the universe... Now now, Stub, stay still. Easy.'

Jonah glanced up at me while gently easing the chains away from Stub's flesh. 'This is one Biennale that won't go down as a triumph.'

'What was that explosion?'

'That was your friend Keziah scaring the dinosaurs. Now easy, easy, careful. You're all right.'

'I am not "all right",' said Stub. 'It's over, Jonah.'

'My dear friend,' said Jonah.

'I can't do this any more.'

'This is the last one.' Jonah eased the chain off the snake. 'You did good work here, Stub.'

'Not on him,' spat Stub, looking at me.

'Oh don't worry about him.'

'Stiff-necked, stubborn-hearted. I tried so hard.'

'You always do. Now come on, back into the wagon. Don't fight. Easy... Jamie, will you carry the other end of the snake? Thank you.'

The Prophet Jonah and I carried the snake on our shoulders across the amphitheatre, which was a battle zone as evil spirits fought each other and firework-stars fell flaming from the sky, sizzling those dinosaurs that were too busy hunting or being hunted to see them coming. A stream of evil spirits, I noticed, was heading for the exits.

'Now, just gently into the wagon, good.' We lowered Stub into the cart, and Jonah covered him with a blanket. 'Corrie should be here in a minute. She's just picking up Keziah.'

'Is she—?' I asked.

'She's fine,' said Jonah. Then he said to Stub. 'You lie there under the blanket and try not to think of any theology. OK.'

He turned to me.

'Jamie. Thank you for helping.' He held out his hand. I looked at the carnage around me.

'Er—I thought you were rescuing me?' I asked.

'No,' said Jonah.

'What?' I said. 'Why not?'

'Jamie,' said Jonah. 'I can't do anything for you. I'm sure Stub's told you. Later!' he thumped my chest. 'Then we might have a job for you! Ah good, here's Corrie and Keziah.' The second flying machine appeared over the amphitheatre, flying erratically.

Jonah climbed into the cart, picked up the reins and gave them a twitch. The penguin-like creature flapped some fins and yanked them into the air. 'I think it'll calm down once we're gone,' said the prophet, as the reins strained and the craft lifted into the sky. 'We upset them.'

They were gone.

I watched them go, the feeling of frustration and abandonment being replaced by a certain determination. *Right*, I thought. *Only one thing left to try. Whether my body's healed or not. I can't wait any more.*

I stepped quickly over to the forest, hoping to keep out of sight.

A fresh trumpet-blast was sounding over the amphitheatre, this time from the Royal Box. I looked up to see the Toad hastily sweeping the slug off his head, waiting for silence.

I rested my back against a tree and tried to concentrate, concentrate.

All around me, I could hear the fighting stopping. I saw two large raptors drop a half-chewed archaeopteryx. After it fell, it crawled off, dragging a broken wing and mouthing rude words at the raptors.

'Worst is over,' the Toad was saying. 'Worst is over. Stay calm. Limit damage. Don't fight. Worst is over. Bring Gaston and Leopold for judgement.'

Come on, I thought, and wonderfully, the scene started to fade. *Yes, come on.* Fumbled a bit in the dark. *Come on, come on.*

... and in. Wonderfully slipped into my own body, the easiest yet. *Now don't try anything*, I said to myself, *don't touch anything, just stay here. Just stay here and don't move.*

I crouched silently inside my body, listening to my own breathing, which was shallow. I could feel my heartbeat, slow and steady. *Just stay here.* Ever so gently, I probed around in my senses. I was lying on my back with my bed tipped half upright, no surprise there. My arm was resting against my side and I could feel the pressure of my right leg against the mattress. I evidently had a thin blanket on top.

I could hear some humming noises and the distant shuffle of shoes on a hard floor. *Just stay here. Stay here and never leave.*

Very gently, I tried to move a finger, still concentrating hard on not leaving my body. I tried different fingers, the other hand, my toes. Nothing.

Just stay here. My left eye was glued shut. The right, I could do something with that. *Stay here, don't lose it. Keep concentrating.* This was exhausting. Slowly, I tried to haul up my right eyelid and was rewarded with a blurry glimmer of dim light. I let it fall back. *And rest.*

I let some more heartbeats pass, still furiously concentrating on not drifting out of my body again, but I knew I was losing it. It was so tiring.

Then I felt I wasn't going to stay much longer, so I gave up trying and put all my effort into lifting the eyelid, and was rewarded with a slightly larger glimmer of light. The lights went off and I woke up next to my tree. How long had I stayed? Fifteen minutes? My longest yet.

Through the trees I could see Gaston and Leopold standing next to each other with their backs to me. They had reverted to humanoid forms: Gaston in his military uniform, Leopold in his dress kilt.

The Toad was sitting on the throne borne aloft by the four tall beings: the bull, the multi-armed woman with terrible hair, the thing like a sphinx, and the large black dog. The Toad had a staff in his hands. Many monsters were gathered in a semicircle around him, looking at Gaston and Leopold.

'Gaston Aubrey Ellwood Pterosauria d'Turville.' His great eyes glowered down at the stiff figure. 'You borrowed from me. Then you rebelled. Now disaster has struck. A day we will not easily forget. A terrible day. I take your possessions and I remove my protection and send you to the darkness. At my word, I set my running dogs among you and your possessions.'

Gaston returned his gaze without flinching.

'Leopold Xavier Squamata St Germain. You complied and acquiesced with your co-accused in direct rebellion to the Almighty Toad. Failed to train or control human pets. *Lost* both the spirits in your charge. Here, in Pandemonium! Participated in a terrible setback for the onward march of the glorious reign of the free spirits of the Omniverse. A shock from which it will take many years to recover.

'Yet I find some usefulness in you. I command your possessions to become mine and at my word I allow my running dogs to chew you for a season but I direct that you may remain as my bond-slave. Leopold, welcome to my design team.'

The crowd murmured. Leopold stiffened, then inched his way over to Gaston. He took Gaston's hand and held it, interweaving his fingers with Gaston's, and still looking at the Toad.

'Get off me,' muttered Gaston, trying to pull his hand away. 'You'll make it worse.'

'Your Brightness,' said Leopold, in a slightly higher pitched tone than I think he meant. 'Where he goes, I go. When he suffers, I suffer. I love him and I stay with him and I defy you.' Leopold stole a glance at Gaston, who was looking straight ahead and still pulling his hand away.

The Toad's chin bulged and his eyes, if it were possible, widened. 'Leopold Xavier Squamata St Germain you forsake my protection for his?'

'Here I stand,' said Leopold, squeakily, edging still nearer to Gaston. I thought I heard him gulp as well.

'Stupid creature,' cursed the Toad.

'Love isn't a widget,' murmured Leopold, defiantly.

'Spirits of the Free!' yelled the Toad. 'Regain your honour! Running dogs! Now!'

Gaston and Leopold stood hand in hand, expecting the crowd to attack. But nothing happened. Except that the Toad's throne started slowly tipping. The bull and the wild-haired woman, who were standing at the back, were pushing the throne upwards. Suddenly the Sphinx and the black dog crouched down, and the Toad pitched forward and fell to the ground. Before he could get up, the bull squashed him with a heavy hoof.

The scary-haired woman walked forward.

'We trusted you,' she said to the Toad. She had black teeth. 'We served you. You have done this. A day of disgrace. We wipe away this disgrace now. We, the throne-bearers of the Toad, overthrow you.'

She looked around at the assembled crowd. 'The Toad's privileges and wealth we keep for ourselves,' she said to them, tossing her head. 'As for his person and everything that belongs to Gaston and Leopold—they are yours.'

The assembled crowd seemed to need no further encouragement. Roaring, flying into the air, salivating, they rushed at Gaston, Leopold and the Toad, dragging them down, biting and ripping them with their claws.

I could hear Leopold screaming.

You can imagine how I spent the following hours. When I could gather enough strength, I jumped back into my body and held on there as long as I could. Then I would get exhausted, or lose concentration, and slip back into the habitat.

The evil spirits clearly thought that Jonah had rescued me. Not giving them any evidence to the contrary was highly motivational, and gave me quite an energy boost. So I quickly kept returning to my body.

I saw the spirits eventually tire of ripping and tearing at Gaston and Leopold. The two of them, clothes shredded and flesh raw, body parts missing, shuffled slowly into the sky heading for who-knows-where while the other spirits watched. Two detached hands—one of

Gaston's, one of Leopold's—were lying on the floor, twitching, holding each other.

The evil spirits took a lot longer with the Toad. When they were finished, they wrapped most of the bits of him in the Adamantine chains that Stub had been wearing, pulling the chains tight against his ripped skin.

Rather later, I again returned to the habitat. First Trumpeter was playing above the tied-up bits of Toad. It looked like the Toad, in his constituent parts, was going to be listening to First Trumpeter for a long time. First Trumpeter was not playing *Hail to the Toad*; I rather think he had decided to play his entire repertoire.

Later again, and the other big beasts seemed to have left the habitat, leaving all kinds of crawling, sliding and squirming beings to scavenge the leftovers. The habitat was trashed. Trees had had their branches pulled off. The outside of the cottage had been graffito-ed, the windows smashed and there was a Rayburn-sized hole in the kitchen wall. Smoke filled the air.

Dodging between the ravaged trees, I crept back to my own habitat. Osama's had been ransacked. They'd played what seemed like a game of football on Lord's Cricket Ground, and they'd crashed the space shuttle on the edge of the sea: waves tugged at it. The maglev looked like the rail had been torn up and used for a fight.

On the umpteenth trip back to my body, with the light of morning washing against my right eyelid, I came across a little hollow into which I could tuck my spirit's feet. I don't think it had been there before. I stuck my feet in there and let go everything else, and I stayed exactly where I was—in my body.

Maybe my physical brain had recovered just enough, and now could make space for my living spirit again. Maybe my repeated trips back to my body had helped kickstart things. It didn't matter. I had played every card in my hand, and somehow it had been enough. I was back.

It just didn't feel that great.

BACK TO THE DOME

They call the type of injuries I had 'Traumatic Brain Injury'. One of the symptoms is that you remember what happened before the trauma much better than what happens afterwards. You can also have delusions, get tired easily and suffer depression, and those are the good bits.

I know now that I was in a coma for about a week, until I had lifesaving brain surgery. The whole story in the habitat took place in that week. After I returned to my body, I stayed in Intensive Care for another month, having more surgery and drifting in and out of consciousness, but staying rooted to planet Earth.

I only have the haziest memories of those weeks. Lizzie visited often, as did my parents, who had tied up their wittily named yacht *The Children's Inheritance* in Madeira and flown home. My sister Alison and her Brilliant Children were less frequent (terribly busy, orchestra on Saturdays and the kids have to be with Oh-*Hugh!* on Sundays), which was a bit of a relief as I was getting quite bad headaches. When they did come, Ali wanted to bawl out the nurses, my niece wanted to talk to me to cheer me up, and my nephew's fingers simply itched to be back on the internet.

I spent my few waking hours organizing my bodily functions, which I found comforting and fascinating. Only the right-hand side of my body worked. When I had visits, it took all my strength to keep my eye open and pay attention and grunt. I did try smiling but stopped after I heard Lizzie say, 'I think he's going to be sick.'

After being lost in the heavenlies and surrounded by the spilled-out contents of my own mind, I can't tell you how extraordinary it was to see real things again. Nurses, both female and (somewhat to my alarm) male, seemed so beautiful as they stretched over me, injecting things or taking my blood pressure. Einstein taught us that matter is sky-sized skeins of energy knotted into atoms. I believed that now, when I looked at these godlike creatures of lustrous flesh. Matter, I thought, is an exotic super-concentrate in a sloshing, dreamy Omniverse of waves and spirits. No wonder the demons covet it. How amazing to touch others and be touched.

I began to realize that the accident had smashed up my emotions as well as my body and brain. Extreme feelings now seemed to come at me raw, like a pack of dogs. I was frightened about getting out of bed, anxious at the thought of visitors, angry with my saline drip. I was brimming with frustrated sexual desire and I thirsted for joy or felt sorrow with such a passion that it was as if I'd eaten some more of the habitat's magic mushrooms. I cried a lot, and for no reason.

Lizzie for example, grey-eyed, blonde hair freshly frizzed, perfect oval face and stubby nose, made me cry the first time I saw her. It was such a struggle to understand what she was saying. Or stay awake, for that matter, but I was enthralled during those moments as she gabbled on.

In my heightened emotional state I even forgave her for bringing the latest boyfriend, whom I'm almost sure was genetically a Neanderthal, sitting surly, hairy and ugly on the chair, legs apart, uncomfortable in his boots and leather jacket, sighing heavily.

By about four weeks after leaving the coma, I was doing really well organizing my bodily inputs and outputs, I could tell the day and time, and I had learnt this about my new situation:

1. Lizzie had let the Neanderthal into our shared house. That's my home trashed, then.

2. With that destructive efficiency of which only blondes are capable, Lizzie had written to the half-dozen clients whose websites I maintained. She'd told them I'd be off work for at least six months, but not to worry because I was fully insured. They'd all written back thanking her and explaining how they would necessarily be looking elsewhere for website support, and wishing me well for the future. So that was my business down the tubes.

3. My dad was in the process of sorting out insurances and benefits. Coming from an insurance dynasty, as I did, I had felt obliged to insure everything that moved, which was now proving to be a good thing.

Five weeks after the accident I was a moved to a slightly less-intensive care ward; or more strictly, to a the-nurses-are-busy,-cross,-and-engaged-in-a-feud-with-management ward.

I started learning to talk and bravely went places in my wheelchair. Mostly the toilet, which was exciting enough and occasionally to the TV lounge if no-one else was there. I began to learn how not to pour tea down the left half of my face. Physios (some more beautiful girls) got me to waggle things and said they were pleased. I slept less. Walking, however, was a distant dream and I wasn't even sure I wanted to learn again.

As soon as I could talk I started asking about Keziah. It took me much thought before I realized that neither Lizzie nor my other visitors nor the nurses knew whom I was talking about.

In the darker moments I wondered if *I* knew her or if there was something seriously delusional going on.

I asked about the crash. My dad told me it was with the insurers and the police. We would hear the full story eventually, don't worry, just get better.

Lizzie said the police had come round several times but she had hidden from them. Lizzie has not had good experiences with police officers, since an unfortunate incident with a boyfriend who asked her to look after some of his pot plants. (The pot plants proved to be strange pinnate things that needed surprising amounts of light, but which also needed to be kept in a dark room.) When the police did finally speak to her, she'd been so unhelpful that they'd exchanged the minimum of information. The police had clearly left with the idea that we were a dubious family with much to hide.

The nurses kept promising to find out if anyone else from the crash had been in the hospital. Then they forgot, or went off shift, or became embroiled in some crisis that required much gossipy whispering at the nursing station. And it was a big hospital, suspicious of giving out information.

I think now that they thought I was having delusions and were quietly fobbing me off.

I had the problems that babies and dogs have, of just being on the point of working something out when I was distracted by some bodily function, or by being fed, or by falling asleep.

Still. Over the weeks I did piece things together so that I knew that whoever had crashed into me:

1. Wasn't dead.

2. Had been in Intensive Care alongside me.

3. Had emerged from her coma a few days after I first opened my eye.

4. Had been one of those Traumatic Brain Injuries that recovers quickly and smoothly. The brain disappears into some deep realm of unconsciousness, but then resurfaces, reordered but remarkably well.

5. *May* have been that girl who, a few days later and on a different ward, was excitingly interviewed by the police, who were thinking of a Dangerous Driving charge.

I was completely thrown one day when Caroline walked into the ward.

Thinking back, I wondered if she hadn't already visited me a couple of times in Intensive Care. It would be a Caroline-like thing to do. She seemed to find me at once, unlike most first-time visitors. (Usually I had to endure shocked expressions as people looked round the ward, thought I wasn't there, then recognized me.)

Caroline was accompanied by a large, stocky man who had a creased brown face and a ridiculous, 14-year-old's moustache.

'Hello Caroline,' I said, then added as they approached my bed, 'as you can see, I decided to rent out half my face but I can't find a tenant.'

(I won't trouble you by transliterating what I actually said, but it was something like *Arro Arorine, Av oo cam he, Ah befided oo wen ou alf my ace, bu Ah car fi a nenan*. By now, people were usually picking up what I meant, though it sometimes took a couple of goes.)

'Hello Jamie,' she replied, giving me an invalid's peck on the forehead. 'You're looking tons better.'

'Good grief.'

Caroline pinkened. 'No, really.'

She looked different from my memory of her. I think she'd paid someone (other than a farmer) to do something about her hair. Her clothes were new and—I don't know—slinky.

'I want you to meet Umberto.' She indicated the bulky young man. He had greasy hair and was struggling with unstacking some chairs. 'He's from Mexico on an Advanced Librarianship Exchange Programme organized by the British Council.'

Their shoulders touched unnecessarily in a way that implied that, as the representative of all that is fine in British Librarianship, she wasn't undercooking the welcome.

'Umberto,' I said, shaking his hand once he managed to disentangle the chairs. 'I understand from Caroline that librarians are novel lovers.'

Caroline sighed and translated the pun into her fluent Spanish, and possibly mentioned the need to humour me, whereupon Umberto seemed to say, in Spanish, *I understood it perfectly. I just didn't find it that funny*.

'Very good,' he said in English, and we talked for some minutes about inconsequential things, mostly haematomas and footballers.

'You know,' said Caroline eventually. 'I wear this ring and most people notice it without me having to say anything.'

The cogs in my head slowly turned. Did that mean she was—

'Engaged?' (I think I actually said *en – age?*). Good grief. *To him?* I tried to smile. 'That's great.'

What I was thinking was, *but Caroline, I was half-hoping that you and I might have had another go.*

We talked about their wonderful news for a while. Honeymoon in Cuba, possibly. Then we had an unsatisfactory talk about Gabriel García Márquez.

I believe he wrote *One Hundred Years of Solitude.*

I did most of my crying at night, secretly.

Having suddenly become an unemployed cripple was a big part of it. Caroline's foolhardy descent into greasy Mexican cuisine hadn't helped my fragile emotions. Caroline was a classic novel: the small print gave you a headache sometimes but she was utterly engrossing. Now she'd been removed from the shelves.

Alongside these heaving emotions was the suspicion that my character was in even worse shape than my physique or my circumstances. It was just possible I wasn't all that good a person. I hear you protesting, but no, it's true. My week in the heavenlies had not been entirely a glorious display of bravery and decency. It was conceivable that I was vain, cowardly, proud, chauvinistic, insensitive and totally self-absorbed. Naturally, I put these worrying thoughts out of my head whenever they fluttered in.

The police interviewed me shortly before I left the hospital for a specialist Brain Injury Rehabilitation Clinic in the Fens.

'So what were your memories of the accident?'

'Aw, it was just one of those things,' I replied. 'Two people were just being a bit careless. I maybe wouldn't have crashed if I hadn't been reaching into my glovebox for a bon-bon. I don't think it was anybody's fault. Maybe she misjudged the speed of the lorry that she was overtaking. Maybe the lorry didn't see her and speeded up. The sun was low. I just think it was one of those things.'

'How do you know the driver was a she?'

'Because the accident replays itself over and over in my head. I could tell you what she was wearing.'

I wasn't going to incriminate Keziah. Neither would the police tell me much about her. I think the police tired of trying to interview me, and they left.

Two months after the accident, I was moved to the King George V Centre, a former TB hospital now fitted out with beds and physiotherapists, set in gardens in the Fenland countryside. From here they hoped to get enough bits of me working that I could go home and be depressed there, at a considerable saving to the stretched budgets of the National Health Service. I had, presumably, by now consumed all the tax I'd ever paid and was adding to the National Debt.

They gave me a single room, a garden to look out on and—joy of joys—wireless Internet access. Lizzie brought my Mac over, miraculously managing not to spill nail-polish remover into it while it was in the back of the wheeled skip that was her—our—replacement car.

I still wasn't walking, but the left side of my body was occasionally twitching with life, Frankenstein-like. Enough fingers worked for me tenderly to lay my hands on my Mac's holy white keys and comfort-surf.

Three days after I arrived at the King George V Centre, Keziah quietly stepped through the door.

I was reading *Wired* at the time and for a second I was completely disoriented. I stared at her almost with a look of panic. She was dressed in a dark business-suit, with a grey camisole top—smarter than I'd ever seen her. Just come from court, perhaps. The pale face, the full turned-down red lips, the green eyes, the shoulder-length thin black hair, the eye-liner, the endless not-quite-being five feet tall: unmistakably it was *Mordant & Co, Solicitors*. Perhaps she was ever so slightly less scrawny; but then, I'd hardly seen her in the flesh before. She looked uncertainly at me, her back still against the door.

I felt tears stinging my eyes and dripping down my cheek.

'You know me, don't you?' I said uncertainly.

'Of course I know you, you dork. I brought you some bon-bons.'

Tears were rolling down my face. She looked unusually ill-at-ease too, trying not to stare, as people did, but staring nonetheless.

'Good practice for the left side of my face,' I said. 'Chewing.'

'They're from the Old Fashioned Internet Sweetshop,' she said. 'I looked it up on your hospital site.'

'That's about all that's left of my site,' I said. 'Thank you.'

'Least I could do.'

I blew my nose. 'Would you hold my hand?' I asked.

With a puzzled look, even a glare, she sat down on the red chair next to my bed, put the bon-bons on the bedside cabinet (National Health Service chipboard, brown top, Gideon Bible within) and obediently took my hand lightly in hers.

'I usually ask people to hold my hand,' I said, truthfully. 'Touch is so wonderful. I hope you don't mind. Please don't be sympathetic.'

'How are you?' asked Keziah. Our conversations were always cursed with awkwardness.

'I'm told there are stages in loss,' I said. 'You start with Denial and end up with Acceptance. I can't remember the middle bits and I'm not sure what stage I'm in. It's either Denial or Acceptance, I think. I cry a lot and my hand shakes.'

'Will you—'

'Get better?' I'd had this conversation with so many visitors now that I didn't need to wait while they edged their way to the main point. 'They never say. What they do say is, Yes, you can almost fully recover. Yes, you can go on recovering all through your life. Either way I think that's a No. I'm shooting for a full Yes. You?'

'I'm fine. Miraculous recovery. Happens with brain injuries.'

'Not with mine.'

We subsided into awkwardness again.

'In the end they didn't pursue the Dangerous Driving charge,' said Keziah. 'It never came to a plea. Too much conflicting evidence.'

'I gave them a statement,' I said. 'That might have confused them a bit.'

'It seems that your evidence contradicted the forensic evidence and they can't trace the driver of the Polish truck. There's doubt over whether he accelerated when I tried to overtake. So it would never work in court.'

'Good,' I said.

'I was preparing to plead guilty,' said Keziah.

'So what happened?'

'In the end the Crown Prosecution Service suggested I did plead guilty to a lesser charge. I ended up with a fine and some points on my licence. There was no request for compensation from the victim.'

'I know. I told the police. The victim is insured up to the eyeballs. The victim's dad ran an insurance broker's, and the victim's dad's son gets to have all the insurance policies he can eat.'

'Still. You didn't need to be kind. I completely deserved prison and it would have been OK.'

'Upsets the natural order. You can't have lawyers in prison.'

'When I was facing the original charge I was bailed not to make any contact with you. That's why I've been so long.'

'You didn't die,' I said.

'No.'

'Happy about that?'

'Yes.'

'How come?'

'It's a long story.'

Outside, the first sunshine of spring was licking the trees. Narcissi were poking up like periscopes, seeing if it was safe for the rest of the garden to come out.

'If you gave me twenty minutes to get ready, you might be able to wheel me round the garden a few times?'

'I'm not *that* heavy,' I said, twenty-two minutes later.

'It's uphill,' complained Keziah, as she pushed.

'I expect it's the wheel sticking,' I said.

She parked my wheelchair and sat on a bench beside me, both of us looking over a patchwork of Fenland fields—some black and ploughed, others ankle-high with winter wheat. It was one of those fragile early spring days that are warm if you stay in the sun and the wind doesn't blow.

'All I remember is, I was doing my performance in front of all these dinosaurs, and your habitat exploded. Then they all started fighting each other.'

'It was you who put me onto it. The rain. Start drinking the rain.'

'You were certainly doing *that* when I left. Why did you start jabbering about Swedish pop groups?'

'*Abba* is the Aramaic for *Daddy*. It's a word people use for God. You never forget Sunday School,' Keziah was looking steadfastly out at the Cambridgeshire mud. 'I felt *held*.'

'Held?'

'Held. In a good way. Just held and loved. Do you remember the first time you visited my habitat?'

'I try not to.'

'In all the chaos, there was a park, and the five-year-old me sitting on my dad's shoulders while he pretended to be a horse.'

'I'll take your word for it. I was mostly trying to get out as fast as I could.'

'It was there. Because it's always been there, through everything. It was from a time before everything went wrong in our family. And *this* was like *that*, being hoisted onto God's shoulders. No words. Just joy. Just love. Like he'd been waiting for me all these years.'

'Because rain was falling on you?'

'Because mercy was falling on me. Always had been. Always is. I'd just always brushed it off before.'

'The return of the prodigal lawyer.'

'Yes. This mercy was everywhere, of course, when you looked. Mushrooms growing. Even a hint of it when First Trumpeter played for us that day, do you remember? Even the evil spirits must have glimpses of it.'

'Why didn't Stub just tell us? "Drink the rain"?'

'Would you have listened?'

'No, but you might have.'

'I think he knew that my heart had to make a journey first. When I understood myself—what had been done to me, what I'd done to myself—only then did I properly despair.'

'So why did you explode?'

'I didn't. Corrie Bright—you remember Stub telling us about her—told me it was Angels with Party Poppers. When they saw what was going on with me they gatecrashed the habitat. This sort are like teenagers, only in a good way. Clubbing. Setting off fireworks. Lit up the whole Omniverse for a few moments.'

'Like a nova in the sky,' I said.

'That's a star, right?'

'Yes. Well a supernova, which is a big nova, is a giant star blowing up. You can see them all the way across the Universe. Certainly frightened the dinosaurs. Then Corrie Bright picked you up?'

'Yes, and Jonah came for Stub.'

'But not for me.'

'No. I tried to get them to. I couldn't understand why they left you behind.'

'Neither could I.'

'They said, "Never save a drowning man until he's gone under for the third time." You'd obviously only gone under for about the second time.'

'Charming.'

'I told them all about the Biennale. How you were likely to be torn apart by dinosaurs and so on.'

'Thank you,' I said.

'But Jonah said, "It'll do him the power of good." He mentioned that it was easier than, for example, spending three days and nights in the belly of a great fish.'

'I suppose he would know,' I said, but I was still piqued.

'So anyway, Miss Bright and Jonah flew out of the habitat with Stub and me in their carts.'

'How did you get past the blue fear-demons?'

'They were flying around in confusion because of the Angels. When they saw us coming they all herded together to let us pass. We flew right out of the satanic realms altogether. That part of the heavenlies is called Pandemonium. John Milton had an idea of it, when he located it as the palace complex in Hell. It's bigger than that but that's where our habitat was.

'So we flew up into the heavenly realms proper— which is enormous, a lot bigger than the space taken up by Pandemonium. It has plenty of problems of its own, bureaucracy mostly. I'm sitting next to Miss Bright— who's this really old lady, but she drives like a lunatic— flying through the heavenlies.

'I looked over my shoulder. I thought our habitat had broken up. My part of the landscape was following us. It was huge, and it was being pulled through the sky by this thing that looked like a penguin. Miss Bright explained that it wasn't my part of the habitat at all. It was the real thing. I'd been building a model of it all this time. I'd kept seeing it in my dreams. My memory-storage: my soul.'

'You were being followed by your soul?'

'Yes. It turns out that wherever you are in the heavenlies—where your spirit is—your soul tries to get near. When we were locked up in the habitat, our souls were orbiting the habitat, bumping against the Pixellated Fear, trying to link up with us. Which of course made it easy for Leopold to dig around in them and for Stub to work on them.'

'So the soul and the memory storage are the same thing?' I asked.

'They are,' said Keziah.

I was beginning to think about the consequences for *my* soul. Presuming I had one, which was not something I'd given much thought to. What was that watertight Dome that I'd visited in my dreams? Stub had shown me the sign outside it: '*Jamie's Myth—a creation of Jamie Smith Fantasy Productions*'? That haunted landscape around the Dome, so polluted and out-of-whack, soiled by the presence of the Dome? What—come to think of it —was that cliff-edged landmass that nearly ran me over when I flew to the edge of the habitat? Were they all the same thing? Was that my soul?

'Miss Bright explained that all the time I was in the habitat, I was making a model of my own soul. That's what everybody does all the time, she told me. If anyone lives anywhere for any length of time, soon their home comes to resemble their soul. You know, it might be homely, or cluttered, or super-tidy, or cosy or cold. And so on.'

'I built a playground.'

'Yes, and I built a wasteland. So I kept looking back over my shoulder as we flew through the heavenlies. My soul is a delta wing like you suggested—built for flight. It was being pulled by this strange penguin creature—called a Pengub, incidentally—and it was doing a victory roll, barrelling through the skies being splattered with the Golden Rain. It looked happy and free. It *was* happy. *I* was happy.'

'You?' I asked. 'Happy?'

'I know,' she said. 'But I was. Of course, I forgot to mention, this Golden Rain was pouring on us all the time. It's a weather feature, tipping down out of the high heavenlies.'

'So it wasn't rotting you?' I asked.

'No, I was lapping it up. So was Miss Bright. So was Jonah—we were flying parallel with each other at that point. Only Stub was hiding from it.

'We arrived at where Jonah and Miss Bright have their base, which is a staff restaurant and leisure facility. They don't have an office, apparently—another long story. They looked after me. Miss Bright spent a long time talking everything through. I had plenty of sleep and shed quite a few more tears and had some good meals.'

'They have food?'

'Mostly muesli,' said Keziah.

'Oh.'

'Or Afghan, Indian, whatever you like.'

'Don't scare me like that.'

'My soul was outside, and it was being washed by the Golden Rain. Which I wasn't sluicing away so much. I was letting it in. New things were growing and maybe the old volcanoes weren't so fierce. Miss Bright was explaining it all.

'Of course, they were pleased with me because that's what they do. Therapists. I was one of their success stories, I suppose.

'I had a long time of healing—it's T12 up there, twelve days pass for every one of ours. So three earth days after you woke up—which was over a month with Miss Bright and Jonah—I was healed enough to drop back into my body.'

'What are you doing now?'

'I called my sister Jemima and we cried. We met up a few times, and we cried some more.'

'You've done plenty of crying.'

'Lot to catch up on... Now the court case is over, and now I've seen you, I'm handing over my clients for another month and going to Africa to meet my mother and mend some fences.'

'Your mother didn't come over even when her daughter was in a coma?'

'She didn't.'

'Lot of fences.'

'One big one. I'll still be commuting to the heavenlies. Jonah and Miss Bright recruited me into the CANSORT.'

Keziah was still looking out at the fields. 'Jamie. They want you to join them too. Like me, you've now got the ability to leave your body when you want. But you've still got a body that you can use on earth. Not many people can do both things. It's a kind of gift.'

'We can commute, like they do.'

'Better, given that Corrie Bright is quite restricted and Jonah's body is under the desert in Mosul.'

'They're offering me a job?' I asked.

'Yes. Both of us.'

'Oh great.'

'I'm not sure I can explain this, Jamie,' said Keziah. 'I've seen things up there. What happened to us wasn't random.'

'True. It was mostly because you were driving like a suicidal maniac.'

'It was an accident but it was also a chapter in a story.'

'Oh goody. I'm enfolded in a Higher Purpose. Very Milton.'

'Knowing you, I don't think it'll be *very* High a Purpose,' said Keziah.

'You may have a point... What's Jonah like to work for?'

'Cynical. Weary. Lovely.'

'And Corrie Bright?'

'Batty, stern, emotionally limited, intellectually brilliant. Kind. Goes surfing in Number Space for a hobby.'

'You can do that in the heavenlies?'

'Yes.'

'Have they got a thing going?'

'Good grief, you're so obsessed...'

'Only asked... of course they don't. Sorry. And this work. Presumably you can do it... when you're asleep on earth and things.'

'Yes. The fact time passes at different rates helps too.'

'Hmm. Do they pay us?'

'No. It's fun, though.' Coming from Keziah, this was roughly like a full orchestra playing the Hallelujah Chorus. 'They have things in mind for us. Mixing and baking a new world, you know, that kind of thing. Gardening in the rain.'

Since we last met, then, Keziah has started using words like 'fun' and 'happy' and seems to mean them. I, meanwhile, have been ambushed by big sad emotions.

'We'd be colleagues,' I said, as much to avoid analysing the preceding thought as anything.

'Yes,' she said. 'There is that.'

'Perhaps there's a website or something that would help,' I said.

'Just you not being so irritating might help.'

We pondered this.

'I'm still not ready, though, am I?' I said. 'That's what you've come to tell me. I'm welcome to work for them—which is kind to be offered—but I've still got to go under for the third time.'

She gazed out over the Fens and sighed.

My sleep patterns are all out of whack, partly because I spend so much time asleep during the day, tired out meeting the insatiable demands of the beautiful physios.

That night I lay awake for a long time, pondering everything.

I made a decision.

Very gently, I unhooked my spirit's feet from their comfortable resting place in my body. This was very brave, actually. I felt my spirit bobbing upwards, held in my body now only by willpower. Then I thought of my soul, and up I went.

And I was in the Dome-land, on my soul. In the polluted landscape of my heart.

I swooped around a bit and saw it all, much as I had seen in my dreams—a great, flying island, with mountains and valleys. A town full of people whom I didn't much want to bother with. The Dome trying to keep me and my friends isolated, but poisoning the whole land, like a rich settlement in a poor country. The rain falling, firmly kept out from wherever it might do some good. Well, hardly worth pushing the metaphor.

As in the dream, I flew past the sign at the Dome's entrance:

JAMIE'S MYTH

and stood inside, surveying it for the first time as its owner.

This Dome needs opening up to the elements. Then I can work on the wastelands outside, rebuilding and irrigating and restoring.

Pretty thought.

Tricky job.

I couldn't bring myself to throw open the doors to the Dome all at once. Even the Golden Rain itself (sloshing and beating against the outside of the Dome) perhaps was too much of a good thing.

Nor was I honestly sure what I might be getting myself into. My soul, the world, the Omniverse, splattered endlessly with mercy and tenderness and joy? It was a novel picture of things, and not one that I could immediately square up with everything else I knew.

Worse, it was a letting go, a surrender.

Definitely a good idea not to overdo things at first.

I stood and looked at the Dome, its high curve stretching over me. With a careful sequence of thoughts, I created a small openable window at the very top, and connected this window to a long series of metal rods and gears, ending in a handle.

I took the handle and moved it half a turn. Rods creaked, gears ground, metal strained. At the top of the Dome, the tiny skylight opened half an inch: a tentative, reversible, agnostic opening to the possibility of grace.

I thought I felt a little zephyr of moist fresh air briefly against my face.

Someone was knocking on the Dome behind me. I turned and saw a familiar cadaverous figure in his Sam Spade hat and raincoat.

'Stub!' I said.

He signalled me to meet him at the entrance to the Dome. I walked over, keeping an eye on him as he traced a parallel path round the outside of the Dome. The entrance was bolted and barred, so I had a tedious job of unlocking. Finally I opened the small door and poked my head through the polythene hangings.

'Hello sir,' said Stub. 'Jonah and Miss Bright and Keziah wondered if you'd like to join them for a meal. They said they've ordered murtabak specially.'

'I see.' I felt a sudden pang of anxiety. 'What am I letting myself in for?'

'Murtabak, sir,' said Stub. 'And probably curry sauce.'

'Quite. But what else? Pain, danger, fear? Commitment?'

'Why not take it a step at a time, sir?'

Because that's how wars start, and disasters happen, and people get into things they regret, I thought.

'I suppose I could give it a go.'

I walked out, and left the door to Jamie's Myth slightly open.

'Are you better, then?' I asked Stub.

'Still hanging on,' he replied.

'Why don't you take your coat off? This rain is good for you.'

'Not for the likes of me, sir,' said Stub. 'Come on.'

THANKS

Many thanks to Jeremy Andrews, Ivan Baker, Annabel Bloxham, Andrew Bowker, Paul Harvey, Richard Hornby, Hugh Osgood, Gareth Owens, Corin Redsell, Daphne Spraggett, Andrew Weighill, Andy Willis and Cy Winskell. They all read drafts and provided insight and encouragement, some, like Corin and Gareth, spending hours reading and commenting.

My long-time publisher and friend Jeremy Mudditt saw an early draft but lost his battle with cancer a few weeks before *Paradise* was published. I'm sorry he never saw the published copy.

Sam Richardson freely gave his time and creativity to produce such a fine cover. Carlina Lampezuda graciously gave permission for me to use her photo *Stone Clouds* for the cover picture. (I recommend a look at her Flickr site.) My colleagues in WEC International allowed me to go part-time so I could write fiction.

Thanks most of all to my wife and children. Their contribution goes far beyond the scope of a little acknowledgements paragraph.

You can follow news of further titles at www.fizz-books.com or www.glennmyers.info; or at 'Paradise - a novel' on Facebook.

Lightning Source UK Ltd.
Milton Keynes UK
08 February 2011
167164UK00001B/70/P